Can a broken engagement ignite the spark of true love?

Sylvia Dowder had almost made it to the altar when her fiancé unexpectedly became a viscount, and dropped her like a stale crumpet to make a more "suitable" match. Though Sylvia's heart has been crushed, her spirit has not. She puts her wits and social savvy to use as a secret gossip columnist—and as the Everton Domestic Society's party planner to the ton. Luckily, she's not in danger of ever falling for an aristocrat again…

Especially not one like Anthony Braighton, Earl of Grafton. Raised in America, Anthony sees no reason to marry when he can enjoy all the perks of being an eligible earl. Determined to convince his family he doesn't need a wife, he hires Sylvia to act as hostess and decorator for upcoming parties. Yet Sylvia is as adept at captivating his interest as she is at beautifying his home. And despite this Everton lady's aversion to titled men, some attractions can't be denied—and love rarely does go where it's told …

Visit us at www.kensingtonbooks.com

Books by A.S. Fenichel

The Demon Hunter Series
Ascension
Deception
Betrayal

Forever Brides Series
Tainted Bride
Foolish Bride
Desperate Bride

The Everton Domestic Society
A Lady's Honor
A Lady's Escape
A Lady's Virtue

Published by Kensington Publishing Corporation

A Lady's Virtue

The Everton Domestic Society

A.S. Fenichel

LYRICAL PRESS
Kensington Publishing Corp.
www.kensingtonbooks.com

Lyrical Press books are published by
Kensington Publishing Corp. 119 West 40th Street New York, NY 10018

Copyright © 2018 by A.S. Fenichel

All rights reserved. No part of this book may be reproduced in any form or by any means without the prior written consent of the Publisher, excepting brief quotes used in reviews.

All Kensington titles, imprints, and distributed lines are available at special quantity discounts for bulk purchases for sales promotion, premiums, fund-raising, and educational or institutional use.

To the extent that the image or images on the cover of this book depict a person or persons, such person or persons are merely models, and are not intended to portray any character or characters featured in the book.

Special book excerpts or customized printings can also be created to fit specific needs. For details, write or phone the office of the Kensington Special Sales Manager:
Kensington Publishing Corp.
119 West 40th Street
New York, NY 10018
Attn. Special Sales Department. Phone: 1-800-221-2647.

Kensington and the K logo Reg. U.S. Pat. & TM Off.
LYRICAL PRESS Reg. U.S. Pat. & TM Off.
Lyrical Press and the L logo are trademarks of Kensington Publishing Corp.f.

First Electronic Edition: March 2019
eISBN-13: 978-1-5161-0586-1
eISBN-10: 1-5161-0586-9

First Print Edition: March 20019
ISBN-13: 978-1-5161-0589-2
ISBN-10: 1-5161-0589-3

Printed in the United States of America

To Dave Mansue, for believing in me even when there was nothing to believe in and for being proud of every tiny accomplishment. Thank you for knowing that staring out into space is sometimes the same as working and for loving me with all my quirks and the random thoughts I share at the oddest moments.

To my dear friend, Karla Doyle, for having the wicked sense of humor that inspired Sylvia.

Acknowledgments

Whenever I write a book it is with the love and support of fabulous friends. Thanks for all your support: Gemma Brocato, Juliette Cross, Kristi Rose, Janna MacGregor and CD Brennan. You ladies make my mornings bright and keep me rolling.

Special thanks to Debbie and Chad for all the support and cheering on. No one has ever had better friends.

Chapter 1

Late again, Sylvia Dowder ran down the stairs at the Everton Domestic Society as if her skirts were on fire. It was impossible to read her handwritten pages while moving at such a pace, but she needed to send her article to the *Weekly Whisper*'s editor before the day was out. She'd been late last month and nearly lost her post at the newspaper.

At the bottom of the stairs, she noted her failure to sign the article. Quill in hand, she dripped ink on her brown skirt, leaned on the banister and scribbled Mable Tattler at the bottom. She would ask Gray to have a footman carry it to Free Market Square. Jumping down the last step brought her up against a wall that toppled her to the floor.

Stunned, she lay still with her papers strewn around her and the light from the transom windows blocked by whatever had felled her.

A masculine, ungloved hand reached toward her. "I'm terribly sorry, miss. Entirely my fault. Are you hurt?" His accent was strange, American perhaps.

Having no gloves on, she was hesitant to touch him, but there was no help for it. She couldn't remain on her back like a turtle. The warmth of his skin traveled up her arm, and her cheeks heated. His fingers were strong and rough. This was no gentleman's hand. She stood as he eased her to her feet. "Not at all," she said. "I was distracted."

He towered over her. At her full height of barely over five feet, she craned her neck and was frozen by the most stunning pair of golden eyes, olive skin and full lips. She blinked to focus on the whole rather than the parts. "Anthony Braighton?"

He bowed over her hand, which he still held firmly in his. "Lady Serena or Sylvia? I'm afraid I don't know."

The mention of her twin's name brought reality crashing back on Sylvia. She pulled her hand back and made a curtsy. "A common mistake, sir. I am Sylvia Dowder. My sister is still living at home."

Cocking his head, he gawked at her. "And you are now living here at Everton House, Miss Dowder?"

"I have joined the Society." While he seemed only curious, it still rubbed her wrong, and she forced herself not to defend her decisions. Anthony Braighton was just a rich gentleman from America. His opinion didn't mean anything.

"Because of Lord March?" The problem with Americans was they said exactly what they thought rather than keeping a conversation polite.

Sylvia bit down on the inside of her cheek. The last thing she wanted was to recount the demise of her engagement to Hunter Gautier, the current Viscount of March. She had been so close to the altar before disaster struck. No. She wouldn't think about that anymore. "My reasons are not your concern, Mr. Braighton. If you'll excuse me, I have to see the butler."

His eyes were wide. "Have I been rude, Miss Dowder? I assure you, it was not my intention. I only meant to convey that March's treatment of you was abominable and no one blames you."

Despite his effort to make things better, his mention of what everyone in London knew of her life and failure only exacerbated her mortification. Still, she could see he was sincere, if mistaken. "There is no harm, Mr. Braighton. I am uninjured."

"I am pleased to hear that. It seems I have a bad habit of offending the English with regularity." His smile created the most charming dimple in his left cheek, and his eyes sparkled with mischief.

If she were honest, she did not mind looking at Anthony Braighton. Best not to be too honest. "I am made of tougher stuff than most."

"Indeed." That dimple deepened, and he raised an eyebrow. Looking at the pages in her hand, he said, "I'm keeping you from something. Forgive me. I was on my way to see Lady Jane Everton."

Curiosity over what troubles might bring a rich young man to the Everton Domestic Society warred with her need to have her article delivered to her editor before her deadline passed. Her training as a lady won the battle. She gestured toward the hallway, which led behind the stairs. "Lady Jane's office is the first door on the right."

"Thank you, Miss Dowder. Very nice to see you again."

"And you, Mr. Braighton. If you will excuse me."

He bowed, and she rushed from the foyer to find Gray, the Evertons' aging butler.

Gray shuffled through the servants' door into the dining room when Sylvia found him. "Hello, Miss Dowder. How may I help?"

How the man managed to stay upright was a mystery, as was his age. No one seemed to know, and Sylvia didn't have the courage to ask him. She admired his fortitude and tried not to giggle at his wild tufts of white hair when they protruded in every direction.

She folded her parchment into a small packet. "Can you have a footman deliver this to Mr. Cane at the *Weekly Whisper*'s office? It must get there before three o'clock."

Taking the packet, he nodded. "I'll see to it, miss."

"Oh, Miss Dowder, there you are." Jane Everton stood in the entrance, her dark hair pulled into a severe bun and her hands clasped in front of her gray skirt.

"Did we have an appointment, my lady?" Sylvia prayed she hadn't forgotten.

"No. However, if you have a few minutes, I would like to speak to you."

The notion that her crashing into Mr. Braighton had become known spiraled her stomach into a knot. Surely, he wasn't upset because she'd been preoccupied and bumped him. After all, it was she who had tumbled to the floor, not him. "Of course, my lady."

Following Jane out of the dining room, through the foyer and past the stairs to her office, Sylvia practiced her apology for the incident. Not that she was very sorry, but it was easier to make amends than fight a tyrant most of the time. Perhaps she was fussing over nothing and Anthony had left the house already.

Besides the masculinity of the room, there was always the warm smell of cherry tobacco, which Lord Everton favored, and the fresh-cut flowers he had delivered nearly every morning for his wife. Today a large vase full of tulips decorated the table to the right of Lady Jane's desk. Seated next to the table, Anthony Braighton waited.

When they entered, he stood.

Jane rounded the desk. "Miss Dowder, this is Lord Anthony Braighton."

Heart pounding, Sylvia made a curtsy. Anthony Braighton's sister was a countess, but he held no title. At least she didn't think he did. "I am acquainted with Mr. Braighton, my lady."

Both of Jane's eyebrows rose. "Oh, well, I suppose that is not surprising as your backgrounds likely afforded you the same friends. Please be seated, Miss Dowder. Lord Braighton has recently become the Earl of Grafton."

"I apologize, my lord."

Anthony waved off the apology. "My cousin passed away without an heir, and now it seems I am an earl." He turned to Lady Jane. "Indeed. Miss Dowder and her sister were at several house parties and balls, and we do indeed share many friends."

"Will that be a problem?" Jane asked.

"Not for me." His gaze fell on Sylvia while he waited for her reaction. Golden eyes surrounded by dark lashes, it was hard not to be mesmerized by his stare.

Clearing her throat, Sylvia realized this was one of those times when keeping quiet could be very detrimental. "If I might ask, my lady, what exactly are we talking about?"

"I apologize, my dear. Lord Grafton has just signed a contract for a hostess to assist him with some necessary events required by his new status and title. I thought you might be the perfect Everton lady for the assignment."

"What type of events?" Her chest tightened. Why it should worry her to spend extended amounts of time with Anthony Braighton, she didn't know, but trepidation shook her from the inside out.

Sitting forward, Anthony rested his chin on his hands, elbows propped on his knees. It had been several years since she'd last seen him, and he was no longer lanky, but tall and filled out. "My mother insists I host at least one dinner party then a ball this season. She would prefer I find a wife, but I intend to prove to her that marrying is not necessary. A respectable lady of the Everton Domestic Society can handle all the details of a hostess."

Jane said, "If you would like to find a wife, I can suggest another lady who can help with matchmaking."

His expression soured. "I'd really rather not."

Sylvia was sure he had more to say on the subject of his not marrying, but he simply gave Jane a warm smile.

"It seems a simple enough task. I'm sure I can manage to plan a dinner party and a ball if his lordship has a guest list in mind." Sylvia had helped plan many events with her mother and sister. This would not be an issue.

"I do. There are a few other things I require." He pulled his lips into a line, and Sylvia wondered where their fullness disappeared to.

Jane raised a brow. "I'm sure we won't be shocked, my lord. What do you require?"

Standing, he paced to the window and ran his hand along the table to the left. "I inherited the Collington townhouse. It's on Grosvenor Street. My great-aunt Daphne has lived there a long time and I offered to purchase a new home for myself, but she insists she'd rather move to the dowager's cottage. The townhouse is nice, but very formal. I've never been comfortable there. I need some assistance with the decor. Are you able to help in that area as well, Miss Dowder?"

Once Jane nodded her approval, Sylvia said, "I'm sure I can be of assistance, my lord."

He turned, and the strain had eased, leaving his lips full again. "Do you think we can schedule the dinner party for one month from now? If I don't do something soon, Momma will drive me to madness."

It wasn't easy to keep from laughing. Sylvia had met Mrs. Braighton once and found her petite and charming. The fact that her strapping young son was afraid of her was much funnier than was polite.

"It's all right, Miss Dowder. You may laugh. I know I'm a coward where my mother is concerned. Still, I'll not let her bully me into marriage. Not yet." His smile was sweet, and he ran his fingers through his shock of dark hair.

Swallowing her laugh, Sylvia stood. "I will be happy to help you, my lord. Lady Jane, do we have a dowager available? I fear this short schedule will require a lot of my time to be spent at his lordship's townhouse. I'll need a chaperon."

Jane went through the ledger on her desk. "Lady Chervil arrived home yesterday. I'll go and see if she will consent to the assignment." Jane stood and walked out of the office, leaving the door open.

At a loss for what to say, Sylvia tugged on the lace along the bottom of her bodice.

A shadow passed in front of her, and she glanced up to find Anthony staring at her. "I know you said you didn't want to speak on why you joined the Everton Domestic Society, Miss Dowder, but may I ask if you are still speaking to your family?"

Normally she would have said it was none of his business, but there was genuine concern etched in the lines around his mouth. That mouth was a distraction that Sylvia could hardly afford. "My sister and I are still in regular contact. As twins it would be difficult if not impossible to sever the ties. Mother is less understanding about my choices, but I go for tea with her every week whether she likes it or not."

"That must be very difficult for you?"

Refusing to show any weakness, she lifted her chin. "I manage. My mother and sister are only concerned with finding Serena a husband this season. They feel it is the last hope. As their attentions are focused there, they leave me in peace."

"Why are they not focused on finding you a husband as well?" While impertinent, the question was softly asked and sincere. Yet there was no pity in his expression. None of the censure a failed engagement and a life of spinsterhood usually garnered.

Swallowing her disappointment had become a regular meal. "Mother feels I already wasted enough of their time and money. I don't disagree, and I'm happy here. At least here I can do as I please and wri—do some good." She closed her mouth before she said too much. She'd nearly told him more than was safe. What was it about Anthony Braighton, Earl of Grafton, that loosened her tongue? Whatever it was, it had to be controlled.

He leaned down until his distracting lips were inches from her ear. "You are not to blame for March's abominable behavior."

Sylvia's heart raced, and she drew in a quick breath. He was too close and the scent of fresh-cut wood and something delectable swamped her senses. She ducked under his chest and around to the back of the chair. Her cheeks were on fire and she was sure she was blushing like an idiot. It would not do.

He rose to his full height and watched her.

"Mr.—I mean, my lord, I am under no delusions." There. She had sounded quite sure of herself.

He bowed. "I'm glad to hear it. I would hate to think you had lost your confidence, Miss Dowder. I remember you and your sister to be young ladies full of life and quite funny at times. Yet I have seen none of that wicked sense of humor since my arrival at Everton House."

Missing the times that she and Serena would poke fun at customs and people would not change her situation. She found her humor was best kept anonymous in her new column. People of society rarely liked a girl with a quick wit. "My sense of humor is intact, my lord. This is a place of business, and jocularity is not always appropriate."

He stared at the chair she used as a wall between them. "The Sylvia Dowder I met at some ball years ago, or Wharton house party two years ago, would never have said such a ridiculous thing. In fact, she loved to poke fun at exactly those kinds of attitudes."

Pulling her shoulders back, she pushed down the hurt of the last six months. "Lives change and people grow up, my lord. You should know that. Look at you. Four years ago, at the Millar ball, you scoffed at our English titles and customs, and now you've gotten yourself a title, a country estate, a townhouse, and a plan to have your very own coming out of a sort. Have you not changed just as much, if not more?"

Stepping back, he raked through that thick mane of hair again. He slumped into a chair and closed his eyes. "It is the last thing I wanted or expected."

She sat across from him and watched the worry return to his sharp features. His cheeks were high and his jaw strong and square. He was by far the most handsome man she'd ever seen. Hunter had been fine to look at, but Anthony was beautiful and exotic with his tiger eyes and olive skin.

Opening his eyes, he said, "My cousin was a bit of a stuffed shirt, but I never wanted his title or responsibilities. I certainly did not wish for my aunt Daphne to suffer the loss of her son. But the title fell to me, and if I refused, my family would lose the title entirely." He sighed long and low. "I had hoped to spend time in Italy. My momma's family has a beautiful estate and vineyard there. I had other plans too."

He made Italy sound like a fairy tale place and made being a noble sound miserable. It was unfair to compare him to Hunter, but she couldn't help it. Hunter had been so keen on having become a viscount, he'd barely spared a thought for the loss of his brother. "You could still go. Your title will not take that much of your time. I'm sure you already enjoy many of the benefits of being an earl."

His shrug was youthful like the Anthony she'd known before. "I suppose that's true, but Momma and my aunt are determined I marry and produce an heir. I have no desire to marry a woman I barely know and have nothing in common with. For Momma's sake I plan to stay here in England for a while. Perhaps by next winter, I can go to Italy. When you come to my house, I will give you a sample of my cousin's wine. It's really special."

"I would like that. I have never had Italian wine." They spoke like old friends, yet she hardly knew him. A few balls and a house party were not the stuff of confidants. Yet, here they were chatting about their lives with the ease of school chums. She almost laughed at the notion she might have attended school with a man. Besides, Anthony hadn't studied in England.

"I shall make it a point then." He smiled, and it made her breath catch.

"Did you attend university, my lord?" Still in her fantasy of being his school mate, she longed to feed the image.

His laugh was round, warm, and one might like to crawl inside the sound and stay a while. "I know you English think we Americans are all heathens, but I did attend the University of Pennsylvania. It's not been around as long as Cambridge, but it is a fine institution of more than sixty years."

Covering her giggle with her hand, she struggled to keep the amusement at bay. His pride and indignation made him sound almost an English gentleman.

"Why are you laughing?"

Unable to stop it, she let the full chortle out. "I was musing about our easy conversation and how we sounded like old school chums, but you sounded like a gauntlet had been thrown down."

"There is the Sylvia I remember." His smile lit his eyes, and the fire behind them burned through her.

Swallowing, she sobered. "Of course, I would never be allowed to attend university, but the notion is intriguing."

He crossed his arms and studied her. "I understand Bradford Academy in Massachusetts admits women, and Washington College in Maryland too. I thought I read about a woman in Sweden earning a degree, though I can't remember in what field."

Part of her was amazed that he knew such things. She would be even more shocked if what he said was true. Men did not follow the accomplishments of women. And yet… "Are you serious? I was only joking. I have no intention of becoming even more conspicuous by trying to go to university."

He frowned. "I only meant that if you wanted to study, it is not impossible."

"You would not say that if your sister took a notion to thwart society and do something outrageous." Her job was to be his Everton lady, not to spar with him at every opportunity. Yet, it was the most fun she'd had in years.

"I beg your pardon. I would support Sophia in whatever venture she chose. I'll admit that when I was younger, that might not have been the case, but I see no reason a woman can't do or be whatever she chooses."

"As long as it's someone's wife or mother." The words slipped out before she could stop them. She clamped her hand over her mouth. "I'm sorry, my lord. I had no right to speak to you that way. If you wish to have me replaced as your Everton lady, I will tell Lady Jane immediately."

During the long silence that followed, he studied her, shook his head and frowned. "I can't decide which sex you are harder on, Miss Dowder, mine or your own. Not all men are tyrants and not all women imbeciles waiting for a man to solve all their problems. You, of all people, should know that."

Her mouth was agape, and she had to force it closed as Lady Jane strode into the office with Mrs. Mary Horthorn in tow. "Lady Chervil apologizes but feels too exhausted for such a long and demanding assignment at this time. She's been reveling in the country with Lord and Lady Devonrose for over a month. However, Mrs. Horthorn is thrilled to help. Mrs. Mary Horthorn, the Earl of Grafton, and of course you already know Miss Dowder."

Mrs. Horthorn was thin as a rail. A good wind could blow her over. She favored a white cap with lace hanging to her shoulders and her gray hair in ringlets around her forehead. Kind and goodhearted, she often brought stray cats and dogs into the house until she found them homes. It happened so often that a pen and dog house had been built near the greenhouse in the garden. A warm smile accompanied Mary's mild expression. "I'm happy to be of service."

"It is a pleasure to meet you, Mrs. Horthorn. I'll admit when Lady Jane said a dowager would be required, I took the term more literally." Another man might have sounded haughty, but Anthony's comment held only curiosity.

Lady Jane said, "While some of our dowagers are literal titles, we use the term to describe a function. Mrs. Horthorn will act as chaperon and confidant to Miss Dowder. We do not send our ladies out with the possibility of ridicule. All social customs are expected to be adhered to."

There was that smile again. It was enough to drive a sensible girl into Bedlam. Ordering herself to keep her wicked mind at bay, she said, "I'm pleased to have you with me, Mrs. Horthorn. We shall have such fun decorating his lordship's home before we must get to serious work of dinner parties and balls."

Mary grinned.

Jane raised one eyebrow.

Unfettered by an English upbringing, Anthony laughed out loud. "I'm glad you see this as something fun, Miss Dowder. For me, it would be torture."

"You will not get off that easily, my lord. I will need your input. I cannot just rush out and purchase this and that without knowing what you want in your home. You must be comfortable in it once complete." Sylvia was pleased with how businesslike she sounded.

"I hadn't thought of that. I will have to live in the place after all the nonsense of parties is finished. Of course, I am at your disposal until the project is complete."

Jane went behind her desk. "I shall add both ladies to the contract, my lord, and they will begin tomorrow if that is satisfactory."

"Yes."

Sylvia asked, "Will you be available to give a tour of the house at eleven, my lord?"

He wrinkled his nose. "So late. Can we make it at nine?"

"That is not very fashionable for paying a call, my lord. As this is a business appointment, I shall be at your home at nine tomorrow morning."

"Until then." He bowed, and the glint in his eyes sent that warning bell ringing in the pit of Sylvia's stomach.

Chapter 2

Anthony had never liked waiting, but why he should be so anxious about Sylvia Dowder's arrival was a mystery. He had always thought she and her twin sister were spirited young ladies. It had been a shock to learn she'd been thrown over by Lord March. After seeing Sylvia at Everton House, Anthony wanted to give the newly raised viscount a sound thrashing. Being given a title is no reason to behave like an ass. March had broken a promise and it was unforgivable.

Pacing the foyer, he contemplated the black and white marble floor. The great clock struck nine, and just as the last chime sounded, the door knocker struck.

Anthony didn't wait for the butler to make his way from the servants' level. Rushing to the door, he pulled it open. "Miss Dowder, Mrs. Horthorn, welcome to Collington House."

Half a smile lifted Sylvia's full lips. "I realize you are American, my lord, but even you must realize it is uncommon for an earl to open his own door."

Wells, the butler, tugging on his waistcoat, rushed toward them. His stoic tone faltered for the first time. "My lord, a hundred apologies for being tardy. It is early for callers."

"It is my error, Wells. I invited the ladies from the Everton Domestic Society for a business meeting this morning and neglected to mention it."

In his normal monotone, Wells said, "Ladies, may I take your outerwear?"

Removing her peach pelisse, she revealed a pretty lavender day dress. She was like something out of a fairy tale, but with a wicked smile filled with mischief.

She thanked Wells, as did Mrs. Horthorn, and then they stared at Anthony.

Their expectant looks brought him out of his daydream. "Pardon me. Shall we tour the house, or do you require refreshment?"

Smiling as if amused by some joke only she heard, she said, "It was a short ride over from Everton House. At this hour there are few carriages on the road. If you please, we would like to get right to business."

"Of course." He longed to know what she was thinking behind that smile and still admired her directness.

Sylvia stared up at the thirty-foot ceiling in the foyer capped by a crystal chandelier that caught the morning light. Polished to a high shine, the wooden railing of the curved staircase enrobed the space. Her gaze swept down to the white marble with gray veins, then along the black accent tiles that formed geometric shapes in the floor and walls of the entry. "It's quite grand. This was Lady Collington's home?"

A pang of guilt tugged at his chest. "Yes. My great-aunt. I tried to get her to remain here, but she wouldn't hear of it. To be honest, I've never really understood the way people are thrust out of their homes due to entailments."

"It is the way of things," she said. "Women rarely inherit, and sometimes a cousin becomes the lord of the manor, thrusting a widow and daughters into the cold."

"I have not thrust anyone into the cold." His neck heated that she might think him so cruel. "My cousin's widow and daughter are comfortably living in the townhouse he purchased when his father died. I have arranged for them to have funds for the rest of their lives. I am not one of your thoughtless peers."

Wide-eyed, she gaped at him. "I did not mean to imply that you were. I only stated the fact that many families are displaced by entailment laws. It is very nice of you to take care of your cousins and aunt. Are you certain you can afford such an ongoing cost?"

"Am I to understand that it is rude for me to inquire about your status with your family and within the Everton Domestic Society, but you may inquire as to my finances?" He liked the way she colored the most delightful peach and it traveled down her chest, where it disappeared into the lace around her collar. Shaking himself, he brought his gaze back up to those warm blue eyes.

She checked with Mrs. Horthorn, who only shrugged. "I apologize. You're right, of course. The question was impertinent. It was only out of concern that your generous nature might leave you in the poorhouse."

Slightly off balance, charm beamed from Sylvia, and Anthony longed to see if her skin was a warm as it appeared. He shook off the notion. She was here to prove to his mother that he didn't need a wife. Getting doe-eyed over a slip of a girl was not in the plan. "My cousin invested wisely, and he left enough to care for his family. I am quite solvent in my own right, Miss Dowder. Your salary is secure."

Narrowing her eyes, she said, "You're teasing me."

He bowed. "Indeed."

"Perhaps you should commence the tour, my lord." She hid a smile behind her gloved hand.

"As you wish." He took her through all the downstairs rooms, including the ballroom, two parlors, dining room, breakfast room and study, before they trudged upstairs and saw the lady's parlor, several bedrooms and the master chamber.

Mrs. Horthorn cleared her throat. "It is unseemly for us to be in here."

The dark wood and dark fabrics that adorned Anthony's bedroom was a theme throughout the dour home. "I don't see how Miss Dowder can fix it, if she hasn't seen it."

Blushing but serious, Sylvia shrugged. "You are here and there's nothing sordid about our being in this room, Mrs. Horthorn. You realize, my lord, there is nothing wrong with this house as it is. It has been well kept and the furnishings are quite exquisite."

"It depresses me. I visited here several times when my aunt lived here, and the only room that is tolerable is the one Aunt Daphne updated for my sister, Sophia, when she came to live here."

Nodding, Sylvia sighed. "You mean the room with the lovely rose and cream colors."

"The rest of the house is a bore." He sat on the edge of his maroon-draped, four-post bed, and the air went out of him. If this was what an earl had to live with, he might have to let the crown take back his title.

Sitting in one of two brown overstuffed chairs near the hearth, she put her hands in her lap. "You are the one who has to live here. If you don't like the decor, we shall change it. However, I want to point out that the bedroom your sister lived in is not that much different from this one. Really it is only that the colors are lighter."

He sat up straight. "I don't want my house to be covered in rose damask, Miss Dowder."

Hiding her giggle, she looked more like the girl he'd known before that idiot March betrayed her. The sweet lightness was fleeting, and her expression turned serious. "No. But perhaps it is only a matter of heavy drapes and dark colors. If we had those bed curtains removed and changed the window drapes to a light gray, replaced the rug for something lighter and maybe these chairs, you might like this room more."

Hope blossomed inside him. "You think I'm mad not to like it as is, don't you?"

Ignoring the slight nod from Mrs. Horthorn, he focused on Sylvia as she ran her finger down her jaw to her pert chin.

"I think you must like the place where you live. This house is magnificent, but it is on the formal side. I think, with a few small changes you could be happy here."

Goodness, he liked her more than was comfortable. "Are you always so positive?"

Cocking her head, she gazed toward the window. "Not always, but this is a small problem. It is fixable. There are other things in life that are not so easily corrected as a rug or wall covering."

No matter how much he wanted to know what she'd meant, it would be rude to ask her to elaborate. He held his tongue. "If you would start with this room and my study, I would be eternally grateful."

"I will take care of it. May I enlist your staff for some of the work?" She stood and smoothed her skirt. The gesture was feminine and graceful.

Anthony was going to have to get this obsession with Sylvia under control. He couldn't understand what it was about her that intrigued him. She was pretty. Her brown hair caught the light, revealing gold flecks, but there were many pretty brunettes in London. She hadn't even shown much of that wicked sense of humor he'd liked so much when they'd met before, yet he knew it was in there clamoring to come out. Just an idle curiosity about a lady of breeding taking a position at the Society. Once he knew more about her, his interest would fade in short order. "The staff is at your disposal. I will inform Wells to help you in any way."

With a nod, she and Mrs. Horthorn preceded him out of the bedroom and down the stairs. Stopping at the front door, she accepted her pelisse from Wells. "Do you want to wait until the renovations are complete before going forward with the dinner party, my lord?"

He didn't like his new title but hated it more when she called him my lord. Perhaps he could get her to stop. Not yet, but soon. "I don't see that the two rooms we are beginning with must be used during a dinner party. If you feel something can be done with the parlor and the dining room, then perhaps a short delay."

"I can order fabrics for new curtains and we shall pull the old ones down at least. The rugs will take longer as we must import them." She tapped her chin again.

Noting she did this whenever she was deep in thought tickled him almost as much as his being able to solve the rug problem. "I have several rugs in a storage facility at the port. Perhaps we might find what we need there. They are waiting on one of my ships to transport them to Philadelphia, but as they belong to me already…"

Her eyes widened. "I thought you only transported spices, my lord."

"Mostly, but I hope to expand more and more. The textiles go over very well in America. You might find some appropriate fabric for drapes in storage as well. I will write to my man at the port and arrange an escort for you if you like. You cannot go there without some protection. The docks are no place for ladies." A knot formed in his belly, and he wished he hadn't mentioned his stores. The idea of any harm coming to either of the ladies because of him was unbearable.

"How exciting. I can check with Lady Jane and see if Everton's can supply an escort. There is no need for you to go to much trouble. I can make time next week to go to the warehouse." Bright with the idea of a new adventure, her eyes were mesmerizing.

Running his schedule for the following week through his mind, he planned to cancel several appointments to be at the warehouse. He would not have anything unpleasant occur. "I have the guest list for the dinner party if you have time to discuss it."

She checked the clock in the foyer. "I suppose I have a few minutes before my next appointment, my lord."

Following her into his study, he was lured by the gentle sway of her hips. Could she know how alluring she was? He guessed the episode with March had damaged her confidence. Fury at March staggered him.

"Are you all right, my lord?" Mrs. Horthorn asked.

Getting himself under control, he forced a smile. "Yes, madam. Thank you."

"It's just that you looked as if you might be planning to do someone harm."

Once again, his easily read facial expressions had betrayed him. "I assure you, I am well. I had a thought and unfortunately have no ability to hide my emotions without an effort."

Sylvia cocked her head as she sat by his desk. "What was the thought?"

"Miss Dowder," Mrs. Horthorn admonished. "That is not your business."

"Of course, you're right. I apologize."

"No need." There was little point in lying, as he was unskilled at it. "I was thinking of Lord March, and how foolish and ungentlemanly he is."

Her shock registered with wide eyes and bright red cheeks. "I…um…" She drew a long breath. "There is no need for you to be distressed by my past, my lord. Hunter has made his choice, and while not what I had planned for my life, I am quite happy at the Society."

"I'm glad to hear it, but I still think March should pay for his behavior." The only question was how to make the blackguard pay.

"You are not responsible for my honor or virtue, Lord Grafton. My parents had their chance to have a say and chose to honor the wishes of a peer. As a new member of the peerage, you might do well to follow their lead."

He laughed. "Are you worried I will make an enemy of March? No need. Any importance he retains is in his own head. He is not as well liked as his brother was, despite being the more outgoing of the two."

Sylvia cocked her head. "Is that so? Then perhaps I am better off not married to a man who is scorned by society even if it is behind his back."

Bowing, Anthony agreed. "You would have made Hunter Gautier tolerable."

She laughed but stifled it too quickly. "You had better show me that list, my lord."

Disappointed not to hear more of her laughter, he rounded the desk and pulled the guest list for the dinner party from a pile of papers he'd been sorting through earlier. "Miles Hallsmith is a particular friend of mine. He always makes a party more fun with his quick wit. The Duke and Duchess of Middleton are good friends as well. You will like Millie, and you have much in common."

Sylvia brightened. "She was an Everton lady. How nice it will be to meet her."

"I'm glad you think so." Making her smile sent a jolt of joy through Anthony. "My mother will attend, of course. Shall we invite your parents and your sister?"

A long sigh seemed to weigh her down. "That is very kind of you, my lord. I would love to have my sister come, but Mother can be difficult."

"I'll leave it to you to decide then."

"If you are sure it will not be an imposition, I will extend an invitation."

"Not at all. Invite anyone you wish." It was very comfortable planning an evening with Sylvia, but liking his Everton lady was not part of the plan.

"Very good." She rose and brushed out her skirt. "I will go to your warehouse on Monday then come back in a few days to speak to your cook about the meal."

Already anticipating seeing her in a few days, he still longed to keep her. "We could talk about it now if you like."

Her smile was warm and touched her eyes in a way that made him long to hear her thoughts. "I have another appointment this morning, my lord. What is a good time to go to meet with your warehouseman?"

An early riser, he preferred to get as much done in the morning hours as possible. "You might try the same time as you arrived here this morning. The working classes tend to get an early start," he said, attempting to sound like all the boring peers he'd met since arriving in London.

"I like the morning. The world seems fresh and rejuvenated." Walking to the front door, she bid him good day.

It was time for him to get to his own work. There was a stack of papers on his desk waiting for his signature, yet he stood at the window and watched as Mrs. Horthorn climbed into the carriage, leaving Sylvia to walk in the opposite direction. Fascinated, he pulled on the coat he'd just removed and followed her at a safe distance.

It was harder to follow once she climbed into a hack, but the busy hours of midday were approaching, and the carriage could not move fast. They entered the business end of town before she stepped out of the carriage and entered a building.

Anthony remained across the street, obscured by the crowd and the shadows of a doorway, until she was safely inside. He crossed the street to the door where she'd disappeared. The sign above read: The Weekly Whisper, Mr. Cole, Editor. The *Whisper* was a newspaper, but what could Sylvia be doing there? Did she have a secondary assignment from the Everton Domestic Society? He hated the jealousy tugging inside him. He must be losing his mind if he was jealous of his Everton lady spending time with another client. He should walk away and see to the matters of his import company. Miss Dowder would be at the warehouse on Monday, and maybe then he could find out more about her activities.

His feet wouldn't obey, and he stayed rooted to the spot outside the *Whisper*'s offices.

An hour later, he wished he'd brought his umbrella along as a light drizzle made him feel more foolish than curious. Then the door opened, and Sylvia stepped onto the street. She carried an umbrella, surveyed the darkening sky and opened it before heading back toward Everton House.

She hadn't seen him, and it occurred to him to just remain behind and let her walk on. Yet his feet and mouth would not agree to the safer, more English staid response. Anthony fell in step behind her. "I cannot help wondering why a fine lady, such as yourself, would take a hack to this area then spend more than an hour in the office of a newspaper."

With her eyes wide, she studied him a full beat before blinking. "Are you following me, my lord?"

"I was curious why you didn't return with Mrs. Horthorn."

The drizzle became a steady rain.

Dry under her umbrella, she narrowed those sharp blue eyes. "I can't see how that is any of your business."

Anthony flagged down a hack. "It is not, but I am still curious."

The carriage stopped, and he held the door open for her.

Frowning, she stepped in.

He sat across from her.

Those eyes were wide and shocked once again. "It is not proper for you to ride in a carriage alone with me, my lord. I realize you are American, but you must know that."

He called up to the hack to take them to his townhouse on Grosvenor Street. "Don't you find all these rules tedious, Miss Dowder?"

Amusement danced behind her eyes and she smiled. "That is not the point, my lord. They are still the rules by which we live."

"Like the fact that I must call you Miss Dowder and you call me my lord. Wouldn't it be simper if you called me Anthony and you granted me permission to call you Sylvia? Wouldn't that be the beginning of a friendship."

She patted her hair into place and tucked a wavy piece behind her ear. "We are not friends, my lord. You are the Earl of Grafton, and I am in your employ. I will do what you have paid the Everton Domestic Society for. Then we shall part ways and probably never see each other again. In fact, once our business is complete, the only time you will see this face is when you meet my sister, Serena, at a ball or event."

He forced the muscle in his jaw to relax. It always tightened and ticked when he became annoyed. "I think in order to be the hostess for my parties and whatnot, you and I will have to form some kind of friendship."

Her smile returned. "Perhaps, but I think my lord and Miss Dowder will have to do for now."

"Then perhaps you would tell me what you were doing for over an hour in that office."

The carriage crawled through the wet, busy streets, and Sylvia gazed out the window. A few moments went by, and Anthony worried how far he could push her before she asked for someone else to take his assignment. Not that it should matter to him which Everton lady played hostess or redecorated his home. Still, he hated the idea of another lady or being set aside by Sylvia. He too watched out the window.

"If I tell you, you must promise to keep it to yourself, and I will require one of your secrets that I will keep." She peered directly in his eyes.

A bubble of excitement spread through him. "I agree. In fact, I will tell you my secret first."

She nodded. "What is your secret?"

"I do not want to be an earl. I have never sought to join the ranks of English peers, and I hate that it was thrust upon me. If I could, I would give the title over to my cousin Lavender, but I'm told that a woman cannot carry the title. I tried to refuse it, but my aunt Daphne was appalled at the idea that I would let our family title revert to the crown or go to some distant cousin no one had ever met. I love my aunt and could not disappoint her, so here we are. I told only my momma. My aunt assumes I came to my senses and am happy with my new designation, when in truth, I hate it. Though I'll admit, the attention in ballrooms is very nice." Power and title were everything to these English.

"I sympathize, my lord, but you said as much at Everton House, so it is not really a secret. At least, not to me."

She was right; he had disclosed more at their meeting than he had to the people closest to him in six months. The way she looked at him or perhaps the sweet tone of her voice pulled information from him. "Here is something no one knows. I am going to live in Italy. I'm not sure when I will leave or how long I will live there. I think I may stay forever and make wine."

She stared at him. "You would run away?"

Of course, she couldn't understand. No one in all of England could fathom his desire to escape and live his own life. "I would follow my own path. In the meantime, I have secured the title for my nephew or a son of my own, should I ever have one. I will hire a steward to see to my tenants and holdings here."

Her gaze never wavered from his. "Now, that is a big secret. You do not want the thing that most men will envy you for. But won't you miss your family and the friends you have made here in the last few years?"

"Of course. I'm not heartless. I have not left yet because I love my family, and I have been tempted to jump on the next transport several times. I preferred enjoying London when no one paid me any attention and my responsibilities were not so grand. Enough about me. Now tell me your secret."

She drew a long breath that pushed her small breasts up near the edge of her dress. "I write a weekly article about the goings-on at balls and in parlors for the *Weekly Whisper*."

"You write gossip in the paper?"

"Only harmless gossip. Though occasionally I right a wrong when someone deserves it." Crossing her arms over her chest, she dared him to contradict her.

"What is the name of your column?"

"Merryweather Mirth by Mable Tattler."

"You wrote that bit about old Henry Cornwash falling in his pudding at the Harbinger dinner party. I laughed for half an hour when I read that. Henry can't hold his brandy."

"And he's a nasty drunk who embarrassed little Emily Marsden and made her cry that same night." Her cheeks pinked as she justified her attack.

"So, you avenge the downtrodden?" He'd never met a lady who had employment before, and now it seemed that Sylvia Dowder had not one job but two. She was fascinating.

Frowning, she turned back to the weather. "I do what I can, my lord. I think that is enough secrets for one day. Don't you?"

He leaned back against the cushion. They had made their way out of the busy section of town and now rolled freely toward his townhouse. "I suppose we must leave some for another day."

The carriage slowed to a stop, and she glared at him. "What makes you think I will share any more of my secrets with you?"

Stepping down, Anthony considered her question. He turned back and said, "It seems to me you and I both needed a confidant, Miss Dowder. I predict that when you see how well I keep this secret of yours, you will be happy for someone to talk to. I further predict that in a short time you will be calling me by my Christian name."

She crossed her arms and frowned but made no comment.

Once the door was closed, he gave the driver directions to Everton House and watched until it rounded the corner. He would be behind on his work for the day, but somehow it had been worth it. Sylvia Dowder, Everton lady, intrigued him, and his curiosity had to be satisfied. He never dreamed she would be going to her second place of employment. It was an idle curiosity and nothing more, but it had been fun to exchange secrets. What other news did Sylvia Dowder hold close to her breast? It was none of his business. She was right that once their business was complete, she would move on to another assignment and it was unlikely they would meet often or at all. Still, he enjoyed her wit, and the way her mind worked when they had met before she joined Everton's.

Deciding the next few months would be fun rather than a chore, he left his coat and headed to his office. A fire in the hearth helped him shake off the cool rain.

Only the day before, he'd been dreading the entire process of showing himself to his contemporaries as a new earl, and now, it would be a laugh. His gray day turned around by a pair of blue eyes and a wicked smile. Sylvia Dowder had changed his perspective. What else would she change before they parted ways?

Chapter 3

Every Tuesday Sylvia did her daughterly duty and went to tea at her parents' townhouse. Anthony was right about one thing, it was better to have told someone her secret than to keep it bottled up. For her entire life, she had enjoyed keeping secrets with her twin. Now it was difficult to keep that relationship the same. She loved her sister, but their lives were taking different directions and it was harder to relate. When they had been young and looking for husbands together, it had all been a laugh. Those days were gone.

She climbed the stairs to the townhouse where she had come out to society and spent many seasons. Before she could strike the knocker, Elijah, the butler, opened the door. "Good day, Miss Sylvia. Your mother and sister are already in the parlor."

With a smile, she stifled a sigh. "Thank you, Elijah. I hope you are well."

"Tolerably, miss." He never smiled, but she saw the amusement behind those gray eyes.

"Are all the servants in good health?" There were some people and things she missed about living at home. She rarely heard about the staff and missed many of them.

"Mary, the under-maid, was down with a cold last week, but has recovered. Everyone else is in good health and spirits. They wanted to line up to greet you today, but the lady of the house said it was unseemly to do so in this case."

Mother didn't want any attention taken away from Serena. Sylvia could understand that. Her sister should get her due after all the years taken up with Sylvia's courting and wedding nonsense. And since it all came to nothing but scandal, it was time Serena was put forward. "I would have loved to see everyone, but Mother is right. There is no need to make a fuss."

There was almost a frown before he righted his expression to the benign butler she'd grown up with. "As you say, miss."

Sylvia walked with Elijah to the parlor door, which he opened. "Enjoy your visit, Miss Sylvia."

"Thank you."

Mother and Serena turned from their conversation when she entered. Mother frowned.

Jumping up from her seat, Serena grinned brightly before running over and dragging Sylvia into her arms. She was a vision in a pale-yellow dress with lace on both the sleeves and neckline. "Oh, Sylvie, how I have missed you. You look just the same."

"You look lovely, Serena. Is that a new dress?" Hugging her twin was like lifting a heavy weight from her shoulders. Everything inside Sylvia eased as if she were home.

"Mother and I have been to the modiste and ordered all new dresses and gowns for my season."

"Enough, Serena. There is no need to run about like a common girl. We do not kiss and hug like farmers. Where are your manners?" Mother's sharp reprimand cut through the joy.

"It is only family here, Mother." Sylvia should have kept quiet, but her mother's constant need for propriety forced her hand.

"Family lives under the same roof. As you have chosen to leave us behind and behave like a servant, I see no reason to treat you like family. It is enough that you are afforded the honor of taking tea with us." Felicia Dowder could be cruel when she felt wronged, and in the case of Sylvia leaving home after her ruined engagement, Mother was hurt, and this type of backlash was not unusual.

Still… "If that is how you feel, our weekly visits can be suspended. There is no need for you to toil with the servants."

Gertrude brought in the tea and gave Sylvia a smile. No one spoke until the petite gray-haired maid left the parlor.

"You are here and still my daughter, regardless of how you choose to live. I know I did my best with you. I explained about men. If that Walter Gautier had just stayed alive for another few months, you would be a viscountess." It was the best Felicia could do.

Sylvia made a curtsy for Mother. "I'm sure Lord March would have liked to remain among the living. I'm sure being married to Hunter would have been an unhappy state, since now we know his character. However, I am grateful to come to tea, Mother. I do love you and would hate to think I would never see you again."

"Unhappy? You would be married…"

Serena gasped. "Come and sit, Sylvie. We have the most delightful treats with our tea. I think Cook made your favorite biscuits too."

"That was very kind." Sylvia sat on the divan next to Serena, who gripped her hand too tight, almost desperately.

"What is new at the Everton Domestic Society?"

"I have a new assignment. I am to be hostess for the new Earl of Grafton. He needs some assistance with a few parties and the like." The mention of Anthony sent a bubble of excitement through Sylvia that she squashed down as quickly as possible.

"We heard that Anthony Braighton had earned the title after his cousin's death. I felt quite sorry for Lady Collington. She has always been kind to me." Serena rarely had a cross thought about anyone.

Mother, on the other hand, was not as benevolent. "An American with an English title is an atrocity. Don't get any ideas about an earl, Sylvia. Men are all the same. He will ruin you and toss you aside just like March. These men only care for possessions, and we have only enough to dower Serena after your disaster. All those years wasted keeping you in finery so Hunter would propose. All that money that might have been used to dower you both had you secured him more quickly. I should have demanded a special license after your engagement."

"First of all, Hunter did not ruin me. He only created a small scandal and behaved badly. You could not have known he would betray us. Second, there is nothing between Lord Grafton and me. I work for him, nothing more. As far as him being American, he lives here now, and his father was English. Besides, he came by the title honestly. He was the next male heir. I cannot think how they could have denied him his due." There was no need to defend Anthony, yet she couldn't help herself.

With a huff, Mother sipped her tea. "How do you manage to play at hostess without ruining what's left of your reputation?"

The bite and implication of the question sent the hair on the back of Sylvia's neck on edge. "I have a widowed lady who works with me to keep everything above board. You know that, Mother. I have explained the workings of the Society to you."

"That Society of yours is an abomination. Stealing nice girls away from their families with hope of independence and money of their own. I should have chained you to the house, locked you in the bedroom, and your poor father…" Felicia dabbed fake tears with a bit of lace handkerchief.

The scathing reply on the tip of Sylvia's tongue was stopped by Serena. "Mother, Sylvie and I are going to walk in the garden. You mentioned letters you needed to write. We don't want to keep you from that task. We know how much you enjoy your letter writing."

Looking at the small lady's desk in the corner, Felicia took a long breath. "Very well. I know you girls want to catch up on gossip. Sylvia, I would like it if you would accompany us to the Wainwright ball on Friday. Your sister has several suitors who will be attending, and it would be nice if the entire family supported her."

While her mother's expression resembled a woman who'd eaten bad fish, the pleading in Serena's eyes made Sylvia cave in. "I will be there. Thank you for the invitation."

"Try to look like a lady."

"I shall do my best." Sylvia's chest burned with a thousand scathing remarks.

Serena took her hand and yanked her out the door and toward the back of the house. Once in the garden, she kept hold but stopped pulling. "It does no good to provoke her. You and I know she is wrong about nearly everything, but why argue when you can just enjoy the good weather?"

Slipping her arm through the crook at Serena's elbow, Sylvia gave a squeeze. "You are right. She knows just how to fire up my temper, and you have always been the sweeter twin. I wish I could have just rolled on with my life after Hunter broke off our engagement. It would have been simpler."

"Maybe, but you would have been unhappy."

"I thought you would want me to stay at home and cry in my pudding." Sylvia held her shock at bay. Serena had wept openly when Sylvia had told her she was leaving home.

Leading them down a crooked path that led to a gazebo where they always sat and shared their secrets, Serena sighed. "I would never wish you to be miserable, Sylvie. When you told me you were leaving, I was selfish. I wanted you to stay for me. However, in the months since you went to Everton Domestic Society, I have noticed how happy you seem. Your life is not what we expected, but it seems fulfilling and exciting. I'm not like Mother, no matter what you may think."

"I never thought you were like her." Sitting on the bench in the gazebo, Sylvia faced Serena and took both her hands. "If I could have gone on as before, I would have done it for you. I just couldn't. Mother was so disappointed and blamed me for Hunter's behavior. I couldn't take it."

"I know." Like lifting a shade up, Serena smiled and shook off the unpleasantness. "I'm so happy you will be at the ball on Friday. I have two prospective suitors: Lord Stansfield and Sir Henry Parker. They are both very nice, but Lord Stansfield might be too stuffy."

"How do you mean?"

With of cock of her head, she gave a stare that meant it should be obvious. "I cannot marry anyone who would forbid me from seeing you, Sylvie. I'm not saying Stansfield would do that, but I need to find out before I let Mother get her claws into him. He is an earl, and I can't forget what March did to you."

A tight knot formed in Sylvia's chest. It hadn't occurred to her that her sister's husband might reproach her choices to the point of keeping them apart. "I would appreciate it if you would not marry anyone who would be so cruel, and not just because I would hate to be separated from you, Serena. A man who would keep twins apart is not a nice man. I hope you will marry someone kind and caring, maybe even someone who loves you."

"Love would be nice, but it might be too much to ask at our age." She shrugged and laughed.

While she and Serena were identical twins, a few people noted subtle differences. It was easy to fool a new nanny when they were young. After a time, they would notice Serena's left eyebrow was slightly higher, or that Sylvia had a small scar on her jaw where she had fallen from a horse and hit a rock. Serena's smile was a bit wider, and she tended to show more teeth. These were little things, and people rarely could tell them apart. As Sylvia watched Serena, she realized they were more different than she'd ever thought. For all his betrayal, Sylvia had loved Hunter, and he'd broken her heart. At the very least, she thought she loved him. In retrospect, it was more wanting to be in love than being in the state.

"I'm not sure I could do without love in my marriage, Serena. Are you sure you can?"

"I love you, Sylvie, and that is enough. I needn't love a man and have him hurt me the way Hunter hurt you. They are unfeeling and unkind by nature. I would do best to find one I can tolerate, and who leaves me to live my own life. That is all I want." There was no deception in Serena's expression. She fully believed what she said.

"It makes me sad that my experience and Hunter's deplorable behavior have soured you on love." A dull ache started in Sylvia's gut. This was all her fault. She should have been a better fiancée. Then the person dearest to her would not be in this state.

"Don't be. It was a valuable lesson. The same thing will never happen to me. Not only will I never allow any man to touch my heart, I shall demand a short engagement. I'll be married and out of this house before the season is out. Mark my words." Serena gave a definitive nod, indicating there was no talking her out of her goal.

"Then I shall stand by you as you are married, Serena. It will be a wonderful day and the beginning of the life you wish for."

The conversation turned to gowns for Friday's ball, and an hour later, Sylvia took a hack home without ever seeing her mother again. It was just as well. Even at the ball she would have to politely greet Felicia then avoid her.

* * * *

Several times between Tuesday and Friday Sylvia considered not going to the Wainwright ball. Ultimately, she couldn't disappoint her sister and when her parents' carriage pulled up to Everton House, she was dressed in a green gown that was darker than was fashionable for a debutant but not so dark it would turn heads. The color made her think of springtime and how the new leaves fill in the winter branches.

She removed her pelisse, and her mother said, "I thought you might wear something more appropriate, Sylvia."

"You look lovely," Serena said before Sylvia and her mother started a row in the foyer.

Mother pursed her lips. "I see Sir Henry is already here. Perhaps you might introduce your sister once he seeks you out, Serena."

Taking Sylvia by the hand, Serena hurried them into the ballroom.

Within two minutes, a tall fellow, with golden hair cropped short and a navy coat that showed off his broad shoulders, navigated the crowd and found them near the hearth. He never glanced at Sylvia but studied Serena before he bowed. "You are looking very lovely this evening, Miss Dowder."

"Thank you, Sir Henry. May I introduce my sister, Miss Sylvia Dowder?"

There was a moment when his face, which was generally handsome, grew ugly, then he bowed. "A pleasure to meet you, Miss Sylvia."

Perhaps she had imagined it. He was the perfect gentleman in every other way. "Nice to meet you, Sir Henry. I hear only nice things about you from my sister."

"I'm sure Miss Dowder is too kind. Though I am pleased to hear she has a good opinion of me. To that end, Miss Dowder, might I ask for the first dance?"

Serena blushed. "Yes, I would be delighted."

After a bow to them both, he took long strides toward a group of young men on the other side of the room. After a moment, the men turned and looked in their direction.

"I think they are talking about us," Sylvia said as lightly as she could manage.

"Hmm. I think Sir Henry is not as much of a gentleman as he pretends to be." The blush was gone from Serena's cheeks and replaced by a narrowed gaze.

"Serena, you can't toss off men because they disapprove of me. In the ton you will be refusing them all. I shall never be liked by men of good standing because of my choices." She would not allow any of these people to hurt her, and she would try to keep them from injuring her sister as well.

Before Serena had time to respond, Anthony Braighton bowed before them. "Miss Dowder, Miss Sylvia, it is good to see you both."

If he had not spoken with his American accent, he could have easily passed for the most dashing Englishman in the room. His dark hair shone in the candlelight, and his warm skin was just a shade lighter than olive. He was all grace and charm in a black jacket and tan trousers. His very fine legs were well defined, and every woman in the room turned to watch him. "I did not expect to see you here, my lord."

"William Wainwright is a good friend of mine. He asked me to come at his mother's behest." He pulled a sour face that made her giggle.

Serena turned sharply at the sound then looked at Anthony. "I have been wanting to congratulate you on your new title, my lord, and to tell you how sorry I was to hear about your cousin's passing. I hope your aunt is not suffering too badly."

"Thank you, Miss Dowder. My aunt is the strongest person I know, but it is hard on her to have lost my father and now her son. She complains that an entire generation has fallen before her eyes and yet she still remains." Caring and sorrow burned behind his eyes, and it endeared him even more than his charm and wit.

Sylvia shook off thoughts that would do her no good and could lead to disaster. "It is fortunate she has you and your sister to comfort her."

"My momma also spends a lot of time with Aunt Daphne. She is well attended, and as I said, very strong. Miss Sylvia, may I ask for the second dance? I'm afraid I promised William I would dance with his sister for the first."

Saying no would be the prudent thing to do. "You have no obligation to dance with me, my lord."

His smile could melt the most hardened lady. "Dancing is never an obligation. It is a pleasure."

"I—thank you, my lord." She had no other choice but to curtsy and accept his invitation.

With a bow, he walked away. The music was about to start, and he found Lillette Wainwright and took the floor.

Serena raised a brow. "Now I wish I had said no to this first dance, Sylvie. I think I want to hear more about the newest earl in England."

"There is nothing to tell. Go and dance. Here comes your partner." Sylvia had no idea what she would tell anyone about Anthony. He was the most unusual man.

Determined not to watch her sister dance or Anthony turn about the floor with Miss Wainwright, Sylvia surveyed the room for someone she knew and was happy to discover the Countess of Marlton smiling at her from across the room. Sophia was always nice to her, and despite her being Anthony's sister, she would make a good distraction.

As Sylvia approached, Sophia's smile brightened. She and Anthony looked very much alike with those arresting golden eyes and dark hair. "Miss Sylvia Dowder, how wonderful to see you. How are you?"

"I'm surprised you can tell me from my sister, my lady. Most people cannot." Sylvia curtsied. There was something wonderful about the naturalness with which Americans approached every conversation. It put her at ease.

"I will admit that I guessed based on your gown. Your sister tends toward paler shades. I understand you are to help my brother with his venture into earldom."

People of the ton rarely took note of anything other than their own concerns, or perhaps something they could gossip about. It was nice to be noticed for herself. "His lordship is my assignment and I will do what I can to help him."

"I think you will do very well, Miss Sylvia. You have always impressed me as a woman with a keen sense of humor and a sharp mind. Anthony needs to be amused, or he gets distracted. His new title has given him more attention from the ladies than is healthy, I think." She glanced over the dancers and grinned.

"He seems capable of amusing himself, my lady. I am only hired to arrange his parties and decorate his house to suit him better, and I have no wish to control his social life." Sylvia couldn't say why the implication that Anthony had a short attention span annoyed her. Sophia was his sister, and she very well might be teasing.

"My brother is out of his element, is all I meant. He will do well for himself and those entrusted to him. I have no doubt." Her smile never dimmed. "I understand your sister is all the rage this season."

"I hope she will have an offer soon. It is what she wishes." Finding Sir Henry and Serena striking a fine figure of a couple as they danced made Sylvia ponder the unpleasant look that had crossed Sir Henry's face.

Sophia inched closer. "I'm pleased you have not mourned the loss of Lord March. I never thought him good enough for you."

Taken by surprise, Sylvia didn't know what to say. "That is kind of you to say."

"It is the truth. His brother was a bore, but a good man. It is tragic that he was not of a stronger constitution. The younger brother has proved himself to be untrustworthy, and you are far better off without him."

"I wish my mother shared your opinion, my lady." Keeping quiet would have been prudent, but the Countess of Marlton had opened the door, and Sylvia would not be still.

Instead of the censure she'd expected, Sophia's grin brightened. "You will do well, Miss Sylvia. I have noted ladies who choose the Everton Domestic Society are made of strong stuff. I have no doubt you will succeed."

The music ended, and Anthony escorted his partner to her friends before walking toward them. Several ladies stopped him to flirt, and he obliged each one. It took him several minutes, but he finally managed to join Sylvia and Sophia. "Are you talking about me?" His bright teasing tone lightened Sylvia's mood.

Sophia slapped him on the shoulder with her fan. "You are not the center of the world."

"Yet I should be." He exaggerated a sad face complete with puppy dog eyes and protruding bottom lip. It was adorable.

"You will have to be satisfied with being the center of Momma's world, Tony. The rest of us have our own lives to live."

He bowed dramatically. "Where is Daniel?"

At the mention of her husband, Sophia's gaze softened, and a warmth entered her eyes. "He and Tom went to White's. I came on my own as a favor to the hostess."

The master of ceremonies cleared his throat and announced a waltz.

"Miss Sylvia, I believe I have this dance."

She placed her hand on his sleeve and followed him onto the dance floor. His unique scent made her want to lean in and take a deep breath. The inappropriate thought made her cross. "You did not need to dance with me, my lord. I am in your employ."

"Do you think you might call me Tony or Anthony while we dance?"

"Why would I do that?" She swallowed down the thrill of being offered his familiar name.

Tightening his hold on her, he pulled her an inch closer. "Because if you are to act as my hostess, we are going to become friends, Sylvia. I have given this a great deal of thought since the carriage ride the other day. You are determined to remain professional and I respect that. However, I feel there is something to be gained by the familiarity of being on a first-name basis. I'm not asking you to shout it across a crowded room, but as my sister enjoys a friendship with Thomas Wheel, you and I might call each other by our names in private."

The entire conversation was outrageous. He whirled her effortlessly around the dance floor to the beat of three and they never missed a step. Yet, they spoke of something simply forbidden between two adults of opposite genders. "It would be highly out of order."

He shrugged. "You are already unusual just because you have chosen a profession over finding some sot to marry. Why not go just a tad further and call me Tony? No one would know, and it would be the second secret we shared."

"Tony." Wanton and wrong, it fell from her lips. She couldn't help wishing she could call it across a room full of peers.

His white teeth shone with his broad smile. "It sounds splendid coming from you, Sylvia."

"Sylvie," she said. "My good friends call me Sylvie."

Rubbing his thumb back and forth over the back of her hand sent a charge up her arm, and it spread through her like a fire out of control. She swallowed down whatever had come over her. "What day would you like to have the dinner party?"

Immediately missing the soft innocent caress, she was sorry she'd turned the conversation toward business. She should have just enjoyed the dance and kept her mouth shut.

As he thought, his gaze wandered and lost focus until he spoke. "I was thinking that Wednesday after next might do if you think you can manage it by then."

"I will need to come and speak with your cook, housekeeper, and butler to make sure you have the proper staff for a party. I'm sure that will be enough time."

"Good. If you come later in the week, I have something I want to show you after you speak to the staff. The weather has been very fine, and I have an open carriage, so our traveling together will be completely within your silly English rules." He turned her too quickly, and her breast brushed his lapel.

Her breath caught. "Where are we going?"

"It's a surprise. I promise it will only take a couple of hours; then I shall bring you directly back unscathed." His reply came quickly and with a serious note.

"I trust you, Tony." The strange thing was she meant it. He was honest and direct. Unlike any man she had ever known, there was no hidden agenda with Anthony Braighton. He was exactly what he seemed. Incapable of lying, since everything he thought was clear in his expression. It was not very English, and she liked it more than she should.

His cheeks pinked just enough that one had to study him to notice. "I'm delighted to hear that."

When the music ended, she longed for a few more bars, so she could stay in his arms. Then she immediately squashed the sentiment and curtsied to him before thanking him for the dance. She found Serena talking to a tall man by the hearth.

Lord Stansfield was handsome, but not in the conventional way. He had brown hair and eyes, and there was something rugged about him. He had not shaved for the evening, and when Sylvia approached, he blinked several times before seeming to understand. "You have a twin."

Serena hid a giggle behind her gloved hand. "Yes, my lord. Most people know that I have a twin sister. This is Miss Sylvia Dowder."

His eyes narrowed before he bowed. "You are the one who has taken up with the Everton Domestic Society."

With a curtsy, Sylvia met his gaze. "I am employed there, my lord."

"Fascinating. And how do you find the work?" He leaned on the mantel then realized it was not appropriate and stood up straight.

"It is quite satisfying and challenging." She raised her chin and kept eye contact. Not even the earl, who might become her brother-in-law, would turn her into a coward.

"Will you continue there indefinitely?"

"I have few options, my lord. Many Everton ladies remain with the Society until they retire or become dowagers, a designation given to women who assist the ladies. If I am still with them when I am of an age, I will likely choose to keep helping people." She saw no disgust or dismissal in Lord Stansfield, only curiosity.

"I'm sure you will help many people if you are compassionate like your sister." His lips twitched, and half a smile appeared.

Serena had been silent, but she took a step closer. "Since we have been courting, my lord, I think it important I tell you, I will not be kept away from my sister, no matter what she decides to do with her life."

He looked from one twin to the other and back at Serena. "I would think a man who attempted to erect such a wall would be a fool."

The tightness in Sylvia's gut eased, and Serena's shoulders relaxed.

He bowed to Sylvia then turned to Serena. "I believe I have this dance, Miss Dowder."

She watched them join the quadrille. He wasn't what she expected. Perhaps a bit rough by the ton's standards, but he wasn't the stern man Serena described. In fact, he was reasonable, and she liked the Earl of Stansfield far more than Sir Henry. It was nice Serena had choices.

Anthony handed her a glass of wine. "It's not very good wine, but it's all that is available. I thought you might like a glass."

"Thank you." She sipped the watery vintage. "Do you know a lot about wine?"

"It is one of my greatest passions. My family has a vineyard in Italy. I spent a few summers there tending the vines and learning about wine." He watched the dancers.

"That must have been wonderful. I think I would like to travel someday. Perhaps I can save enough money to do so in a few years." It was wonderful to speak of such things and know he would not think her a mad woman. Somehow, she knew he would be amiable to a woman deciding to travel.

"You will need to hire someone to protect you. When you are ready to go, come and see me. I have some contacts and can help you with your plans."

Liking Anthony Braighton was not against any rules, but she had never thought of a client as anything more than that. Anthony was succeeding in becoming her friend. She would have to search the *Everton Companion, Rules of Conduct* for any advice in such cases. "That is very kind. Most men would think the idea foolish. In fact, most women would as well. If you are still in England when I'm ready to travel, I shall seek your counsel."

Worry marred his expression. He was so easy to read, it must be embarrassing for him more often than not. "I think we have established that you and I are not like most people." He nodded toward the dance floor. "Your sister could do worse than Stansfield. He's a good man with a lot of money and good sense."

"I only met him for a moment, but I liked him. He seemed thoughtful, a rare commodity among the ton." Sylvia liked the slight blush in Serena's cheeks as she talked to Stansfield. She always tried to look disinterested but was failing with her current suitor. Maybe that was a good sign.

Lady Nelda Abernathy's voice carried across the crush of people. "You will come to no good, Eliza. Flirting only leads to ruination. I am ashamed of you, and you will break your mother's heart."

Tears streamed down Eliza Pollard's blotchy cheeks, and her pale hair came loose from its chignon. "I only said I would dance with him, my lady."

"He is a scoundrel, and you must know better."

Eliza's gaze shifted around the onlookers. "Please, keep your voice down. I have done nothing wrong."

"Don't you dare tell me how to behave. Harlot!"

Tears coming in earnest, Eliza rushed for the ballroom exit toward the lady's retiring room.

Anthony dipped his head and whispered, "I think I have had enough bad wine and marriage-mart mommas for one night. I will see you Monday, Sylvie."

"Good evening, Tony." It was far more intimate than was proper, despite their being in plain sight of half of society. A thrill ran up her spine. It wasn't a crime to share secrets, but it felt a bit wicked, and she liked it. She had to force the grin building inside her from her lips before anyone else realized her wanton thoughts.

With a stern look in Nelda Abernathy's direction, Sylvia rushed after poor Eliza. On her way up to the lady's retiring room, she glimpsed Anthony escorting an actress who had arrived with Sir Edward Grant out of the house. It shouldn't matter, but a vise tightened around her heart and bile rose in her throat. Shaking herself back into a reality where Anthony Braighton was just her client, she continued up the stairs.

Chapter 4

An Everton footman, who was particularly strong of figure, accompanied Sylvia and Mrs. Horthorn to the Braighton warehouse near the port. He took his assignment very seriously, and Anthony was glad to see someone capable watching over the ladies as they perused the textiles.

Anthony approached the stack of rugs, where several of his workers were peeling back layers for the ladies to get a better look. "Miss Dowder, have you found anything you like?"

The footman grumbled and stepped between Anthony and the women.

"It's all right, Bertram. This is Lord Grafton. He is our client."

Bowing, Bertram stepped back. "I apologize, my lord."

"Not at all. You're a good man with a rather large responsibility. I'm pleased you take it to the extreme." Anthony meant every word. It was good to know the Society had their ladies' safety in mind.

"Indeed, my lord. I shall not let any harm come to my charges." Bertram resumed his guard duty.

Joining the ladies, Anthony repeated his question.

Her smile bright, Sylvia bubbled with glee. "I have tagged no less than six beautiful rugs that will be stunning in your house. I spied so many fabrics on the walk back here. I can't wait to put my mark on those for new curtains throughout. You are going to be very happy, my lord."

Watching her enthusiasm started a thrill bubbling inside Anthony. He couldn't remember anyone else's delight giving him so much joy. This Everton lady was driving him insane, and he had no desire to stop the madness. "I'm glad you are finding my stores useful."

"I cannot believe how many beautiful things you are shipping off to America when you could easily sell all of this here in England." She shook her head at the next rug, and Pete pulled the next one over.

"I do sell some here when they come in from the East, but these were designated for Philadelphia. I assure you your countrymen are not being slighted for the savages in America."

She peered up with her mouth open, and he longed to kiss those full lips. "I did not mean to imply the people in Philadelphia didn't deserve such beautiful things. Only that it is a great expense to ship the rugs and fabrics, and they would be accepted here."

"I am teasing you, Miss Dowder. My country will get their fair share of beautiful things, and England has already met the quota." Flustering Sylvia could become a bad habit. He stifled a sigh.

She gave the most darling huff and hid her smile. "I suppose I deserved that. Would you like to approve the rugs here, my lord, or wait until they are in your house?"

"I trust you, Miss Dowder. I have no doubt that whatever you pick will be what I am looking for to lighten the mood at Collington House."

"As you wish," she said. "Peter, I think we are done here. Can you arrange for the rugs I've picked to be delivered this week?"

Pete was one of the toughest men Anthony had ever met, but he blushed at her regard like a schoolboy. "I will see to it myself, miss."

"Thank you. You are too kind."

"Do you want to look at the fabric now, miss?" He clutched it in one hand then combed his fingers through his thinning hair.

"Yes. Please." She walked back toward the front of the warehouse. Mrs. Horthorn, Pete, and Bertram trailing, and Anthony took up the rear. "You know, my lord, you need not be here. I can handle all of this, and Bertram will keep us safe."

"It is my warehouse and you are in my employ. I feel quite determined to see that no harm comes to you, and while I know Bertram is fully capable, I would feel better if I saw you safely into your carriage."

She waved a hand. "As you wish."

An hour later, the bolts of fabric were loaded into the Everton carriage. Sylvia would see that they were delivered to a seamstress she had contracted to make the curtains in short order.

* * * *

Three days later, Anthony watched the exchanges between his staff and Sylvia. Cook, the housekeeper, Mrs. Colms, and the butler, Wells, fell all over themselves to help her. They liked her immediately and wanted to do whatever they could to make her job easier. It was the most animated he had ever seen the stoic butler. She got a better response than Anthony, and he was the earl.

"My lord, you will need two more footmen. Her ladyship kept a minimal staff, as she did not entertain. I would think an additional maid might be in order as well. Will that be a problem?" Sylvia looked up from the long wooden table below stairs, where she sat with his staff hashing out what needed to be done to host a dinner party in less than a week.

They all stared at him and waited.

"I have no objections. In fact, you may all take your orders from Miss Dowder while she assists me for the next few months. She knows better than I what we need at this time." He shouldn't like to have someone else ordering his staff about, but Sylvia slid into the role seamlessly.

"Thank you, my lord. Not having to check every small decision with you will make this process go faster. In fact, you needn't remain below with us if you have other tasks this morning." She returned her attention to the list in front of her, and he was dismissed.

At the top of the stairs, he went to his library where an oversized desk filled one corner of the massive room.

The library loomed around him. He was still staring at the hundreds of books, lost in thoughts of Sylvia, the staff, the ugly decor, and what he planned when she'd finished with the staff.

As if thinking of her made her appear, she knocked gently on the inside of the open door. "Am I interrupting some deep thoughts?"

He stood. "Just daydreaming and wondering how you will make this room tolerable."

She stepped farther inside and glanced around. "Do you need a desk that large?"

"No one needs a desk this big." He leaned on the edge of the massive piece.

"The curtains will be here on Monday next. A lighter fabric will go a long way. I will order you a smaller desk. Then we will move the furniture around to create two smaller groupings for conversation and reading by the windows. The rug is quite nice and might do once we change the rest." She continued to examine the room.

Everything she said made sense, though he couldn't picture it. He liked the way her expression turned confident when she talked of hiring footmen and changing curtains. "Did your meeting downstairs go well?"

"Yes. You have a fine staff, if a little shorthanded. Wells and Mrs. Colms will handle the hiring. They know the best people. You can meet with your new staff in a few days and make sure you like each of them. Now, what did you want to show me, Tony?" She propped her fists on her slim hips and appeared about to do battle. The stern set of her jaw and intense stare were probably meant to warn him off.

He couldn't help laughing. "Don't look as if I'm kidnapping you for nefarious purposes, Sylvie. I just want to show you something. It's only an hour or so by carriage."

Narrowing her gaze, she remained cautious. "Very well. We had better go then. Cook said to tell you the basket you requested will be in the carriage."

Mrs. Horthorn sat waiting in the foyer. When they exited the library, she gathered up her sewing.

He escorted them out the front door to his carriage, a large Grafton coat of arms emblazoned the side. It was an open carriage, which was more appropriate for escorting a lady. "It's a nice day, and the ride is a pretty one, ladies."

Once he handed them both up, he sat facing them.

They headed north out of town and chatted about nothing. Mrs. Horthorn gave her opinion on gardening and foods she liked.

His excitement grew as they turned down the lane to Riverdale. A canopy of oak trees shaded the lane until the yard opened before them, and the pretty, white manor appeared like something out of a dream.

"Where are we, my lord? This is lovely." Sylvia's blue eyes were wide and filled with wonder.

He had an urgent notion to kiss those parted lips. Pushing the stupid thought aside, he said, "Welcome to Riverdale. It was left to me as one of the Grafton estates. There is also a large estate in the lake district, but this one is prettier in my opinion. It was little used while my cousin held the title. I've had it cleaned and hired a small staff. Would you ladies like a tour?"

"Of course, but why have you brought us here?" Sylvia asked as he handed her down from the carriage.

"I was thinking it might be nice to host a small house party here. Just a few friends to get away from the city for a week. I wondered if I might add that task to our arrangement?" Waiting for her response, he held his breath. It shouldn't matter. He could get a different lady to play hostess for him. Yet he hated the idea of his Everton lady abandoning him for another assignment.

"I don't think that will be a problem, my lord. Who were you thinking of inviting?"

"Just a few friends. You may include your sister and mother in the party if you please. I would be happy to have them here." He sounded a bit desperate, and it didn't appeal to him. "If this is too much to ask, just say so, and I'll speak to Lady Jane."

She took a step back and frowned. "Are you dissatisfied with my work thus far, my lord? I have barely begun, and I think once you see how well the dinner party goes, you may change your mind. However, if you wish for another lady to take my place, you need not trouble yourself. I can speak to Lady Jane this evening and see who else is available."

Something was wrong with him. It was the only explanation for his idiotic behavior. Perhaps he needed to rest and forget all this earl business. Shaking his head, he tried to clear away the stupidity floating inside it. "Forgive me. I only meant that I might be asking too much of you. I am sure you will continue to do an excellent job."

"Perhaps you might give us a tour of the house now, my lord." Her smile didn't reach those eyes that entranced him more than he wanted to admit.

Making things uncomfortable between them was the last thing he'd wanted to do, but there was something about her that turned him into an imbecile. Taking her advice, he led them to the front door, where a footman waited. "I haven't hired a butler here yet. However, this house does not require redecorating. The furniture has been covered and is of a more casual design than the other houses. I'm quite comfortable here at Riverdale."

The French country style appealed to him with the lighter woods, blues and whites. One could breathe there. And if he wanted to flop down on a settee and stretch out his legs, he did so without worry that the piece wouldn't support his weight. It was a sturdy home with good light and warmth. Eight bedrooms, two parlors, a small card room, dining room and gentleman's smoking room brought them back to the foyer.

"It is a very pretty house, my lord, and if you want to host a few guests for a week, we can make it a happy party. I wonder, if you like this so much more than the townhouse, that you don't live here instead. It's close enough to town, after all." She walked out the front door.

A maid and two footmen were setting up a picnic to the right of the drive, where several trees offered shade.

"Lovely," Mrs. Horthorn said as she strode over to where a blanket had been placed on the ground for them to sit and eat.

At a slower pace, he strolled with Sylvia. "I had thought of it, but Momma insisted I reside in London and act the proper earl. Since I have no clue how to be an earl, I agreed for the time being."

"You are very malleable where your mother is concerned."

"Italian men have a very close relationship with their mothers. I can't tell you why, but I've never met one who wouldn't throw himself on a spike for his momma."

Her laugh sang on the breeze. "You admit that rather freely. English men would hide this from public ridicule."

"There is little point. I adore my mother. You will too. Angelica is an angel, but with teeth. She is the main reason I haven't gone through with my plans to escape England." He stopped so they wouldn't get to the servants and Mrs. Horthorn too soon.

Stopping and facing him, she smiled. "I'm sure she is wonderful. Still, if you love it at Riverdale, I think you should consider making this your home. But perhaps, once I've changed the Collington townhouse, you might like that just as well. If they are both not enough to hold you here, then you can follow your heart to the vineyards. There is no need to decide anything today, Tony."

It must be a bout of insanity, but he craved hearing her asking him to stay. He shook off the desire to be wanted by Sylvia. She had her own life and it had nothing to do with him.

"Would you like to invite your sister here?" He longed for her to say yes.

Shaking her head, she sighed. "Perhaps we can invite my family to the ball in London. My sister comes with my mother, and I am not ready to spend a week in public with Mother's censure."

"Are the two of you going to eat? This chicken is wonderful." Mrs. Horthorn had already dug into the basket and was happily nibbling her food.

He sat, and they all watched a butterfly flit around the longer grass. "I thought after that terrible wine at the ball yesterday, I would treat you to a good Italian wine."

The footman struggled with the cork.

"Give it to me, John. If you'll get the glasses, I'll open the bottle. Remind me to give you a lesson before the house party."

"Yes, my lord. I would like that. I'm afraid my experience is limited." John blushed and stared at the ground. Then he rushed to a small table where they had staged various things for the picnic.

With a few quick turns of the steel worm and a firm steady pull, the cork was freed from the bottle.

John returned with three glasses, and Anthony poured the wine. He didn't drink his while he watched Sylvia take a sip.

A drop of the rich red beaded on her bottom lip before the tip of her tongue peeked out and licked it away. She closed her eyes and a low hum rumbled in her throat.

Body on fire, Anthony had to close his eyes for a moment but couldn't resist looking at her again. The satisfaction on her face was enough to keep him aroused for a week.

"Can I assume you like it?" He tasted his wine and let the fruits and spices awaken his palate.

She opened her eyes, and there was wonder inside. "Is this your family's wine?"

"Yes. My cousin in Italy had several cases sent to me as a gift when I became an earl. It is the only good thing to come of the title thus far." He meant it as a joke, but truth was truth.

"It's wonderful. Much more flavorful than the glass you brought me at the ball. I had no idea wine could be so warm and spectacular. I think they always water it down in ballrooms."

"I'm sure you're right," he agreed.

The conversation dwindled as they drank and ate. He liked watching her expressions with each flavor, and the way she noticed how the wine changed with a bite of food and the food with a sip of wine.

Before his thoughts took him over, he changed direction. "I read an article in the *Whisper* this week. Did you see it? It was about how Lady Abernathy's scolding of young ladies in their first season had grown to sinister proportions. Yes. That was what the author said, sinister. I laughed for ten minutes."

Pink cheeked, Sylvia popped a berry in her mouth.

Mrs. Horthorn dabbed the corners of her mouth with a linen napkin. "I saw her attack two sweet girls in the park just three days ago. She's a menace, and it's no surprise she's been called out on her bad habit. Perhaps she'll think twice before she ruins another girl's day or makes them feel small in the ballroom. Not even Nelda Abernathy wants to be thought of as a villain in the public eye."

"What do you think, Miss Sylvia?" he asked.

"Sometimes people get what they deserve, my lord. Usually, among the ton, nice women are ruined by stupid gossip. Occasionally, it's nice to see one of the gossipers take a fall. Of course, that is just my opinion." She ate another berry and lifted her chin.

"Yes. I thought you might say so." It was impossible for him to hide his amusement.

She narrowed her eyes at him and gave her head a shake.

"I wonder if you might like to walk to the creek, Miss Sylvia? Mrs. Horthorn would still be able to see us. It's just across the meadow." He pointed across the green meadow to where the trees marked a gentle stream.

"Oh, yes. You young people should get some exercise. I'll help clean up our picnic and enjoy the shade." Despite saying she would tidy up, she pulled her sewing from her large bag, composed of fabric scraps, and settled against the tree.

Anthony offered Sylvia a hand up. She had removed her gloves to eat, and her flesh was warm and soft in his hand. A jolt of energy shot from his palm down his body from the moment the pads of her fingers met his skin. Only their hands had met, but he felt the touch to his toes, and in places between that he quickly had to control.

Her sharp gaze met his. Had she felt it too? Was desire the same for a woman? Yes, it had been desire. She was a beautiful woman. Of course, he desired her. Many men would. It didn't mean anything, and nothing would come of it even if it did. He had no desire to marry, and Sylvia was not a woman to dally with. She was a lady in every sense of the word. But perhaps if he were older and ready to settle down, she might be just the kind of woman he would choose.

Pulling her hand away, she frowned and crossed her arms.

They walked toward the trees.

"What is it you want to say, Tony? I know you have something in that mind of yours that was inappropriate for Mrs. Horthorn to hear. If it's about Lady Abernathy, she got exactly what she deserved. I'll not apologize for it." She unfolded her arms and put her fists on her hips.

"I didn't think you would. What I'm after is another secret." He should leave this alone, but it was too delicious to know her secrets. He wanted more.

"You already know more than you should." She'd lowered her voice, speaking more to herself.

"Tell me why you and March didn't marry." He noted her flinch and regretted any injury he might do her, but his desire to know the answer outweighed his good sense.

"I thought you already knew. I thought everyone in London knew. Despite my publicly calling off the wedding, it seemed everyone assumed Hunter had abandoned me when he became a viscount." The sharp bite in her voice was a contrast to her usual melodic tones.

"That is the gossip, Sylvie. I want to know what really happened." He inched closer as they walked. The bubbling stream grew closer and sang a higher tone than the breeze through the grass.

She clutched her hands behind her back. "Why do you want to know?"

"We are friends. At least I believe we are becoming friends. I think you keep things pent up inside, and that does you harm." He took hope from the fact that she didn't move away.

"There is no sense talking about the past or wanting things that are never to be."

"The past colors our future," he said.

She stopped at the edge of the stream and sighed. "This is very pretty. This place suits you."

"Are you changing the subject?"

She gazed at him, her blue eyes swimming with memories. "The gossip is all true. Hunter came to me to ask me to end our engagement because he felt himself too good for Miss Sylvia Dowder now that he's a viscount. It was a terrible day, and I don't know why you insist I relive it."

Checking back toward the picnic, he confirmed the servants had gone and Mrs. Horthorn was engrossed in her sewing. Anthony pulled her into his arms. "I never want to hurt you, Sylvie. I'm sorry the man you loved turned out to be an ass."

She'd relaxed against his chest for a moment before pushing away. "I was lucky he did. I could have ended up married to a man who thinks more of his social status than his honor. Hunter Gautier is no gentleman. He made my mother cry, caused a hideous amount of gossip, which I pray does not hinder my sister from finding a husband, and destroyed any faith we had in love."

The mention of love caused something in Anthony's chest to tighten. "Then you did love him?"

Whenever she gave a question a lot of thought, she tipped her head to one side while pulling her bottom lip through her teeth. She was adorable. The urge to nibble that lip himself was dangerously needy.

"I thought I loved him. Perhaps I loved the idea of being married, leaving home, and having my own life. I used to dream of a house in the country and filling it with children. Hunter was my way to make my dreams come true." Kneeling, she reached out and let the water run over her fingers.

"You could still have all of those things. Being an Everton lady is a choice. You are lovely and not very old. You could find love, Sylvie."

She stood and backed away from him. "Love is for fools, Tony. Anyone who tells you differently is lying. My sister recently reminded me of that fact, which our mother has tried to instill in us for years."

It cut him deeply to hear her say it, even though it was a sentiment he had believed from time to time in his life, until he saw his sister's happy marriage and thought about what his parents had shared. "I will not try to convince you since I can see your mind is set. Though, I know you are wrong." He held up a hand to stop her from expounding on her beliefs. He was sure she could give a dozen examples of miserable marriages, which he couldn't bear to hear her tell. "Let us agree to disagree on this point for now."

She shrugged, and the fire went out of her. Maybe she'd wanted him to try to prove her wrong, or perhaps she was just ready for a good fight.

He liked a good debate too. "Tell me something else."

As they walked along the stream, the sun illuminated golden streaks in her hair. The urge to feel if it was as soft as it looked forced him to grip his hands behind his back. Every moment with her was an exercise in restraint. Though he wouldn't give back one instant of her company.

"Yes?"

"What did you do when that ingrate March told you he wanted you to break off your engagement?" Anthony would have beaten him soundly.

"I tossed him from the house after a sound setting down."

He faced her. His heart ached for her as much as it would for a member of his family. She had become important to him in a very short time. He wanted to be her friend, have her trust him. Though, it made little sense to push the issue. "Did you cry, Sylvie? Did that pig make you cry?"

"No. Once he was gone, I fainted." She laughed but there was no humor in the hollow sound. "It was the first time I have ever done so. Very embarrassing. I'm glad only my mother and sister were present."

Giving in, he brushed a stray curl behind her ear. It was like fine silk. He trailed his knuckle along her cheek. "I have an unnatural urge to go this moment, find March, and whip him until he faints."

This time the smile reached her eyes. "You are being silly." She took his hand away from her face but didn't release it immediately. "I am not your responsibility. In fact, I am only your employee for a few months. Perhaps soon, you will flee England, and live your Italian dream. I will be nothing more than an odd memory."

Standing by the water with his hand in hers, he wanted there to be more between them. More than that, he wanted her to want more. He shook off the ridiculous notion and let her hand fall away. Forcing his voice to a light bantering tone, he said, "But we are friends, and I do not like for my friends to be wronged. Besides, you will always be much more."

"Thank you." She curtsied and walked toward where Mrs. Horthorn continued with her sewing.

Anthony followed. "Do you think we might escape here for the house party after the ball? I should love a few days with close friends much more than a large party of people I hardly know."

She nodded. "But let's get through the dinner party first and see how that goes. I will send the invitations tomorrow. Your cook seemed very competent, and the entire staff was looking forward to entertaining. It seems Lady Collington has not had a large group at the house in some time."

"Aunt Daphne tends to have a very busy schedule of parties to attend. She didn't need to throw balls and dinners. Perhaps someday, when I am of an age, I can do the same."

There was that laugh again, and his heart beat a bit faster. Damn.

Sylvia said, "If you live as long as your aunt and become as influential, you will be a lucky man."

"Indeed."

Mrs. Horthorn rose when they approached. "You have a fine place here, my lord, but I think you had better be taking us back to town. We told Lady Jane we would return for supper."

"Of course." Bowing, he strained to think of some reason to detain them longer. He would have to settle for seeing her again the day of the dinner party.

A sweet sigh pushed from Sylvia's lips. "I like it here very much, but of course you're right, and we should get back. I will come by early on Wednesday and see that everything is in order for dinner. I have no doubt it will be a success."

"With you at the helm, my mother can have no complaints."

A wicked grin lifted her lips. "And of course, it is she that we are trying to impress. I keep forgetting that."

"Don't tease. My momma is tiny yet formidable. You will see. She is not a woman to be disappointed." His attachment to his mother was normally a subject of embarrassment, but he enjoyed the teasing coming from Sylvia. "I'd better call for the carriage."

When he dropped the ladies at Everton House, it pained him to watch her go. Ridiculous. White's Gentlemen's Club was just the distraction he needed.

The club was crowded. Since receiving his earldom, Anthony had been avoiding White's. Too many well-wishers who often wanted something else.

From the corner of the room, Miles Hallsmith waved him over. "Grafton, you look like you would rather be somewhere else."

"I think maybe I would. Since I became an earl, everyone wants something from me. At least it seems so." He sat in the chair adjacent and waved at a footman for a brandy.

"I was about to have some dinner. Would you care to join me? I promise you if I wanted something from a man with a title, my brother is higher on the list than you." He laughed. Miles's brother, the Viscount of Thornbury, was a complete imbecile who would have spent all his family money and alienated all of England if it wasn't for Miles.

"Thank you, Hallsmith. I would like that."

"I heard a rumor about you tonight." Miles leaned forward and lowered his voice.

A knot tightened in Anthony's gut. "Only one?"

"They are saying that you've hired an Everton lady."

"And is that so terrible?" If he had to defend every decision he made, it was going to be a long life among the ton.

Miles ran his hand through his shock of red hair and grinned. "You know, my sister, Phoebe, was with the Everton Domestic Society for a while. She did very well there. It got her away from my brother and mother when she needed it. I was proud of her for venturing out on her own. It seems a cruel fate for a girl past her prime, by society's standards, to be forced to wither away doing nothing for the rest of her life. I think the Society is a brilliant idea."

"But your sister didn't remain at the Society. She married, and quite well, to the Viscount of Devonrose." The idea of Sylvia remaining alone her entire life, even as an Everton lady, churned something inside him. It was all March's fault, yet the idea of her ending up as that idiot's wife was no better comfort.

"Phoebe's situation was unique from what I know. Most of the ladies have fine careers with the Society, and some retire with a nice pension or become escorts to younger ladies when the rigors of service become too taxing." Miles put his empty glass on the table. "What have you hired your Everton lady for?"

It warmed Anthony from the inside out to think of Sylvia as his Everton lady. "She is going to help with some changes at Collington House and act as hostess for a few events. In fact, you should be getting an invitation to a dinner party shortly."

"Excellent. I love a good party, especially if there is good food, and lovely ladies to flirt with."

Anthony laughed at Miles's enthusiasm. "I'm sure both will be available."

"Am I permitted to ask who the lady is?"

Unable to think of a reason to lie, when Miles would know in a few days when he arrived at the dinner party, he said, "Sylvia Dowder."

Frowning, Miles made fists. "March is a cad. That girl waited over three years for him to propose, and then two years with a contract. I know she claims to have cried off, but I don't believe it for a moment. He's just the type to cast off a lady when it suited him, and it was too late for her to recover."

"I hardly think it's too late. She's still lovely and not old." Anthony's temper flared.

Raising an eyebrow, Miles smiled. "You like Miss Dowder?"

"No. I just believe her family life forced her hand, and she might regret not attempting another season. She's hardly old enough to be on the shelf."

Miles laughed. "I can see your interest is small. If I'm correct, Miss Sylvia Dowder is near to turning twenty-five. Her sister is making a last attempt, and it is unlikely her family has time or funds for them both to have yet another season after March's abominable behavior. Still, if you like her, maybe all hope is not lost."

"I didn't say that I liked her. I don't like her. I just need her to help with a few events." It came out in a rush and he was powerless to control it.

"Yes…your interest is mild at best." Miles's words dripped with sarcasm. When the footman came with their brandy, they decided to have the drinks brought to the dining room.

Anthony was glad for the distraction and change of subject.

Chapter 5

Yet another letter from her mother had arrived explaining how Sylvia should come to her senses and return home. She sat at her desk and penned a return letter, but the old argument would fall on deaf ears.

"Am I disturbing you, Miss Dowder?" Lady Jane asked from the threshold.

Happy to put the letter writing aside, Sylvia turned toward her employer. "You know Serena was born three minutes before me, and all my life I have been Miss Sylvia and she Miss Dowder. I rather like the change as an Everton lady."

A hint of a smile lifted Jane's lips. "It is an honor well deserved. I should tell you that your sister is in the front parlor and seems quite out of sorts."

"Oh, no." Sylvia stood. "Are there tears? I hate it when she cries. In fact, she can talk me into almost anything when she sheds those giant tears of hers."

Hiding a laugh behind her hand, Jane said, "None when I left her. Just a lot of hand wringing and pacing."

Sylvia drew a deep breath. "Well then, I had better go down and see what brings a fine young lady into Everton House in such a state. Surely Mother has put her up to something and she is distressed."

"I'm certain you will handle the situation with your usual grace, Miss Dowder."

"Thank you, my lady. I will do my best." On the way down the stairs, a few scenarios played out in Sylvia's head. Her sister might have come to beg her to return home. Perhaps Hunter had come to his senses and wanted her back. Well, she wouldn't have him. She pulled her shoulders back and pushed through the parlor door.

Serena stood in the center of the room, a deep crease between her eyes, and her back straight and rigid. At the sight of Sylvia, the air went out of her and she rushed toward her. "Sylvie, thank God you are here."

"Where else would I be? What on earth is wrong?"

"Mother and Sir Henry have been talking about me without my knowledge. I think she intends to marry me off without my consent." Serena blurted out the information in one breath then drew another. "I don't know what to do. He is not terrible, but I was just starting to like Lord Stansfield."

The idea that Mother would go behind Serena's back to secure a husband was repugnant. "Why would she do such a thing? What does Father have to say on the subject?"

She tugged Sylvia's arm, and they sat on the brown divan. Plucking at the cuff of her glove, she sighed. "Father would not listen to me. He said that Mother would do what was best for my future."

"Do you think Stansfield will offer if given enough time?" Perhaps Mother knew or saw something Serena didn't.

She shrugged. "He likes me, and I liked that he was not put off by your occupation. We spoke of the theater and books. He is very well read and not nearly as stuffy as I first thought. His eyes are kind."

It was nice to see some warm regard from Serena. Clearly, it was not all about finding a rich husband. She wanted one who she could care for and would care for her. "When do you see Sir Henry again?"

She made a sour face. "We are to attend a play in four days. I had to beg Mother to let me go to your dinner party. She said it would not get me married, since Henry would not be there. She's gone marriage mad, Sylvie. She thinks Stansfield will not offer because he is above me and I will end up in your situation if I pursue a man so far above my station."

"You are a daughter of a gentleman. Besides, either one of them would be lucky to have you. You are the sweetest, kindest person I know." She hugged her sister and kissed her cheek.

"Thank you, but I think as my twin, you are required to think so." Serena laughed and took Sylvia's hand. "The problem is I have not had enough time with Lord Stansfield to know if he might wish to offer. I think him a little shy, and that is what I mistook for stuffiness at first. Each time I see him, he is more appealing."

Sylvia had already sent out the invitations to Anthony's dinner party, and it was not her place to add to the list. Perhaps she could ask a favor though. "Let me see if I can help put you and Lord Stansfield in the same room. I can't promise you anything, but I will do my best."

Smiling as bright as the sun, Serena was a vision. She squeezed Sylvia's hand. "I knew you would make me feel better, Sylvie. You are always the kind voice in my head that tells me everything will be all right."

"And everything will. Mother cannot make you marry anyone you do not wish to marry. Do not let her bully you." Hating the idea of her sister being trapped in a marriage without affection forced her voice into a stern tone.

Taking a breath, Serena pulled her shoulders back. "I will be more like you and cleverer than Mother."

"Good girl."

The clock struck eleven, and Serena jumped up. "She will wonder where I am. I must get home. I told her I was going for a walk in the park. Jenny promised to keep my secret."

Serena rushed into the foyer, and Jenny, the girls' maid, appeared from the servants' stairs, ready to rush after her mistress.

"Hello, Jenny," Sylvia said.

Stopping, Jenny tucked her wild red hair under her cap and made a hasty curtsy. "Oh, miss, it's good to see you. You look fine."

Gray held the door, and Serena stood half outside with the same worried look she'd had when she arrived. "Jenny, we must get home."

Sylvia watched them rush down the steps and into the carriage before Gray closed the door. "Gray, can you ask if the carriage is available for an hour or so? I have an errand to run."

"Yes, miss." He ambled down the stairs.

* * * *

What had seemed like a great idea an hour earlier left her stomach churning as she stood outside Anthony's townhouse. "Mrs. Horthorn, this might have been a mistake."

"Hardly, my dear. I think it is very sensible to help your sister while still attaining the goals for which you were hired within the Everton Domestic Society. There are no rules against it, and if his lordship doesn't mind, I see no conflict." She tugged on her white cap and plastered a serene expression on her face as the door opened.

Wells glared an instant longer than was polite before saying, "Miss Dowder, we were not expecting you today."

"I know, Wells. Is his lordship at home? I would like to speak to him." She hated the hesitation in her voice and cleared her throat.

Mrs. Horthorn huffed. "I would like to be allowed entry, so we don't look like a pair of vagabonds standing on the stoop."

Despite Wells's calm demeanor, the house was in an unusual frenzy.

Footmen and other men of questionable background were hollering and carrying rugs and other goods from room to room. Sylvia had never seen such chaos. "What on earth? That rug you are holding, young man, should go into his lordship's dining room. Peter, you have the desk for his study. How in the world did you end up with that? It should have been delivered tomorrow by the furniture maker."

Pete put down the desk, reached back to rub his lower back, then pulled his hat off and blushed. "Miss, I can't tell you how it happened, only that the rug was wrong, and the old desk is still in place. I was told to put it in the grand parlor, but I've not found a door marked as such. In fact, I have no idea what rooms are what."

Sylvia hid her amusement behind a gloved hand. "Leave it there for now. In fact, Wells, have everyone stop moving about like mice looking for a cube of cheese. Where did all these people come from?"

Perspiration dotting his forehead, Anthony rushed down the stairs. "Miss Dowder. Thank all that is good you are here. I am at a loss. Rugs, curtains, a desk. I don't know what plan you had in mind."

"I had planned for it to arrive tomorrow and the next day at the earliest. I'm sorry, my lord. If you will gather the men, I will take over. The old rugs and your desk must be taken out first."

"Stay here," he commanded. "Wells, see that the ladies are secure. I will gather our resources."

"Yes, my lord." Wells stood in front of them, practically backing them into the front door, while they waited for Anthony to call all the footmen and delivery men into the foyer with their wares.

Once he had them all there, he narrowed his gaze. "This is Miss Dowder. She will oversee this transition. I expect each of you to treat her with the utmost respect."

A chorus of "Yes, my lord" sounded.

Sylvia stepped around Wells. As she spoke, she pointed to the different rooms. "You may all put down whatever you have here. Now if two or three of you would load his lordship's current desk onto the carriage that brought all of this, that would be a help. Peter, the rugs in the master's chamber, dining room, and two parlors should also be loaded and taken for storage. His lordship can decide what to do with them later. Perhaps a donation or sale."

With an awkward bow, Peter said, "Yes, miss."

The footmen carried the great desk out through the back door, and men went to do her bidding. If she were honest, she found great satisfaction in ordering burly men about the house. Hiding her thrill, she waited while Wells made sure no damage came to anything else while rugs were rolled and carried here and there.

Anthony eased into the space next to her. "You look pleased with yourself, Sylvie."

"I admit it, this is fun." She fought the tug on her lips.

"I'm relieved you are here, but I was not expecting you today. Is there anything amiss?"

The knot of worry returned in her chest. "I have a favor or request, but it can wait until we have this all sorted out."

Mrs. Colms rushed up, tugging her cap. "Oh miss, the divan and chairs you had recovered for his lordship have just arrived as well. It is all too much."

"Do not panic, madam. Just have them wait at the back, and when we get the new rugs down, they can carry them in. I suggest a small gratuity for their patience." The old furnishings had been in place so long, none of the staff was used to so much change. Sylvia should have prepared better and been ready for the early delivery.

Harried, Mrs. Colms nodded and rushed back toward the servants' entrance at the back of the house.

"Wells, can you tell our driver to come back for us in three hours? I cannot take up the Everton carriage indefinitely, and this will take some time."

Before the butler could comment, Anthony said, "I will see you home."

"I would not wish to inconvenience you, my lord." If her request was not well received, the ride home could be most awkward.

"It is nothing," he said before nodding to Wells in silent communication.

With no other choice, Sylvia allowed her carriage to be sent away.

Pete returned after having all the rugs removed. "What's next, miss?"

She pointed to the largest rug. "This one goes in the study."

He and one of the Grafton footmen lifted the rug and walked through the double doors.

Sylvia followed and told them where to place the cream-and-blue rug. She did the same in each room, placed every piece of furniture as she imagined it when she first saw the rooms. It was nearly the dinner hour by the time the last was put in place. Standing in the middle of Anthony's bedroom, she admired the warm golds of the rug and how well they would look when the new curtains of a slightly lighter shade arrived for the bed.

She'd decided to leave the deep red curtains on the windows. Once the rest was changed, they would look rich and luxurious.

It was a good view, overlooking the garden and the city beyond. A light breeze tickled her skin, and she had a fleeting thought of jumping out and running away. It wouldn't do. It was a fine day in London, and the birds sang out happily before the sun went down. She was no coward, and it was only a small favor. The worst that could happen was that he would say no. Or perhaps he would think her impertinent and vulgar. It shouldn't matter what Anthony Braighton thought of her, but her chest hurt at the notion of his bad opinion. There was no one else in the room when she voiced her anxiety, "Perhaps I shouldn't have come."

"Why not?" His deep, warm voice filled the room behind her.

She spun toward his voice, and he stole her breath. His dark hair was tousled from running his fingers through it. Bright golden eyes captured hers and held her in their depths. He filled the doorway, his head nearly touching the header. He had not been this stunning when they had first met at a ball nearly four years earlier, but those years had turned a lanky youth into a fearsome giant of a man.

His question hung between them.

Drawing a full breath, Sylvia lifted her chin. "I only meant that the favor I wish to ask is not that important."

Those full lips of his drew down in displeasure. "Where is Mrs. Horthorn?"

She stayed near the window, but the breeze no longer cooled her. Heat bloomed in places she rarely thought about. "She's having a cup of tea with Mrs. Colms."

Narrowing his eyes, he nodded and stepped inside. "Why shouldn't you have come, Sylvie?"

"My lord…"

"Tony. You call me Tony. Remember?" He crossed his arms over his broad chest.

She sat on the windowsill. "You are not obligated to grant me any favors."

"What could you possibly ask that I would deny?" He crossed the room and reached out for her hand.

Having removed her gloves to keep them clean while she worked, the skin-on-skin contact spread warmth through her like a forest fire. "It's about my sister."

He stared a long time at where their skin met before capturing her gaze again. "She is coming to our dinner party?"

"Yes."

They were too close. His breath grazed her forehead, and she had to tip her head back to meet his gaze. The world faded into nothing, and there was only the two of them. "Can your favor wait a moment, Sylvie?"

"Why?"

"I'm going to kiss you."

It was impossible to breathe. He took up all the air, and her heart pounded in her ears. "Is that wise?"

"Not in the least." Leaning down, he captured her lips with his.

Soft, tender, but strong all at once, he didn't just kiss her, he made love to her lips. Every nerve sang out for more, and she touched his coat at the chest. A long sigh escaped her as she melted into his embrace. Her body trembled, and she was powerless to stop it, didn't want to stop the rush of sensation that flooded her. *More* was all she could think. She wanted more.

Shocked by her own wantonness, she pressed her palm against his chest.

He released her immediately. "I don't know what came over me. If I have offended you, Sylvie, I apologize. Though I refuse to say I am sorry for the kiss."

"No. It was…"

Running his knuckle down the side of her jaw, he smiled. "It was, indeed."

If she didn't do something, he would kiss her again, and Lord only knew if she had the will to stop him. Reluctantly, she stepped back. "I think it's best if we keep our relationship business and perhaps friendship, Tony. What just happened was lovely, but it cannot happen again. You hired me because you do not wish to marry, and I'm no one's mistress, so no good can come from allowing our desire to rule the day."

He glowered at his feet for a long moment, and his jaw ticked several times. When he looked up, his expression was calm and unreadable. Stepping back, he said, "You're right, of course. We are friends. Just look at what you've already done for my home. I may have hired you, but I see you care that I am happy with the home you create for me. I shall cherish what you have done and will do. Ask your favor, Sylvie."

Unable to decipher the tone or expression beyond his words, she had to take him at face value. It would be best if she could forget the way his lips felt, but their touch still burned into her. However, if he could forget, then so could she. She pulled her shoulders back and swallowed down any sentiment. "Serena has two suitors, and Mother is pushing one over the other without consulting her. She would like to get to know Lord Stansfield better. You said he's a good man. May I invite him to your dinner party?"

He chuckled. "I thought you would ask something much more taxing. Invite who you wish. Rutledge Haversham is a friend. I would be glad to have him for dinner, and if he likes Serena, all the better."

"It is impertinent of me to ask." For some reason she needed to justify her hesitation.

His smile was a kind of delightful torture. "You forget I am American and care little for these silly rules. Invite who you want. As long as the people I've requested have their invitations, I will not be displeased."

"Thank you, Tony."

He stared into her eyes a long time before picking up her hand and kissing her knuckles. "I should stay silent on the subject, but that kiss was more than I expected. I don't know why I did it. You drew me in like a magnet, and I had no ability to resist. Even then, I thought it would be a quick kiss that would mean nothing. I want to always be honest with you, Sylvie. I have never had a kiss touch me so deeply, and I'm not at all sure what to do about it."

Pulling her hand free, she walked to the open door. "There is nothing to do. It was a kiss, Tony. You have not ruined me, and no one need ever know that we made a misstep. An accident that will mean nothing in a few days. In a few months, I will complete this assignment, and you will go back to your life as I go back to mine. You will succeed as the Earl of Grafton with the approval of the ton. Perhaps you will have your vineyard, and one day, when you're ready, you will marry an appropriate woman to give you an heir. I will take other assignments and live a fulfilling life with the Everton Domestic Society. Do not make more of this than it is. You have not injured me. I could have stopped you, and I should have."

His eyes burned with anger. "I don't believe you feel that way, but I see your point. I shall not 'misstep' again. I assume you will return tomorrow for the remaining curtain delivery?"

"I will be here after luncheon, my lord."

Impossibly, the anger in his eyes mounted. "I see, we are back to formal address, Miss Dowder. I do not know if I shall be available tomorrow when you arrive. Please feel free to proceed without me."

"Of course. Your presence is not needed to hang some curtains."

"Very well."

She turned and left his bedroom in search of Mrs. Horthorn.

It would have been easy to fix the rift she'd created. All she had to do was call him Tony and lighten her tone of voice. He wouldn't even require an apology, but she knew this was for the best. That kiss had broken all the Everton rules, and her own as well. It had been the most wonderful experience of her life, and it was wrong. Nothing could make it right. Hunter's kisses had been pale compared to the volcano that erupted between her and Anthony Braighton. Keeping him at a distance was critical. The last thing she wanted was to create a scandal that neither she nor her sister could recover from. Becoming a mistress to an earl was no life for Sylvia Dowder. She would not shame herself or her family. Even if his intentions were honorable, he was not long for England, so nothing could come of it.

Chapter 6

"I can't believe the difference in the house, Tony." Sophia, Anthony's sister, ran her hand down the pale blue curtains that replaced the dark brown in his study.

"I wish I could take the credit, but Miss Dowder did a wonderful job." It had been a week since he had seen Sylvia. She'd come to finish the decorating then left the cleaning and hiring to his staff. Mrs. Colms informed him that Miss Dowder had come by to check that all was in order in the morning, but Anthony had gone to a meeting with his banker.

His sister, the Countess of Marlton, had come to town unexpectedly to visit some friends. As she had left her husband and children in the country, she would spend a week with Anthony. She ran her hand along his new desk. "She's done a wonderful job. I can't get over how a few lighter colors have changed the entire look of the house. It reflects you much more now. I wonder what Aunt Daphne will think when she sees it."

"I'm curious as well, but she insisted I take the house and she move to the country. I had to make the place feel more like it's mine." Their great-aunt had said she would come to town for his first ball, so he would hear her opinion of the changes then. She could be quite cutting when displeased, but there was nothing to be done about it now.

Sophia tried to hide her wicked grin but failed as she too was incapable of hiding any of her emotions or feelings. "She will say, Anthony, good gracious what have you done to my house? You must be mad. Be careful or they will begin calling you the Mad Earl of Grafton." She had a knack for mimicry and did a perfect impression of Aunt Daphne.

It was impossible to keep a stoic face. He tried and failed. "I hope you are wrong, Sophie, but we shall see next month when she comes to town for my ball."

She sat in the newly upholstered chair. Her red gown a contrast to the blue and cream surrounded by dark wood. "Will Miss Sylvia be your hostess for the ball as well?"

The ache in his chest at the mention of her name was at once painful and pleasant. "She is my Everton lady. She will help with the ball. I can see no reason for Momma to push marriage on me when I have the Everton Domestic Society to do all the things a countess would do."

"And you still prefer to remain unmarried?" She raised one dark eyebrow.

"Of course, why do you ask?" Sylvia's blue eyes filled with mirth flashed in his mind and he had to shake them away.

Shrugging, she smoothed her skirt. "It is only that since I arrived a few hours ago, you have spoken of Miss Sylvia Dowder more than I have ever heard you speak of anyone. Are you certain you are not smitten with her?"

"No," he answered too quickly. "I mean to say. She works for me. It would not be appropriate to harbor feelings for her. She is doing a fine job and that is all." He sat across from her on the divan and ran his hand over the deep blue fabric. It was stupid, but he wondered how pretty Sylvia would look in the color. It would set off her eyes.

Sophia's smile dimmed, she got up, rounded the low table and sat next to him. "I suggest if you plan to continue that lie, you mask your expressions better outside of this room. But Tony, if you're in love with her, why not explore the idea of a life with her? She's a nice girl from a good family. What happened to her engagement is notorious gossip, but I hope that would not stop you from pursuing a relationship."

Anger flared so strong he jerked away from her. "March is a dog. Nothing he could do would stop me."

When his sister's eyes widened, and her mouth hung open, he knew he'd made a mistake. He'd shown just how much he liked Sylvia when he wanted to quash the emotions and go on as before. Kissing her had been a momentary lapse in judgment that he was determined not to let happen again.

He shook his head. "I only mean, if I was interested, March's behavior would not be an issue."

"You know, Tony, lying to me is one thing, but lying to yourself is not at all healthy." She held up a hand to forestall his denial. "Just the same, I will give you some advice. If you love her, don't be a fool. Not pursuing the woman you love to prove some point to your mother is idiotic. Momma only wants you to be happy. She had a long wonderful marriage, and she wants the same for her children. Believe me, when they sent me away to London, the last thing I wanted was to fall in love. My experience had tainted my idea of what a marriage would or could be. I'm not sure why you are so against the notion, but think it through before you punish yourself and Sylvia."

Sophia had endured more than Anthony could bear to think about at the hands of a family friend. The thought made him sick to his stomach. "Momma and Papa had an ideal marriage filled with love and respect. I see more marriages of convenience since we moved to England than I care to count. I know you and Marlton have more than that, but I can't see myself tied down to one woman for the rest of my life. I like Sylvia. She is smart, funny and beautiful, but that's just the problem. What if I married her or some other girl and all I did was make her miserable? She could end up hating me. Then what; I go find a mistress and she a lover? I think it better to have no delusions. I'm not the marrying type, Sophie. Sylvia Dowder deserves someone who will cherish her and make her happy. I'm not that kind of man."

Staring at him as if he'd just spoken in a foreign tongue, she pursed her lips. Her telling expressions went from shock, to sorrow, then the scariest of all, cunning. "So, if I bring a nice gentleman, Mr. Tucker, to your ball and introduce him to Sylvia, you would not mind. I met him last year. He is wealthy and landed, has a nice disposition and a keen mind. I think he would be a fine match for her and he is not the type who would mind her lack of dowry or the March scandal."

He didn't know what to say. Fear and fury waged war in his gut. Still, if Sylvia liked this Mr. Tucker… "It would be none of my business, if she were to be courted by your Mr. Tucker." He had to swallow the bile rising in his throat.

"I don't believe you, Tony. I think you're in love with her. But since you say you're not, I will bring Mr. Tucker along and test your resolve." She stood and stretched her arms over her head. "Your guests will be arriving soon. You had better put your coat on to greet them."

Taking the coal-gray coat from the back of his chair, he longed to throttle his sister, or at least toss her in the lake as he had when they were children. "You may bring whomever you want. I have no claims on Sylvia or any other woman. I will remain unattached until producing an heir is inevitable. That should give me another twenty years to enjoy myself."

"It just sounds like twenty lonely years to me, Tony." She kissed his cheek and exited the study.

Following her out, he saw Sylvia in every room as they crossed to the great parlor. Even the foyer, where they had made no changes, had her touch as a large bouquet of flowers had been delivered from Everton House earlier in the day. She had thought of everything.

The dining room was like new with cream-colored curtains, which were pulled back allowing the last of the day's light to filter in before the candles were lit. Even the dark table had been covered with white linen and all the china and silver polished to a high shine. Crystal goblets shone like crowns above each place setting, ready to be filled with wine when dinner commenced.

The knocker on the door sounded, and a moment later Sylvia entered the dining room. Stunning in an emerald-green gown, her hair far more intricately styled than was her custom, she patted a curl down around her flushed cheek. Since her mother would be in attendance, there was no need for another chaperon. "I hope everything is to your liking, my lord."

"It is perfect, Sylvie. My sister knows we are friends. There is no need for formality in front of her. There will be plenty of time for titles this evening." Dread crept into his tone despite his desire to prove to his momma that he would be an honorable earl without a wife.

The ladies curtsied. Sylvia smiled. "It's good to see you again, my lady."

There was Sophia's wicked grin again. "I think Sophia will do for me as well if you will permit me to call you Sylvia."

"I would be honored." Sylvia shifted a goblet at the near end of the table then nodded at the arrangement.

"You have done a wonderful job," Sophia said. "The house looks like new. I can hardly believe it is the same home I lived in when I first arrived in London. Of course, my room is unchanged. Aunt Daphne was very kind in redecorating for my arrival."

Sylvia nodded. "That room is so pretty there was no need to make any changes. It is the perfect room for a young lady. We should go to the parlor before the other guests arrive.

"I particularly loved what you did with Tony's room. Such a big change with so little expense. Perhaps I should have you come out to Marlton and update the country home. It can be a bit dreary."

"I would be happy to help. I hope that whoever Tony eventually chooses for his countess will like the master chambers as well. I tried to make it pretty while still keeping it a bit masculine." Sounding very nonchalant about the decor of his bedroom did not keep the blush from her cheeks.

"Only a fool would quarrel with what you have done." Sophia preceded them into the parlor, now with less furniture and lighter colors to offset the dark woods.

The footman lit the last of the candles and left them.

Once Sylvia sat, Anthony did too. "You look very pretty in that color, Sylvie."

"Thank you, but you really shouldn't say such things. I'm not really a guest, Tony. I work for you."

His curt response was cut off.

Sophia said, "Speaking of guests, I noticed there are ten place settings. Who is coming to dinner?"

Anthony agreed it wiser to avoid argument. "Besides Miss Dowder and her mother, we have the pleasure of Lord Stansfield and his uncle Mr. Condon, as well as Miles Hallsmith, and the Duke and Duchess of Middleton."

Sophia clapped. "You will love Preston and Millie Knowles, Sylvia. Did you know Her Grace was an Everton lady?"

"She is a very popular subject at the Society. She was gone before I joined, but many of the ladies and dowagers still speak very fondly of her."

"I didn't know you were friends with Lord Stansfield, Tony." Sophia plucked at her gloves.

"He is an acquittance. I like him, and he is attempting to court Miss Serena Dowder. Sylvie asked if he could join the party tonight, and I thought it a grand idea." The way Sylvia's skin turned from cream to ruby red made his mouth water with longing to touch her and kiss her. It was impossible and inconvenient, but he couldn't deny his desire. However, he could conquer it.

Sophia wiggled her eyebrows. "Oh, I love a good romantic encounter. I have only met Lord Stansfield once, but he seemed very intelligent, and he has kind eyes. You say he is coming with his uncle?"

"Yes," Sylvia said. "Mr. Condon is staying with him for a few weeks, and rather than leave him at home alone, he will round out our party nicely."

"It should be a lively night." Sophia had plucked her glove off, and when the knocker sounded, she frowned and tugged it back on. "I have always hated gloves. The best part about a dinner party is that you can remove them for dinner."

Momma walked in before Wells could announce her. "You have never liked the niceties of being a lady, Sophia. You preferred Philadelphia, where you could break all the rules."

They all rose. Sophia kissed her mother on both cheeks. "True, Momma, but London has its charms, and it did bring me to Daniel."

Momma always smelled of wildflowers. Her cheek was warm and soft and brought Anthony back to his childhood and all the wonderful memories. It also reminded him of losing their father and the responsibilities he now maintained. "You look stunning as always, Momma."

Angelica still wore black every day in honor of her husband, but tonight the dark gown was piped with a yellow that made it less dour. Her long, dark hair was pulled up but curled loosely around her olive skin and the same golden eyes he and his sister had inherited. "I thought it time to lighten up." Her rich Italian accent lilted with more happiness than he'd heard from her in years.

Miles Hallsmith arrived, complimented every woman in the room, then the room itself. "The house looks marvelous, Grafton. I see you in all the changes."

Catching Sylvia hiding her smile shot a warm joy through him. She had managed to put his personality into the new decor. It was a bit of magic, the way she'd accomplished it.

Felicia and Serena Dowder's arrival took a toll on Sylvia's mood. She stole away into a corner and whispered with her sister while their mother chatted with his. He'd grown up with a sister but still had no idea what women whispered about with such animation.

Slapping his back, Miles leaned in. "It's futile to try to figure them out. Just enjoy them and let them be a mystery."

The rest of the party arrived at once. It turned out that Middleton and Stansfield had been at Eton together and remained good friends.

When they all finally went in for dinner, Mr. Condon was seated next to Momma. The two chatted like they'd known each other for years. A knot formed in Anthony's gut, and it would not loosen up.

Between the second course and the fish, the footmen refilled the wineglasses. The Duchess of Middleton touched his arm. "I cannot tell if you are upset that your mother has made a friend, or if you want to kill poor Miles."

He appreciated her whisper was for his ears only. "Neither can I, Millie. It is not that I don't want my mother to make friends, but it would be better if her friends were women."

Millie laughed. "She is a grown woman, Anthony. Try to remember that and tread carefully."

"I'm sure that is sound advice. Whether or not I can follow it is yet to be seen."

"And what of Miles?" She looked down the table to where Miles and Sylvia had their heads together in some deeply amusing conversation.

"Miss Sylvia is not in my charge, only in my employ. I can't dictate with whom she flirts." Despite his sounding unconcerned, he was close to leaping across the table and beating Miles to a pulp.

Millie looked down the table, her gaze intent on them. "He is clearly flirting, but it's Miles's nature to try to please everyone he meets. People like Miles because he says what they want to hear and means it. He is a lovely person, and Miss Sylvia could do far worse. However, if I may point out, Sylvia is not returning his flirtation. She is engaged in the conversation, to be sure, but there is no blushing or batting of eyelashes. She does not touch his sleeve or make long eye contact, nor shy away from eye contact. Her gaze is direct and unfazed, if you want my opinion."

Looking more closely, he couldn't argue with Millie's keen observations. Sylvia didn't give any indication that she was interested in more than conversation with Miles. The band around his heart loosened. "I suppose you are right. You have a keen eye, Your Grace."

"Do not forget, I was an Everton lady. I am trained to know what people want and need. Miles's sister was also an Everton lady. I imagine he and Sylvia have a lot to converse about. But, if they should become smitten, what harm is there in that? He is a gentleman and she the daughter of a gentleman."

The band gripped tighter again. "Indeed."

Her giggle turned his head. "You and your sister should really have learned to mask your emotions better after all these years in England. It is never good to let everyone know what you are thinking."

"Would that it was so easy, Millie. Perhaps then, I could play cards without being trounced. As it is, I keep my money off the gambling tables and my heart on my sleeve." For the rest of dinner, he avoided looking toward Sylvia and focused on his own dinner partners. Instead of getting angry with Condon, he engaged him in a conversation about his farm in the north, and Momma lost interest in talk of crops. Still, Momma's regard for Condon gnawed at him. He didn't know this man or his character.

Stansfield and Serena barely spoke to anyone else, and Mrs. Dowder watched them both keenly, while ignoring Sylvia entirely.

It shouldn't matter to him what happened within the Dowder family, but he disliked Felicia Dowder more and more as the night went on. Her disregard for the happiness of one twin daughter over the other was abysmal.

Instead of the men retiring to smoke and drink, Anthony had decided they would all take their pudding in the parlor. He'd always hated the English tradition of men and women separating after the meal. Being American gave him some leave to do as he pleased, and Sylvia didn't object.

If she had objected, he might have changed his mind. That was more disturbing than he cared to admit.

Felicia strode across the parlor, her expression sour. "My lord, Serena and I must take our leave. Thank you for a very nice evening. It was lovely. Shall I collect Sylvia as well, or will your sister act as her chaperon?"

From her perch on the divan, Mother frowned and narrowed her eyes at Felicia.

Sophia jumped up. "I will be happy to see that Miss Sylvia gets back to her home safely, madam. Do not trouble yourself."

"That is very kind of you, Your Grace," Sylvia said around a deep frown that she forced away a moment later.

"Very well. Come along, Serena." Felicia curtsied and strode out of the parlor.

With little choice, Serena curtsied. "Thank you for a wonderful evening, my lord. I hope we will all meet again very soon." She glanced at Stansfield, who bowed and smiled.

Anthony was even more determined to help Serena and thwart Mrs. Dowder after her horrid behavior toward Sylvia. "I will see you at my ball and perhaps a nice house party away from the city for a few days."

Joy filled Serena's familiar face. Yet as much as the twins looked alike, he couldn't understand how he'd ever mistaken one for the other. Sylvia's eyes held more expression and were a deeper shade of blue. Her lips were slightly fuller and her skin brighter. He must have been mad to ever mistake Serena for his Sylvie.

"Thank you, my lord. I should be delighted by the invitation." With another quick glance at Stansfield, she rushed after her mother.

It wasn't long before the rest of the party broke up. By midnight only his mother, sister and Sylvia remained. On the divan, Momma sat with Sylvia. "Is your mother always so short with regard to you, my dear?"

Most English would have been offended, but Sylvia's sad smile said she knew Angelica had been mortified for her. "It was not always so, Mrs. Braighton. Mother has much strain put on her by having two unmarried daughters approaching an unmarriageable age. I have done the unthinkable and lost my only prospective husband then taken myself off the marriage market. All she has is the hope of marrying Serena well and soon. Please don't judge her too harshly."

In her very Italian way, Momma cupped the side of Sylvia's cheek then kissed her other cheek. "You are too kind, and I like that about you very much. I am sometimes judged by my thick accent, and it makes me cross.

You are judged by the actions of a scoundrel who broke his promise, yet you have no malice inside you."

"If you had seen me on the day March ended our engagement, you might have been less impressed. My malice could not be measured by any standard means. I could have beaten him with a stick." The wicked smile he loved lit her up brighter than the remaining candles.

Momma laughed, full and round. "I think he deserved no less. A shame you English do not follow those instincts. In Italy, my brothers would have made him pay for such a slight."

"Between the wine that your son has shared with me and your description, I should very much like to visit your country."

Another laugh from Momma. "You would love it but miss the niceties of England. This is home now. Though America was wild and exciting when my husband was alive. I think Anthony will take me to Italy soon for a visit. I miss my family and would like a long stay."

Noting the longing in Momma's voice, he realized it had been over five years since his mother had been home. He could take her to Italy and check on his vineyard then break the news that he would not return to England. If that was what he truly wanted. "I'll be happy to take you whenever you wish, Momma, and come and retrieve you when you're ready to return."

She sighed. "I'm tired. We can talk about this another day. Miss Dowder, shall I carry you home in my carriage?"

"Thank you, madam, but the Everton carriage is already outside waiting for me."

"Very well." She kissed Sylvia again, stood up and kissed Sophia and Anthony. "You made a very fine party. With Miss Dowder's help, you shall look like an earl yet."

"Thank you." He escorted her out to her carriage and handed her up.

"She is a very nice girl, Anthony. A shame she shall never marry. I hate to think of her alone as she grows older and with no children to comfort her. It is quite sad." Angelica leaned back and closed her eyes.

"Good night, Momma." He closed the door and called up to her driver to take her home.

The image his mother painted haunted Anthony as he returned to the parlor. Sylvia shouldn't be alone. She was smart, beautiful, and had too much to offer a marriage to be left to a life of solitude. But the thought of someone marrying her didn't give him more pleasant thoughts. Miles liked her, and he was keen to marry sooner rather than later. The idea was nauseating. She was everything he said he didn't want, and yet he couldn't resist her. It wouldn't do.

When Anthony returned, Sylvia and Sophia were laughing and talking about the evening.

Getting up, Sylvia smiled at him. "It was a good night. I hope you were pleased. I must get home, Tony. I will talk to you in a few days."

"I have a complaint," he said.

Her eyes widened. "Oh?"

"Did you intentionally have Stansfield bring his uncle to court my mother?"

"That is a question, not a complaint." She propped her fists on her hips.

"The complaint will come depending on your response."

"No, I didn't, but it seems to me your mother can take care of herself. She is a beautiful, smart woman, and if she has made a friend her own age, you should be happy for her."

Sophia stood. "She's quite right, Tony. Momma deserves to be happy. Papa has been gone a long time."

"Sophie, you and I can discuss this in private. This conversation is between me and my Everton lady." He should have let it go. But the idea that she had tried to set up a courtship for his mother gnawed at him.

"As I said, I didn't arrange anything. Lord Stansfield asked if he might bring his uncle, who was visiting, and I could think of no reason to deny the request. Besides, it gave us an even number of guests, which is always a better table. However, if this is how you react when faced with something unexpected, perhaps it would be better if someone else took over this assignment."

His heart dropped. "You're quitting me?"

"I believe I am. I don't care for your tone, and we both know it would be better if someone else took over. You and I have…difficulties working together." She glanced at Sophia and let the sentence hang.

He, too, was unwilling to divulge the kiss in his bedroom. Wanting her, wanting freedom, and hating himself for both, Anthony felt rage he'd rarely experienced well up inside him. "If that's what you want, then inform Lady Jane I will need a new lady in the morning."

"Fine." She stormed out.

"Fine."

Once the door slammed, Sophia stood up and hugged him. "Oh, Tony, what have you done?"

"I did what needed to be done. She should not be matchmaking Momma, and the situation was getting out of hand." A veil of dread spread through him despite his claim to have done the right thing.

Pulling out of his arms, she narrowed her gaze. "You picked that fight knowing she had not tried to make any sort of match. And what would be wrong with Momma marrying again? She has been alone long enough. Do you want her to grow bitter and lonely?"

"She will never be lonely. She has us." He strode to the long credenza against the wall and poured himself a brandy. Sophia didn't care for brandy or wine, so he didn't offer her any.

Hands on her hips, she stared him down. "I'm going to pretend you didn't say that and get to the real problem. You have fallen in love with Sylvia Dowder and are too much of a coward to admit it. Thus, you have cut off your nose to spite your face. I hope you will be very happy, Tony, but I sincerely doubt it after seeing what a dunderhead you've become."

She was right about his making a mistake, but not the rest. Of course, he didn't love Sylvia. He refused to love any woman. He already had enough responsibility and couldn't take on any more, certainly not another person's happiness. "You may call me as many names as you wish, Sophie. I have done the right thing, and another lady will make no difference in the outcome of the next few months."

"No, just the rest of your life."

"My point exactly."

She mumbled, "Dunderhead," stormed out, and up the steps to her room.

Anthony drained his snifter of brandy and put the glass down harder than he'd intended, snapping off the glass stem. "Damn."

He picked up the broken shards and put them in the glass.

Wells came in an instant later. "I will clean that, my lord. Do not injure yourself."

"Thank you, Wells. I think I had better go to bed before I break anything else."

"Good night, my lord." Wells set about cleaning up the broken glass.

Anthony trudged up the steps. He should feel better, having removed his problem from his life, but Sophia's words and the fierce look on Sylvia's face as she told him another Everton lady would suit him better haunted him. She had been thinking about the kiss and the pink in her cheeks had given her away. He commanded himself not to dwell on the perfection of that moment when their lips met. It didn't mean anything.

Inside his bedroom, the memory was even more intense, and the new furnishings screamed Sylvia. He would never get to sleep. He sat by the empty fireplace and rubbed his eyes. The images remained just as clear.

Chapter 7

The arrival of the *Weekly Whisper* newspaper at Everton House just three days after Anthony's dinner party made quite a stir among the ladies. At breakfast, Lady Jane read aloud the article on the treatment of widows by Mable Tattler.

"Miss Tattler finishes by saying: 'This reporter is appalled by how a woman, who has run her own home, raised children, and cared for an ailing husband, can be treated like a child with no say in her future. The men of England should be ashamed of themselves. These widowed ladies have every right to make their own decisions and pick their own friends. No one thinks a man suddenly an imbecile just because his wife has died. Perhaps England needs to rethink their treatment of widows and women in general.'"

"Good lord," Lord Rupert said from the head of the long table. "Mable Tattler speaks very boldly. The *Whisper* should be careful lest they find themselves put out of business."

Jane folded the paper and placed her palm on it. The morning sun peeked through the sheer curtains, since the heavy blue drapes had been pulled back. "Are you saying you disagree with what she wrote?"

"Of course not. Women are just as, if not more capable than men. We have proved that a hundred times here at the Everton Domestic Society. My point is that a very strong voice for the stupidity of society might be silenced if they do not temper her somewhat."

Sylvia knew he was right, but she refused to be sorry for what she'd written. Anthony had infuriated her, and as soon as she returned to her room, she'd written the article then sent it off to Mr. Cole before she lost her nerve. Hearing her words read back and seeing the nods of approval from the other ladies, she had done the right thing.

With a shrug, Lady Jane picked up her fork and tapped it on the white china. "I suppose you have a point, Rupert, but someone must say that which is truth, or we will continue to make the same stupid blunders indefinitely."

Rupert glanced at Sylvia.

Her heart stopped. Could he know she was Mable Tattler? It was possible, but no one had ever mentioned her posts to that part of town. She had only told Anthony and one other person, and she was sure neither would have divulged her secret.

"Then we shall have to hope the *Whisper* and Miss Tattler survive her latest bashing of the English way of life." Rupert folded his napkin, stood, and bowed before leaving the breakfast room.

His deep voice sounded in the foyer. "Lord Grafton, we were not expecting anyone to call so early."

"I apologize for the early hour, Lord Rupert. I have an urgent matter to discuss with Miss Dowder." Anthony's voice rang with an intensity that only an American could conjure.

Sylvia's heart pounded, and she couldn't decide if it was excitement over seeing Anthony or because he was probably angry with her. Not that he had any right to be upset. She gave Lady Jane a nod and went to the foyer.

Lord Rupert said, "Oh, I was under the impression you would not be needing Miss Dowder any longer. We have made arrangements for Miss Ann Wittman to replace Miss Dowder."

Anthony's hair was standing up on end. Clearly, he had been running his fingers through the thick dark locks. "Yes, well, I still need to speak to Miss Dowder."

"I am here, my lord. What is it you need?" She tried to sound disinterested, but she'd missed his warm voice and unusual eyes these last three days.

His anger shone in his taut lips and narrowed gaze. He could hide none of his emotions, not even the quick jolt of joy that fled his eyes a moment after he'd initially spotted her. "I need a word with you, Miss Dowder."

It would be better if she hadn't noticed the moment he'd been happy to see her. Her own joy she could hide from onlookers, but if she noticed his expression, Lord Rupert might have as well. "Join me in the small parlor, my lord. No one is using that room at this hour."

They excused themselves from Lord Rupert and walked down the hall to the room at the back of the house where private meetings were often held. Sylvia left the door open as they were unchaperoned, though she doubted anyone would disturb them. "It is not usual to call this early, my lord. You must know the house is either asleep or breaking their fast."

"I also know you are an early riser, Sylvie. Do not call me by my title. It only serves to fuel my anger." He rested his hand on the window casing and leaned into the glass. His jacket stretched across his broad back, straining at the seams and lifting to reveal his very fine legs.

Sylvia had to draw several breaths and look away. The burgundy-and-rose rug was a good distraction with its intricate swirls. She followed one along the edge to regain her composure. "I thought you had made it quite clear that our friendship was void after the dinner party. As we are no longer friends, I see no point in the familiar address."

"I was angry, and I may have gone too far. However, your article this morning was badly done." He approached until he hovered over her.

Standing her ground, she craned her neck to meet his gaze. "Do you think so? I thought it rather well written and to the point."

He gripped her chin firmly but without harming her. "How can anyone so beautiful be so aggravating? You know what I mean. I do not treat my mother like a child. I adore her and worry about her. I will not have some lazy sot ruining the rest of her life."

Staring up into his eyes, she saw every fleck of gold, brown, and even some streaks of green. The moment hung between them, and he leaned in the slightest inch, as if he might repeat the kiss they'd shared.

It took a force of will to step away from his touch and to ignore his compliment. "I had the impression Mr. Condon was rather wealthy, and he was certainly charming."

He threw his hands up in the air and turned away. "You know what I mean."

"No, Tony. I have no idea what you mean or think anymore. I thought I did. I thought we were friends, and you liked the changes I made to your house with your tastes in mind. You seemed pleased with the result of your dinner party. Then without warning, you turned on me like a viper. As a result, Ann Wittman, a very smart, nice lady, will be taking my place as your Everton lady. You will like her, and she will do a fine job for you."

"How do I make you understand?" He spoke to himself, low and with his eyes cast down. He fiddled with a vase from the small table near the divan.

"There is nothing for me to understand. I was in your employ, and you did not wish for that arrangement to continue. Luckily the Society has another lady available for you." The knot in her throat threatened to push tears into her eyes. She fought them back with all her might.

Sorrow crept into his eyes as he tugged on his coat. "You think I'm some kind of monster who orders the women in my life about like chattel."

"Why should an earl care what a servant thinks?" It was time she remembered her place and he his.

"You are not a servant, and we are friends." He raked his fingers through his hair, further disheveling his look.

The guilt returned. How could she not feel bad seeing how distraught he was over a few written words that would be forgotten in a day or two? "I have never thought you a monster, just a bit high-handed."

"I don't treat my mother like a child. She is my responsibility. I must see to her happiness. I have people who depend on me. Workers whose families will starve if I don't do my job. People in America who will suffer if I can't be the man my father was. Of course, you don't understand. How could you? You are a woman with no one depending on you for more than a few months. You do your work, make everything pretty, then walk away. It's so easy for you to judge me." His knuckles were white where he gripped the back of the chair.

Maybe he was right. Had she been callous in her judgment? Obviously, he had worries that she had not even thought about. "I did not mean to hurt your feelings, Tony. Well, maybe I did. I'm sorry you are upset, but I don't think anything I wrote was untrue. Your mother is grown and brilliant. She can decide her own fate without you manipulating her and picking her friends. I would suggest you not spend so much time worrying about the fate of others. You work hard. There is no reason to believe any harm will come to those in your care."

He shook his head. "Let's discuss you coming back to work for me."

"I don't think that would be wise."

Lady Jane spoke loudly from the hallway. "Ann, I want you to meet his lordship while he's in the house."

Sitting, Sylvia waited for the ladies to enter.

Anthony stepped away from the chair and forced a bland expression. It did not really work, but she admired his effort.

Lady Jane and Ann entered the parlor, making the room overcrowded. Jane made a curtsy. "Lord Grafton, since you are here, I wanted you to meet your new Everton lady. Miss Ann Wittman, the Earl of Grafton."

Ann made a pretty curtsy before pushing her spectacles up on her nose. "A pleasure to meet you, my lord. Miss Dowder has given me all the details of the ball, and I will come by tomorrow to discuss things. I would have come today, but Lady Chervil will not be available until tomorrow to act as my chaperon."

The silence dragged on for several uncomfortable beats, but Sylvia refused to run back to him. He had decided, and she didn't know his reasons. If he wanted her to come back, it would take much more than admitting he'd lost his temper. That had been obvious. Besides, Ann had been pulled off another client's contract to accommodate him.

"Thank you, Miss Wittman. I look forward to our meeting." Anthony bowed and bid them all good day before seeing himself out.

"That was very odd." Ann sat next to Sylvia.

"Indeed," Jane said. "Is there something you should tell us, Sylvia?"

"No. I told you what happened. He thought I had tried to matchmake his mother and lost his temper. I tried to explain I had not done any such thing. I'm sure this will all work out. Ann will handle it, and I will see that Roberta Fletcher has a marvelous first few balls."

"Well, then it's all settled." Jane rose, and Ann followed her out.

"Ann," Sylvia called out before Ann cleared the threshold.

Smiling, Ann turned back. "Did you need something, Sylvia?"

"You said Lady Chervil is back home?"

"She arrived home yesterday but had some calls to make and said she would rest most of today."

Once Ann left, Sylvia went up to Lady Chervil's room and knocked.

"Come in." Honoria Chervil's voice sang out from within.

Peeking around the door, Sylvia found Honoria in several layers of ruby silk, standing on an ottoman with her lady's maid poking pins in the bottom of what would eventually be a very ostentatious gown. "I hope I am not disturbing you, my lady."

"Oh, Sylvia, do come in. I haven't seen you in an age. Margery, are you nearly done?" Where most of Everton House was distinctly masculine, Honoria's room was covered in lace, silk, and every possible shade of pink. It was an explosion of femininity that was shocking at first glance.

"One more pin, my lady." Poor Margery groaned as Honoria fidgeted and she moved to the next spot.

"Well, stick it and get this thing off me before I melt. Besides, our friend looks as if she has a problem."

Margery glanced back at Sylvia and smiled. "I'll just be a moment, miss."

"I'm fine, really. No rush."

Once the last pin was pushed, Honoria and Margery stepped behind a screen and removed the red silk in favor of a cotton day dress in pale peach with a dozen salmon-colored ribbons flowing from the bodice to her ankles. "Now, if you will excuse us, Margery."

With just one rolling of her eyes, Margery slipped from the room and closed the door behind her.

Honoria sat in one of two pink overstuffed chairs near the window. "Now come and tell me what has put that crease between your lovely eyes, my dear."

"I don't want to trouble you, my lady, but I have no one else to confide in. My sister has her own problems." Sylvia had met Honoria on her first day at Everton's, and they had become fast friends. Unfortunately for Sylvia, Lady Chervil had many friends and was away from London quite a lot. However, when she was in house, it was like having a favorite aunt to tell all her secrets to. It was nice to have a confidant. Sylvia and Serena had shared everything since birth. Not having her twin to tell her troubles to would have been devastating without Honoria's kindness.

"Don't be silly. Of course, you should trouble me. Now, I heard you have been removed from Anthony Braighton's case. Was that his decision or yours?" Of course, she knew the source of Sylvia's problems. Everyone in the house knew of her failure with Anthony.

"I think both. You see, he became angry over nothing and went into a rage, but I think it was really because of the kiss."

Honoria leaned forward, her eyes bright. "There was a kiss? Where did he kiss you?"

"In his bedroom."

"I actually meant, where on you. However, what on earth were you doing in his bedroom?" Most people would have been shocked, but Honoria grinned and clasped her hands at her chest.

"I was charged with redecorating. I had made some changes in the master chamber, and we were alone for a few moments when the maids and footmen stepped out. He kissed me on the lips." The memory of that kiss sent warmth from her toes up, until her cheeks were on fire, and all the places between longed to repeat that spectacular kiss.

"How was it?"

"The kiss?"

"Yes. Of course, the kiss." Honoria huffed and flopped back against the cushion.

"Oh. It was wonderful, but I don't think that's significant. I have broken rules and been sacked. Well, technically, I quit him. He left me little choice after his outburst." Sylvia suspected Honoria was lost in some romantic thought.

For a moment Honoria peered off into nothing with the most pleasant smile on her round face. With a sigh, she patted her gray curls into place. "Let me see if I understand what has upset you so. You kissed the Earl of Grafton in his bedchamber. Then he requested a new lady to replace you."

"I think you are oversimplifying the situation, my lady."

Honoria shrugged. "Perhaps, but doesn't it sound better this way?"

"No, it makes it sound like I kissed him on purpose and deserved to be replaced." A horrifying notion.

"Well, then you had better tell me what really happened when he lost his temper." She crossed her arms and stared Sylvia down.

"He was upset because a Mr. Condon flirted with his mother at the dinner party. He accused me of trying to make a match. I had not and said as much but also said that there was nothing wrong with his mother making a new friend. His sister agreed; then things got a bit ugly and we both said it would be better if he had a new Everton lady. He did imply that we could not work together."

"It sounds a bit contrived, but I would guess he was taken by surprise by how much that kiss in his bedchamber meant to him. What happened when he came here this morning?" Honoria knew everything that happened within Everton House's walls.

"He was upset because I wrote an article about the treatment of widows in England. I admit, I may have gone a bit far without considering his feelings." Guilt knotted inside Sylvia.

Honoria giggled. "I quite liked the piece and found it to be filled with truths. How does he know you are Miss Tattler?"

"He followed me from his house to the *Whisper*'s office one day and waited in the rain for me. He offered me a secret of his own in exchange for mine."

"How intriguing. I don't suppose you would share his secret with me." Honoria leaned forward again, her eyes alight with mischief.

Unable to keep her amusement at bay, Sylvia laughed. "You know I won't."

Sighing, Honoria shrugged. "It was worth a try."

"Do you have any advice for me?" Sylvia knew there was no help for her troubles. Still, a little wisdom from a friend would be nice.

"Did he ask you to return?"

"He was about to when Lady Jane interrupted and introduced him to Miss Wittman."

"Jane has the most impeccable timing." Honoria chuckled. "I think his lordship is probably in love with you, my dear. How do you feel about him?"

No words would push out of Sylvia's clogged throat. "I'm—I worked for him. I like him. He's a good man. I enjoyed the kiss more than I would have expected, though I suspect it was just a product of the intimacy of the room and new decor. I have tried not to think beyond that. However, I'm sure you are wrong about his lordship's feelings. He does not love me.

Besides, he made it quite clear that his reasons for contacting the Everton Domestic Society were because he did not wish to marry."

"I see. Many young men think they do not wish to marry until they meet the right woman." She plucked at the lace around her sleeves.

"But how many go to such lengths to make sure they are not available for the marriage mart? After all, he did come to us to act as hostess and prove to his mother that he does not need a wife."

Honoria tapped her index finger on her chin. "True. It might be best to keep away from him unless you plan to encourage his affections." Honoria stood and glided to her mirror, where she added a third necklace to her already bejeweled throat.

"I certainly will not encourage any affections. He might like to have a mistress, but I am not that kind of woman."

"Certainly not." Honoria clipped on a pair of diamond and ruby earrings that were large and elaborate for any occasion. They were completely inappropriate for early morning at the Everton Domestic Society.

"Fine, then I shall take your good advice. And since Ann will take over, I see no reason to be in his presence. I shall probably never see Lord Grafton again."

Honoria spun to face her. "Oh, my dear girl, you don't actually believe that, do you?"

"I see no reason why I should run into him. It's too bad that my sister will not be able to benefit from my role as his hostess, but that cannot be helped. I will continue as an Everton lady, and Anthony Braighton will be a notoriously single earl until one day he realizes he must produce an heir." The idea of Tony marrying a young woman in ten years or so made her stomach grip in the most unpleasant way. However, the thought of him alone didn't make her feel any better.

Leaning against her vanity table, Honoria gave her the most whimsical smile. Perhaps she was thinking of something else entirely. "You will be surprised then, my dear. I'm sure his lordship will find a way to see you, and I seriously doubt it will take him very long. However, you have another assignment, and Miss Fletcher's coming out into society is equally important."

Sylvia stood and pulled her shoulders back. Of course, she must do a good job for Roberta Fletcher. "I should go and prepare to meet her this afternoon. Thank you for listening, my lady. I don't know what I would do without you."

With a laugh, Honoria hugged her. "You would manage, I dare say. Enjoy your day and come back and see me whenever you wish."

Ready to face a new challenge, Sylvia rushed to her own room and readied herself for her day. No one, not even Anthony Braighton, would keep her from being the best Everton lady she could be.

Chapter 8

Miss Ann Wittman was a perfect Everton lady. She had all the arrangements that Sylvia had made neatly written in a small leather-bound book. Anthony wanted to run her out of his house. He searched for reasons to get rid of her, but she did everything right. She always said the right thing and had the most level, soothing voice.

It was impossible.

"My lord, will you want to serve a great many refreshments at the ball?" Ann asked.

"Supper, I suppose, is customary. We can afford to put out a nice spread, Miss Wittman." His short tone was uncalled for, but he couldn't seem to help it. Hopefully, she would just assume Americans were all rude.

"I will speak to your cook and arrange a nice meal. Miss Dowder already scheduled the master of ceremonies and the musicians. It will be a lovely evening." Ann made another note in her book.

Lady Chervil sat quietly in the back of his study watching him. She had said no more than the polite hello but smiled and giggled from time to time.

Her regard made Anthony uncomfortable. "Lady Chervil, what do you think? Is supper necessary? I know some of the bigger balls have done away with nice food and good drink."

Raising both eyebrows, she crossed her arms over her chest. "Supper is always a good way to impress your friends and sometimes to make new ones, my lord. If you wish to make an impression, I would encourage you to feed the masses."

"And the music? Has Miss Dowder done an adequate job in her hiring?" It would have been wiser to stay away from talk of Sylvia, but she was all he thought about. Somehow a skinny brunette had invaded his mind, and she would not leave him alone no matter how hard he tried to wipe her from his life.

Ann eased back in her chair and watched the exchange. She turned from one to the other with interest.

"It has been my experience that Miss Dowder does more than adequate work. She is smart and well versed in what society wants and doesn't want. She has never failed at any of her other assignments. Yours was the first." Honoria narrowed her gaze, challenging him.

Had he scarred Sylvia's career with his hasty actions? Lord, what an ass he was. "I'm sure the failure was mine, my lady."

Those expressive eyebrows rose again as Honoria studied him. "Ann, why don't you go and speak to the cook and housekeeper. I'm sure you have copious notes to share with each of them. I know Sylvia gave you all her lists."

Ann looked from one to the other. "Miss Dowder was very thorough. My job is quite easy compared to what she has already done. I'll be an hour or so. Will you be able to entertain yourself, my lady?"

Honoria laughed but continued to stare at Anthony. "I shall manage, my dear."

It annoyed him the way these women seemed to have some silent communication about him that didn't include him. Women in general had been vexing for weeks. Once Ann was gone, Anthony sat back behind his desk. "Well, you have me alone, Lady Chervil. I assume you wish to berate me on my bad behavior. There is no need. I have already given myself a sound thrashing."

Her mouth quirked up on one side. "What was it like in America, my lord?"

Taken completely by surprise, he took a moment to process the question. "Um…it's a bit wild, but in good society there are many rules to live by. The land is very green in Pennsylvania. Why do you ask?"

"I have always wanted to go to America but have never had the chance. Now I'm too old to make the journey. It is a shame, but a fact nonetheless. I wonder if any young people think about all they will miss if they wait too long to have what they want."

"As a young person, I can confirm that while we do think about the future, we also always think there will be time." His father lying on his deathbed flashed into Anthony's mind. Charles Braighton had been the strongest person he'd known. Then he'd been gone in a flash. "I suppose we should know better."

"The thing to remember is how important timing is. If you see an opportunity to enhance your happiness, you have to seize it before the moment passes."

"Are you implying that I am missing my moment, my lady?"

Honoria gave him a wistful smile and sighed. "That is not for me to say, my lord. I have heard you desire to remain a bachelor. If that is true, perhaps you will let many opportunities pass you."

"Marrying is not in my plans for the moment."

"A moment too late is a moment gone," she said.

"What exactly are we talking about?" Most women were confusing, but Honoria Chervil left him completely baffled. He'd not felt so lost since his first day at school.

She waved a hand in the air. "Life and youth. I missed going to America and I would hate for you to miss a great opportunity to be happy. That is all."

"And where do you suppose I might find my happiness?"

Staring at the ceiling in thought, Honoria touched her finger to her chin. "I'm not sure, but I think you might attend the Rochester ball a week from Friday."

"Is that so?" His mother wanted him to marry. It seemed Lady Chervil wanted him to marry. He had no idea what Sylvia wanted, but her dismissal of his kiss indicated she did not want him. Not that it mattered. He would not marry until he was too old to have any fun. Then he would marry someone who could sustain their own amusement. He would never become emotionally attached. He had enough people to care for.

Rising, Honoria smiled. "It is my best guess, my lord. I shall go and find Miss Wittman now. After all, I am her chaperon."

"Are you also often Miss Dowder's chaperon, my lady?"

"Actually, I have never had the pleasure of working with Miss Dowder. However, we are good friends and I am quite fond of her. She is one of brightest and funniest young women I have ever known. And since I meet a great many intelligent women at the Everton Domestic Society, it's quite a compliment."

Refusing to debate a point that he agreed with or discuss Sylvia in detail with Honoria or anyone, he bowed. "I'm sure you are right. Shall I show you the way down to the kitchen?"

She waved her hand frivolously again and trotted out the door. "I can find my own way."

Somehow, Anthony had been run down by the passing carriage that was Lady Honoria Chervil. Did she want him to court Sylvia or go to America before he was too old? Since he'd already been to America, he assumed it was the first. It didn't matter what anyone else wanted or if he liked Sylvia more than he'd ever liked anyone. He would not give up his bachelorhood or his dreams.

* * * *

As many times as he swore he would not attend the Rochester ball, he stepped into the ballroom and ignored every pretty girl who tried to catch his eye. Scanning the room, he immediately found Sylvia in a yellow gown. Her hair shone in the candlelight, and when she spotted him, the blue of her eyes brightened.

Perhaps he had imagined excitement in her expression, but he wanted to believe she was happy to see him. Though, he hated how much he'd missed her and had denied his foul mood all week.

He crossed the ballroom, trying to ignore the whispers from the crowd. The Rochester townhouse reminded him of his own before Sylvia's redecorating. Dark drapes hung from bronze poles and gold and blue papered the walls. A breeze blew in from the open doors leading out to the garden.

A round-faced girl with blond hair and a full figure bounced next to Sylvia and whispered in her ear.

Dipping her head, Sylvia replied to the girl but never took her gaze away from his. "Good evening, my lord. What brings you out?"

He bowed. "I was invited."

"Of course. It's only I'm surprised you would attend this particular ball."

It wouldn't do to tell her the truth about why he'd come. "A man in my position must be seen around town. That's what my mother says anyway."

The fake smile she'd plastered on her lips morphed into genuine pleasure, making his embarrassment well worth it. "Pardon me, my lord. May I introduce Miss Roberta Fletcher? Miss Fletcher, the Earl of Grafton."

Roberta stopped bouncing long enough to curtsy, and he bowed. "Nice to meet you, Miss Fletcher. Is this your first ball?"

"Yes, my lord. Miss Dowder is keeping me out of trouble."

"I'm sure she is." He didn't envy Sylvia her charge. "Miss Dowder has a knack for such things."

Sylvia cocked her head. "Indeed? In that case, my lord, perhaps you will stand up with Miss Fletcher. She is free for the next dance."

Being trapped into dancing with a child of perhaps sixteen was not part of his plan for the evening, but perhaps he could turn it to his advantage. "It would be my honor, if you will dance the next with me, Miss Dowder."

A dozen arguments flitted across her eyes, but she wanted her charge to have a good first ball, and an earl dancing with her would give other men leave to do the same. He might be American, but he knew how London society worked. There were very few leaders and far too many followers.

Nodding, Sylvia frowned.

Thrilled with the outcome, as the music started, he offered Miss Fletcher his arm and led her out for the quadrille.

As the dancers gathered, Roberta said, "You and Miss Dowder have known each other a long time, I suppose."

"For some time. Though, we have only recently become friends."

"She was your Everton lady?"

"Yes."

"Hmm. You seemed very eager to see her when you walked in. I wonder that you don't court her." Roberta took her place for the dance.

He was glad it was a dance with little time for conversation. For someone so young, Roberta had a lot to say on a subject that was not her business. He had behaved stupidly by striding directly to Sylvia the moment he entered. Yet it wasn't in his nature to be coy. She was his Everton lady and he would get her to come back. That was all he wanted from Sylvia Dowder.

Courting Sylvia was out of the question. He didn't want to court anyone, as it led to engagement and marriage. No. His life had no room for a wife. He just needed his Everton lady back, and things would be fine.

The dance ended, and Roberta took his arm. "You were thinking about her all through the dance, my lord. It was clearly on your face. Why not court a lady you are obviously interested in? It's far better than being forced to marry someone you don't even like."

"You are mistaken, Miss Fletcher. I have no feelings for Miss Dowder. She has been in service to me as an Everton lady, nothing more."

She wrinkled her freckled nose. "I may be young, my lord, but I'm not a fool. I can see in your eyes and in hers that it is more than that. You are in love with her, and she is in danger of falling in love with you."

"Impossible." Saying more to his new acquaintance would be rude, and he didn't need a girl screaming and crying from the room.

She stopped and faced him. "All things seem impossible until they happen for the first time. Thank you for the dance." With a quick curtsy, she rushed over to a group of girls, who all giggled.

On the other side of the room, half obscured by the curtains, Sylvia hid in the corner. She was watching Miss Fletcher so didn't notice his approach.

"I believe I have the next dance, Sylvie." He held out his arm.

"While I appreciate you dancing with Roberta, I see no point in our dancing, my lord."

"My name is Tony. You promised me a dance, and as it is the only reason I agreed to stand up with your Miss Fletcher, I won't be sent away."

With a sigh, she took his arm. "Why are you doing this, Tony? You wanted a new Everton lady and you got one. You wanted to prove you didn't need a wife, and you've nearly done so. What can you possibly want from me?"

The waltz began, and he took her in his arms. Despite their difference in height, she fit him perfectly and they moved as one around the floor. "I'm not doing anything, Sylvie. I miss having you take care of my hosting responsibilities, and I want to apologize and ask you to come back. It was why I came to Everton House the other day, but I got sidetracked and Lady Jane interrupted."

She met his gaze. "Is Ann not to your liking?"

Sometimes he wished he was a good liar. This would have been a perfect time to tell her Ann had made some grievous error. "Ann works hard and knows how to plan a ball. I have no complaints."

"Then I see no reason to cause everyone more difficulties. I shall help Miss Fletcher with her debut, and Ann will be your Everton lady." She swallowed hard, and he couldn't help staring at the soft bob of her throat and wishing he could run a string of kisses along that movement.

He tightened his hand at her back. "I think it would be better if you came back, Sylvie. I'm sure my ball and house party will be much more successful if you are the hostess."

"No. I'm committed to Roberta now. You know that our personalities do not work well together. It is better this way."

Every word set the vise around his heart tighter. "Is this because I kissed you?"

"Must you always be so blunt?"

"I suppose I must. I am blunt and honest. I realize these are not qualities prided among you English, but I thought you were different." Inside his head, he screamed at himself to hold his temper, but it still simmered just below the surface.

She stopped dancing and stepped back from him. "I am not different. I am an English lady whose father is a gentleman, and you would do well to remember that."

"You are making a scene, Miss Dowder." He offered her his embrace to finish the dance.

Stepping back into the circle of his arms, she held her tears at bay. "I'm a lady, Tony. Whatever it is you want, it doesn't fit within my life and expectations."

He couldn't bear her tears or that he was the cause of them. "I have always treated you with the utmost respect. I admit I shouldn't have kissed you but refuse to regret a moment that was pure and honest. Frankly, it was the sweetest minute of my life. I'm only sorry that you were hurt by it."

Blinking her tears away, she said, "Not hurt, confused and ashamed."

The music ended. "Come back, Sylvie."

"No."

He bowed. "Then you leave me no choice."

She opened her mouth to say something, but he turned and walked away. She would see soon enough what he meant when he arrived at Everton House in the morning. On the veranda, he took several long deep breaths and tried to cool his desire to kiss her senseless.

"That was quite a show," Miles Hallsmith said and handed him a glass of wine.

Taking the wine, he noted a couple sneaking into the shadows of the garden. The burgundy was bold and well formed. He sipped. "What are you talking about?"

"You and the little blonde then Miss Dowder have given the entire ballroom gossip for days." Miles drank his wine and leaned against the stone balustrade.

"How did I do that?"

"Let me see. First you strode with a single focus to speak to Miss Dowder, a lady beyond society's ideas of marriageable. Then you danced the first dance with a young girl of no title who is just out. If that wasn't enough to get the tongues wagging, you then danced the waltz with Miss Dowder and the two of you seemed to be involved in an impassioned conversation." Miles raised one dark red eyebrow.

A long sigh escaped Anthony's lips. "I suppose I could have been more discreet."

Miles's laugh was bold and filled with joy. "My friend, you are the least discreet person I know. I only suggest you mind the lady's reputation. It is already tested by her being in Everton's employ. Making a spectacle of her could make her very unpopular. A lady's virtue is all she has in this society. You would not wish to jeopardize her professional status."

"No. I would not wish to do that. I can't seem to make her see reason." He downed the remaining wine and put the glass on the railing.

Miles lowered his voice. "What are you trying to convince her to do?"

"I lost my temper and asked for a new lady. It was a mistake, and I'm just trying to get her to come back." Lord, he sounded like an idiot.

"Is not one Everton lady the same as the next?" Miles's smile said he knew the answer.

"Evidently not."

"May I ask you something personal, Grafton?"

Anthony would never get used to his title. "Can I stop you?"

Miles shrugged. "Have you changed your determination to not marry?"

"No. Why would you ask that?"

"Well, you want to keep Miss Dowder close, yet you do not wish to marry her or anyone else. Do you plan to make her your mistress?"

"Of course not. She's a lady." Anthony considered calling Miles out for suggesting such a thing. He would never think of Sylvia so crassly. Though, it pained him that he had made her think of herself in those terms. His desires were a jumble of emotions that he couldn't sort through.

"My point exactly. You have fired her but want her back. You approach her as if she is the only woman in the ballroom and have a passionate talk while dancing. You say you will not court her, yet you expect her to return to your home as an employee. I think the lady should stay as far away from you as possible." Miles picked up his glass and walked back into the ballroom.

A glimpse of yellow caught his eye. Turning, he watched Sylvia leave the ballroom and step around the corner of the house.

Miles's warning rang in his ears, but his feet followed her into the shadows. The full moon shone down on her. She was a goddess. "Are you hiding again?"

The nook of the veranda separated them from the rest of the crowd, but anyone who rounded the corner would see them alone together. "You should go back inside, Tony."

"You should walk with me in the garden where we won't be seen."

"Why?" No sign of shock, she sounded weary.

"I want to talk, to apologize for my behavior. Miles was out here and made me see that I have not been a gentleman where you are concerned. I have put you in a dangerous position. Tell me how I can make amends."

"I will be fine, Tony. I have the Everton Domestic Society to protect me, and you have your title. In a few weeks no one will even remember you sought me out." She kept both hands on the stone rail and would not look at him.

Voices carried out from the ballroom. Anthony glanced back to be sure no one was coming around the side of the house. "Will you remember, Sylvie?"

"For the rest of my life." She let go of the stone and looked at him for the first time since he'd followed her. Tears again glowed in her blue eyes.

More voices.

The unexplainable ache in his chest doubled. All his resolve to remain a bachelor seemed foolish. He reached out his hand. "Please, Sylvie, walk with me."

She backed away toward the small staircase leading down to the garden.

Certain she was running away to leave him brokenhearted, when she reached her hand toward him, he leaped forward and took it. Then he hurried into the shadows, so they wouldn't be seen. A niche in the stone wall was partially covered by shrubbery and he eased her into the space. "What is it about you that makes me act this way? I never wanted to be responsible for anyone else's happiness."

She reached up and ran her fingers along the side of his face. "No one can be responsible for another's true happiness. You can only be a good man and do what you think is right. We are each in charge of our own feelings."

Leaning into her touch, he turned his head and kissed her palm. "If my actions have brought you sorrow, I shall never forgive myself."

Her laugh rolled low and warm. "Here I was thinking you wanted to kiss me, Tony, and you really did want to talk."

Every fiber of his body solidified with the mention of kissing her. "I want to kiss you more than I want to take my next breath."

"Then you had better do so before I come to my senses." Sylvia lifted on her toes and wrapped her hand around his neck. Her delicate yet capable fingers threaded through the back of his hair.

Leaning in, he captured those full lips. She pulled him close, and he relished deepening the kiss, feeling her soft sigh against his tongue. When they were both breathless, he pulled back, pressed kisses along her jaw to her ear, her eyelid, her sweet nose. "I'm going to ask Jane to let you come back."

"Tony, this is never going to be a good thing. You can only hurt me, and in ways you cannot even imagine. I know you mean well, but what future do you see?" She pressed her forehead against his chest.

Whenever she was in his arms, he couldn't think of anything but the present. "I don't know. I will promise to keep my hands and lips to myself. We shall be good friends and nothing more as long as you don't request a kiss, Sylvie. If you do that, I can't resist you."

Her silence scared him. "Ann is a wonderful Everton lady. She has done nothing wrong, but you understand me. You decorated my home as well as if I'd done it myself. You turned something I hated into a place I now call home, and I need that in the ballroom as well as at the house party."

Shaking her head, she pressed away from his embrace. "Come to Everton House tomorrow. I suspect you intended to do so anyway and make a big scene to bully Lady Jane into making me come back."

Holding his laughter back, he said, "You see how well you know me."

"Indeed." Playfully she slapped his shoulder. "I'll speak to her ladyship, and you will think of something respectful to say when you arrive."

"Thank you, Sylvie." He kissed the top of her head and breathed in her scent.

"You should go inside. I have been here before and know a way in through the kitchen garden." She pointed to her right.

"Are you sure you will be all right?"

"Of course. Go and don't look so…whatever that look is."

Having no idea what she meant, he tried to have a bland expression. "How is this?"

She laughed. "Very British." Slipping under his arm, she disappeared behind an evergreen. Her whisper filtered through the greenery. "And Tony, I will not ask for another kiss, despite how lovely they are."

Inside the ballroom, he found Miles and more of the wine. "I'm going to White's if you'd like to join me."

"I have had my fill of wine and debutantes for one night. A brandy and some male company might be just the way to end this night." Miles put his glass on the table, and they called for Anthony's carriage.

In the carriage, they were stopped by traffic and a sudden rain shower.

Miles opened the shade and peered out. "Have you decided what to do about Miss Dowder?"

"Yes and no."

Miles laughed. "That clear, is it?"

"My life used to be very simple, and now it is like crossing the Atlantic, and daily, I'm concerned with my survival."

Still amused, Miles tapped out a tune on the wooden frame of the carriage window. "You'll live, my friend. One way or the other, you'll still be here in the morning."

In the morning he would see his Sylvia again. It warmed his soul, and even that terrified him.

The horses jerked forward, and they made their way through the wet streets toward St. James.

Chapter 9

The morning paper had Sylvia seething. Sitting at her writing desk, she reread the article that all but called her a whore. How dare this ninny say she had questionable morals.

A knock at her door forced her to take a deep breath. "Come in."

Lady Honoria Chervil popped her head in, and the rest of her billowed in on the breeze in a wispy dress far better suited to a young girl. "Oh, I see you've already seen the paper. I was hoping to soften the blow."

"I can't believe anyone would say such hurtful and untrue things. I was not loose at the ball. I only danced with Lord Grafton one time, not three as this E. M. Whitewall says. I certainly didn't dance another three with Miles Hallsmith. In fact, I never danced with Mr. Hallsmith. I greeted him, introduced him to Miss Fletcher and bid him a good evening."

Honoria sank into the chair a few feet away. "Did you disappear into the garden for several hours?"

Fury Sylvia hadn't felt since Hunter betrayed her scorched her tongue, forcing her to take several breaths before answering. "Ten minutes to catch my breath from the hot ballroom."

"Could Grafton have gone missing in those same ten minutes?" Honoria raised her brows.

Sylvia scanned the article. "It doesn't say a word about that."

"No. I just wanted to see how you would react." Her voice took on a singsong tone. "And I got my answer."

"The point is that ninety percent of this is fabricated. E. M. Whitewall, whoever she is, has made up a hurtful story about me and I have no idea why."

"You might look at it another way."

"What other way is there to see a fraud?"

Honoria shrugged. "Perhaps she was trying to help you in her own way. It is possible she hoped to force Grafton's hand. Clearly the two of you have feelings for each other, yet you both claim or pretend otherwise. Miss Whitewall may think a little nudge is all you two need to move on to the next natural step."

"Lady Chervil, please do not tell me you are E. M. Whitewall."

"Of course not."

Sylvia was able to breathe again. "Thank goodness. She is wildly out of order, if she is trying to be helpful. Besides, it would never work."

"Oh, I don't know. His lordship is downstairs now, looking ready to do someone harm, and defend you to the end. He has been pacing and ranting to Lady Jane for half an hour about the lies in the paper." Honoria stood and sashayed to the door. "I suppose you had better finish dressing and come down."

It was eight o'clock in the morning. No one, not even a brash American, called at such an hour. Putting the paper aside, Sylvia sighed, then finished her morning toilet and rushed down the stairs.

Anthony's voice carried through the office doors, down the hall, and into the foyer. Several ladies and household staff had gathered at the bottom of the steps to listen to the commotion.

"You should all find something else to do," Sylvia scolded as she stormed past. As the yelling grew louder and she was out of view of the rest of the house, she slowed her gait and waited.

"You can't possibly believe what that woman wrote," Anthony said.

"I never said I did, my lord. You are clearly upset, and for that I am sorry, but I do not control the gossip printed in the newspaper." Jane's voice was steady and as unaffected as always.

"Miss Dowder is a lady through and through." It was sweet that he was so staunchly defending her. Some bit of her resolve to stay away from private moments with him melted away.

"I never doubted that," Lady Jane said.

Sylvia knocked but pushed through before being given leave to enter. "My lord, your call is unusually early."

He turned toward her voice and froze, his eyes wide but filled with regret. "Sy—Miss Dowder, are you all right?"

"I assure you, Lord Grafton, I am uninjured. A little false gossip will not topple me or the Everton Domestic Society."

"Did you lose your post with Miss Fletcher?" He crossed his arms over his chest then put them at his sides before crossing them again.

"Not that I'm aware of." She looked at Jane for confirmation.

Jane sat behind her desk and sighed. "No, but this gossip will make it difficult for the Fletcher family to continue with you as their Everton lady. At least until the next bit of news hits the papers."

"I suppose that's true." Sylvia hated to admit it, but her name in the paper saying she behaved badly at a ball made her a poor choice to bring a young lady out in society. Of course, the ton would get over it and move on to another story in a week or two.

"I will ask Ann to take over. I believe Lord Grafton would like you to return to your former post if that will suit you, Miss Dowder." Jane jotted a note as she spoke.

"I am familiar with the case and am happy to return if his lordship is certain his temperament can bear it. I have not changed and will continue to give my honest opinion, even if it is not what you wish to hear."

He bowed. "I have already apologized, Miss Dowder. I will not lose my temper again. Though, I do admit my mother is a touchy subject. Perhaps you might tread more gently regarding her?"

It took an effort to not giggle at the truth. "I will do my best."

Jane stood. "Good. That is settled then. However, I'll warn you both that if more gossip about the two of you should rear its nasty head, I will have to pull Miss Dowder for her own protection. If she were ruined for society, it would be hard to keep her working. I would hate for us to have an issue of that kind."

"It will not be a problem, my lady." Sylvia cringed. She couldn't afford another scandal looming in the background. One per year, or lifetime, was more than enough. "Shall I walk you out, my lord?"

"Thank you." He grabbed his hat from the chair and followed her.

The foyer was blissfully empty. At the door, he leaned close to her ear. "Are you truly all right, Sylvie?"

"Yes. Just a bit annoyed. I wish I knew who E. M. Whitewall is."

He smiled, and it sent a shock through her that settled between her legs. Something about him turned her into a wanton. "I'm sure Miss Tattler will put things right again. She has a way of putting people in their place."

It was the perfect vehicle to get her revenge. She should go speak to Anthony's cook first, but she had to write a new column before the paper went to print. "Will you tell your cook that I will come to see her this afternoon? I want to settle on the menu, and I also need to speak to the staff about the table setting."

He bowed. "I shall be available this afternoon as well, should you need my input."

"Good day, my lord."

With a quick nod, he was gone, down the steps and into his carriage.

At a run, Sylvia charged up the steps to her room and pulled out parchment and ink. Fire with fire was the only way to finish this. It was a pity she couldn't figure out who E. M. Whitewall was, but it still had to be stopped.

* * * *

Sylvia finished her article and delivered it to the *Whisper* before taking the Everton carriage back to Anthony's house.

"How long do you think this will take, Miss Dowder?" Mrs. Horthorn asked.

"I expect it will be a few hours. Do you have another appointment?"

She held up her bag of knitting. "No. I'll just settle myself in that lovely front parlor, and you do what you need to. I can't see how my services will be necessary for a meeting with the cook."

"Very well. I'll collect you when I've finished." Sylvia went to the kitchen but was informed the cook had stepped out and would be back in half an hour, so she walked out to the garden and thought how lovely it would be to light the path for the ball. She would speak to the gardener about some torches.

"I heard you had arrived, Sylvie." Anthony's low voice warmed her inside and out.

She pointed to the path. "Don't you think some torches to light the path would be lovely for the ball?"

"You mean to keep people out of the shadows?" His smile was wicked and wonderful.

First, she'd practically begged him to kiss her, and now she was ready to swoon over a smile. She must be losing her senses. "I'm sure if people want to find a shadow or two, they will do so regardless of the torches. I just think it will be beautiful from the veranda."

"Then we shall have torches." His expression grew serious. "Have I ruined you, Sylvie? Would you tell me if I had?"

A knot formed in her gut. "No, Tony. It will be fine. I have endured far worse gossip, and this too will be forgotten in a short time."

"You didn't answer the second question." He stood so close to her that as they looked out over the small wilderness of a garden, his pinkie finger touched hers.

"There is nothing you could do about it, so if I am honest, no. I would not tell you, but I think you would know from what others say." Just the tiny bit of skin touching worked a warm haze through her, and she wished she could stand like that all day and keep the contact.

Sorrow, need, and something new etched lines around his beautiful mouth and those unusual eyes. "I am here to do whatever you need."

Was he talking about the ball or something else? She didn't know, but it wouldn't do to assume he'd just offered to fix things if she were ruined, since there was only one way to do that. It was impossible that the Earl of Grafton had just proposed, so Sylvia assumed he meant with the ball. "I'm sure I can manage. I'll just go and see if Cook is back in the kitchen."

It took all her strength not to run as fast as she could away from him. He had just meant to help with the ball. Her heart was pounding out of her chest. In the servants' hall she whispered, "Don't be a fool, Sylvia. Nothing can come of any of this and you wouldn't want it to anyway. You have a good life mapped out for yourself, and he is only an assignment."

"Did you say something, miss?" Cook asked as she tromped down the hall. Her girth nearly the same as her height, she moved well for her size.

"Just talking to myself about the ball. I have quite a lot of ideas about the meal if you have some time?" Sylvia sat at the long wooden table in the kitchen where the servants took their meals, and the cook sat adjacent to her.

"I assume you'll want to start with a white soup." Cook put on a pair of spectacles to look at Sylvia's list.

"Yes. That would be perfect, and I thought roast fowls and a game pie should follow with lamb, savory cake and aspic as well. Can you do a few meringues?" She had a vision of the table with all the silver, candles, china and crystal gleaming around the most beautiful food. No one would turn up their noses to the newest member of the peerage if she could help it.

"I see you want to be makin' a big show for the guests. I can do it, and I'll add a few more sweets to decorate the table up right. I'll not have his lordship looked down upon just because he's an American."

These servants had served and loved Lady Collington, but they had embraced Anthony as their own. He was charming and good to them, that was obvious in their quick loyalty. "That's just it. We must have everything just so and keep those wagging tongues quiet."

With a nod, Cook said, "I'll be doin' my part, miss. Not to worry. The house looks fit for all the finest people thanks to you, and I know it will all turn out well."

"Thank you." Sylvia left the kitchen in search of the gardener; then she found Wells for a quick word about staff and serving. Once she was sure it was all in order, she knocked on Anthony's study door.

"Come in."

She pushed through the threshold. He had one hand threaded through his hair and the other leaning on the desk. His coat was slung on the back of his chair, leaving him in his white blouse, hunched over a piece of paper. She longed to read over his shoulder and run her fingers through that mass of thick hair. It took her a heartbeat to gather herself. "I wanted to let you know Mrs. Horthorn and I will be leaving now."

He stood. "Do you need anything from me?"

"Everything is in order. Ann sent out the invitations, and I think all good London society will be attending your ball. My sister wrote to me this morning to say how excited she is to attend, and both her suitors will be present. That should make my evening more interesting than need be."

He pulled his jacket on and sat when she did. "I hope she chooses Stansfield. I've always thought Parker a bit big for his britches."

"Is that your American way of saying he is a snob?" She giggled. "In that case it explains why Mother likes him so much."

"Speaking of mothers." His smile faltered. "My mother has asked that Mr. Condon be invited to the ball."

Part of her wanted to jump for joy that Mrs. Braighton had found a friend to stave off any loneliness, but the other part worried that this was about to become a fight with the one man she never wanted to fight with. She leaned forward and put her hands on the desk. "What do you think about that, Tony?"

Leaning back in his chair, he put his hands over his face and rubbed before letting out a long sigh. "I want to protect her the way my father would have. I asked around about Mr. Condon, and anyone who knows him or has done business with him says he is a good man with a lot of money. He hails originally from Ireland and is Catholic. My mother was raised in the Catholic Church, and they have much to talk about, both living in England now. I want to keep her safe, but I also want her to be happy. My father has been dead almost six years. Maybe it's time."

"Six years is a long time to be alone." She kept her voice low and even.

His gaze met hers. Whatever he wanted to say, he shook it away and put a typical English mild expression on his face. "It is time I realized my mother is a grown woman who can make her own decisions without my input or direction."

Suddenly she hated that bland expression. It didn't suit him at all. He was fire and ice, not this cool facade that the gentry always put on. What had he been about to say to her about being alone? Why hadn't he said it? "That is very mature of you."

"I'm learning. Anyway, if I had found out something untoward about him, I would have advised my mother of his bad character. Since I can't do that, I'll keep my own counsel and see what happens."

"It will be a grand ball, and your mother and Mr. Condon are only two people. You will have a hundred others to deal with on the night." She stood, and so did he.

"More than I'll want, for sure. Did you need anything else from me?" He rounded the desk.

"Everything is taken care of unless you would like to handle the wine selection."

"I'll not have the sweet watered-down mess that is usually served at these events." There was the fire she loved.

"You may serve whatever wine you wish. Just be sure you can afford the drunkards you will create." She laughed.

He frowned. "I see your point. Perhaps I will reserve the good wine served to close family and friends."

"Another wise decision." She walked to the door.

"Did you write your rebuttal?"

"You will have to wait for tomorrow's paper and find out," she teased him.

Anthony raised an eyebrow. "You would make me wait after all the secrets I have shared with you."

"I have not had a new secret in some time, my lord." Treading on dangerous ground, she should not flirt, but couldn't help herself.

He leaned in. "I will tell you one, if you tell me one."

The heat of him was like a warm blanket she wanted to crawl under and never leave. "I don't think I have any more secrets. Why don't you ask me something and I'll tell you?"

There was that serious Anthony again. "Was March the love of your life?"

The question shook her. "I'm not sure I believe a person has a love of their life."

He relaxed. "If you think that, then he wasn't yours. My parents were inseparable. They could not sit in a room together without one placing a hand on the other's shoulder or letting their fingers graze each other. My sister and Marlton are the same way. Their love is so enormous, everyone who meets them can see it."

What would it be like to have that kind of love? A silly notion, but one she would think about for a long time. "Then your answer is, no. Hunter was not the love of my life."

"I'm glad to hear that. I don't like the idea of you suffering the loss of that kind of love."

Too much emotion flew between them like some thick jungle she'd read about. It would do only harm to fight through that kind of mess. "What is your secret?"

He opened the study door and leaned in until she felt his breath on her ear. "I would marry you to keep you safe, Sylvie."

"What?" She must have heard him wrong.

Mrs. Horthorn stood up from her chair in the parlor across the foyer. "Ready to leave now, Miss Dowder?"

"I, um. Yes. I suppose I'm ready."

"Good day, Miss Dowder." Anthony's expression was serious and intense. She swallowed to make room for more words. "Good day, my lord."

* * * *

It had taken Sylvia longer than usual to go down for the morning meal. The more she thought about what he'd said, the more confused Sylvia became. Would he marry a woman just to keep the gossips at bay? No one in their right mind would saddle themselves with a wife they didn't want for such a silly reason. She must have misunderstood him. Not that it mattered. She didn't need anyone to keep her safe and she certainly didn't want to be any man's burden.

In the breakfast room all the ladies where talking at once, with Lord Rupert grinning from ear to ear at the head of the table.

As Sylvia entered everyone grew silent and gawked at her.

"Good morning," she said. "Is something amiss?" She checked her dress for tears or stains.

"Not at all, Miss Dowder. It seems you have a champion," Jane said, waving the morning newspaper in the air.

"Is that so?" Sylvia took a plate and served herself toast and coddled eggs from the sideboard.

Once she was seated, Lady Jane said, "Oh yes, it seems Miss Tattler was at the ball last week and has taken up your cause. She thrashed Miss Whitewall soundly, saying she saw no imprudent behavior on your part.

She even said that you had only taken part in one dance all evening, and while it was with Lord Grafton, there was nothing improper to report."

Sylvia swallowed a bite of toast. "That was kind of Miss Tattler. I wonder why she would take an interest in me."

On the other side of the table, Ann clapped happily. "She said in her article that she was tired of the mean-spiritedness that is taking over the ballrooms of London. Miss Tattler said that there was nothing to gain by besmirching the reputation of a lady of good birth but no consequence. She went so far as to accuse the gossips of having some design on Lord Grafton, as that was the only reason anyone would be so mean."

Perhaps she had gone too far with that part, but Sylvia had been so hurt and angry at the time, she'd written more from the heart than her head.

Honoria cleared her throat. "A bit rough to say you are of no consequence, in my opinion."

"True though," Sylvia said. "I threaten no one searching for a husband."

Jane put the paper down. "It's a triumph for you, Miss Dowder. I wish I could thank Miss Tattler in person. She has done the Everton Domestic Society a great service."

Lord Rupert coughed. Sylvia caught his eye as he gave her a long look.

Clearly, he knew of her secondary occupation.

Honoria raised an eyebrow. "I'm just glad we shall get through one early morning without an angry earl banging down the doors."

"That is a benefit." Jane sipped her tea. "Speaking of the earl, how are the plans for the Grafton ball coming along?"

"Everything is in order. Ann managed quite a lot of the planning, and his lordship has a competent staff. I have every expectation that it will be a singular event." Sylvia may have shown too much pride in her work, but it was going to be a night remembered by the ton.

"Excellent. I heard from Lady Chervil that the house looks beautiful. She had visited with Lady Collington when her ladyship was in residence and said that you have made a big impact for very little cost. I'm sure Lord Grafton is pleased." Jane smiled down the table at her.

"I hope he is, my lady. The house is beautiful and really only needed some updates and lightening up to suit his lordship's tastes."

With a nod, she changed the subject to other cases and directed her attention to the other ladies at the table.

Sylvia ate her eggs and excused herself.

Lord Rupert stood. "Miss Dowder, might I have a word?"

"Of course." She followed him to the office, where he closed the door and stood facing her a long moment. "Is something wrong, my lord?"

"Miss Dowder, you are a smart young woman, so I'll not dally. It is not my habit to tell the ladies what to do. You are all capable and know your own minds, but don't you think it time you give up your alter ego and let Miss Tattler die?"

Sylvia sank into the chair near the desk. "I had a notion that you knew. I hope you're not angry with me."

Straightening his coat, he crossed and sat behind the desk. "Not at all. I thought your column fun, and most of the time the recipients of your sharp pen deserved what they got. But if you were found out after defending yourself, you would be in a bad position and Lady Jane and I would have a difficult time finding clients who would be willing to use you. I'm sure you can see the problem."

A heavy weight settled on Sylvia's chest. "I can, my lord. I do so enjoy writing the column, but it was in bad taste to defend myself so overtly. My temper got away from me."

"I cannot say that I blame you. That Whitewall woman was cruel, and for no reason."

"My lord, may I ask how long you have known Miss Tattler and I are one and the same?"

He grinned and ran his hand down his trimmed beard, his blue eyes alight with amusement. "On your second week here, you asked for the carriage, but I had already taken it. When I was in town I saw you enter the offices of the *Weekly Whisper.* Once you had gone, I spoke to Mr. Cole and he told me that Miss Tattler was one of his best new writers."

All that time, he had known. "Thank you for keeping my secret, my lord."

"Does that mean you will end your work with the *Weekly Whisper?*"

"I will think about your advice. It is not my habit to act rashly, but it may be time to put Miss Tattler to an end." Standing, she brushed out her skirt.

He stood and bowed. "I'm sure you will do what is best for you, and that is all I want, Miss Dowder. I have only your best interest in mind."

"I know, and I thank you." She walked to the door. "I have some lists to make for the Grafton ball. If you will excuse me, my lord."

"Good day, Miss Dowder."

Chapter 10

Anthony loved his mother and his sister, he was even very fond of his brother-in-law, Daniel Fallon, the Earl of Marlton, but when the three arrived early for his first ball, he'd hoped the knock would reveal Sylvia.

"You were hoping for someone else, Tony?" Sophia winked.

"I'm happy to see you." He wished for the thousandth time he could keep disappointment hidden. Anthony led them into the great parlor with its new lighter decor. A lot of the furniture had been moved to allow people to mill around more freely during the ball. Many people who did not care to dance would visit in the parlor.

"This is much different from when Lady Collington lived here." Daniel sat when the ladies were seated.

"Aunt Daphne is coming tonight, is she not, Anthony?" his mother asked.

His nerves doubled with the thought that his great-aunt would frown upon the changes he'd made. "She said she would be here, but I've not heard from her in over a week."

Daniel glanced around, nodding his approval. "If Daphne Collington said she would be here, then she will. I have no doubt of that."

Their aunt was tenacious and brutally honest. Anthony was also sure she would make an appearance at the ball. There were footsteps in the hall, but it was only the footmen getting ready for guests to arrive. "I have made sure she has a seat to my right for supper."

"Who are you waiting so anxiously for?" Mother looked at the door then back at him.

Sophia raised an eyebrow. "I suspect it is a certain Everton lady that Lord Grafton admires."

Nerves at their end, he said, "You shouldn't believe everything you read in the paper, Sophie."

She mimicked him perfectly before switching to her own soft voice. "I don't read gossip. However, I do know my older brother well enough to see the way he looks at Miss Sylvia Dowder. What I don't know is why you are so hesitant to do something about it."

"There is nothing to do. She is an Everton lady and I have no need to act. She decorated my home and arranges my parties. Nothing more." He leaned on the mantel.

Daniel laughed. "Tony, it's a good thing you don't play cards. I have not seen Sylvia or Serena in many years. I assume they have matured out of their silliness."

Sophia leaned against her husband. "Serena is still quite light of heart, but Sylvia has grown more serious after the March ordeal. I hope he will not be here tonight."

A familiar knot tightened in Anthony's stomach. Ann had handled the invitations, and he'd not thought to look them over. It was quite likely that, as a viscount, living in town, March would have received an invitation. "I really don't know if he will be here."

"Who, my lord?" Sylvia was a vision in a ruby dress. That dress alone would cause a stir, but she looked like every dream he'd ever had. Lightly freckled, her soft skin shone in the candlelight, and her hair was woven with pearls. She was a confection and he longed to take a taste.

His family stood. "Miss Dowder. Good evening."

She curtsied and smiled. "It's nice to see you all again. Lord Marlton, it has been many years."

Daniel crossed and bowed over her hand. "Far too long, Miss Dowder. I was telling Tony how much I like what you've done with the house."

"I'm glad you approve. With that in mind, I should warn you that I arrived at the same time as Lady Collington. She has gone to inspect the ballroom and dining room." Sylvia widened her eyes dramatically. "I fear for my life."

Mother came closer. "I hope she was kind when you saw her."

"I was told that March was an imbecile and I'm better off without him cluttering up my home. Oh, and she approves of ladies finding their own way in the world. I took both comments to be a great success on my part." Sylvia smiled, and Anthony thought his heart might burst from his chest.

It was entirely possible he had lost his mind. "She must like you."

Accepting the compliment, she inclined her head. "Who were you wondering about attending, my lord?"

He'd hoped she'd forgotten but knew she didn't forget anything. "I was saying that I didn't know if Lord March would attend, as I did not check the guest list before Miss Wittman sent the invitations."

A brief wave of panic crossed her face but was quickly replaced by the calm expression English women used whenever they hid their true feelings. "I'm sure he will come if he was invited to an earl's home."

"I'm sorry, Sylvie. I should have been more careful." He should have kept their conversation formal in front of his family, but he wanted her to know she was not alone.

"My lord, I will be fine. There is no need for you to concern yourself."

"Nephew!" Aunt Daphne called before her tall figure ambled in with the use of an elaborate cane. Her gray hair was swept away from her high forehead and piled on top in a stately bun.

"Good evening, Aunt Daphne. I'm pleased you could come," Anthony said and bowed before his mother and sister rushed over to hug their aunt.

She blustered at the open affection, but he caught the hint of a smile. "You have changed the entire house."

"Do you like it?"

She narrowed her gaze and glowered at the redecorated parlor. "It suits you."

Anthony took a deep breath. "I'm glad you approve. Miss Dowder did most of the work, but if you had hated it, I would have had to take the blame."

A slow smile pulled at Daphne's lips. "You are more and more like your father. Well done. The table is spectacular. I should be interested to see it after Cook brings in the food."

"The menu will be wonderful, and Cook has promised me some beautiful puddings," Sylvia said.

Daphne tapped her cane, walked to the divan and sat. "Miss Dowder, that gown is very forward for an unmarried woman. You'll not stop the gossips dressing like that."

"I have decided they may gossip all they want. I will not change for anyone." Sylvia lifted her chin.

Mother grinned, as did Sophia.

Daphne nodded. "You might go and check the seating. I thought I saw old Pemberhamble is seated next to Cynthia Watlington. That dunderhead will eat the girl alive."

Panic flushed Sylvia's face. "Excuse me." She made a curtsy and rushed from the room, skirts in hand.

"I like that girl." Aunt Daphne studied the door where Sylvia exited. "She turned out well despite a difficult beginning and a mother with little affection. I worry about the other one, but there's nothing to be done but hope for the best."

"I like her too," Mother said. "She's tough but not overbearing. She'd make someone a fine wife. A shame she's on the shelf."

Daphne made a derisive sound. "Don't be so sure, Angelica. Good women like that do not last long without some smart gentleman snatching them up. Even with the March scandal, I think Miss Sylvia Dowder will marry. Perhaps she'll meet a nice gentleman tonight. Ballrooms are always the best place to find a husband."

Sophia said, "It is where Daniel and I first met. I had Miss Ann Wittman add Mr. Edward Tucker to the guest list tonight. I thought he might be a nice match for Miss Dowder."

Anthony had forgotten about Mr. Tucker. He didn't know whether to berate his sister for inviting him or toss him from the house the moment he appeared. Both would be satisfying, but he would do neither. The night was not starting out well.

Daniel kissed her hand. "You took my breath away, and a few minutes later, I wanted to throttle you with your request for me to dance with Elinor, and you were flirting with Thomas. However, I thought you had given up matchmaking."

"I most certainly was not flirting. I was talking him into dancing with Elinor to save her reputation after Michael had ruined her. I'm not matchmaking, just creating opportunities for two nice people."

Daphne laughed, and everyone turned at the rare sound. "It all turned out, as you two are married these six years, Thomas has a fine wife, and Elinor is married, to a duke no less."

"Indeed," Sophia agreed. "Shall we go and greet your guests, Tony?"

Keeping his temper and expression under tight control proved more difficult than being a proper earl. How the English always appeared so benign was a mystery.

They went to the foyer, where people had started to arrive. Each unmarried man who entered made Anthony think about what Daphne had said. Would this man or that one dance with Sylvia? Would she fall in love with one of them? By the time the initial crush had entered and he could break away from the front door, he was cursing himself a fool. He couldn't stand the thought of his Sylvia with another man.

She'd been at the other end of the receiving line, but only to make sure all went well, and the staff handled boots, swords and other items unsuitable for the ballroom with the proper care. She disappeared into the crowd long before he could snatch her up and tell her he wouldn't stand for her marrying someone else.

The master of ceremonies was arranging the musicians and listening to the tuning of each instrument while Anthony was lost in his thoughts.

Miles slapped him on the back. "Let me guess what or who you are daydreaming about."

"Hallsmith, I think I've made a terrible mistake." Regret, worry and panic set in until Anthony thought he might be sick.

Laughing, Miles gazed around the room. "I'm sure there is still time to fix things. After all, she's only across the room."

Sure enough, Sylvia was on the other side of the ballroom with her sister and Lord Stansfield. The three had their heads together and smiled at whatever was being said. "She must think me a fool."

"All men are fools, and men in love are the biggest fools of all. Women know this, and she will forgive you. Or she will tell you to go to Hades. Either way, what choice do you have?"

Miles was the most likable person Anthony had ever met, and he still wanted to murder him. "You are not helping."

"If you love her, you had better tell her before someone else whisks her away for a dull life of marriage and babies."

"You think it would be dull?" It was one of Anthony's fears. How would he find things to talk about for the rest of his life? How would he keep her happy?

Expression serious, Miles shook his head. "I think if you marry a woman like that, who you love, and who loves you, it cannot be dull. However, if she married the next man out of a sense of duty or fear, she will be miserable the rest of her life and so will you. Of course, that's only my bachelor opinion, and what do I know?"

Serena said something to Sylvia, and Sylvia turned white.

Searching the room, he found March had entered with a blond woman on his arm and a smirk on his face.

Miles grabbed Anthony's shoulder. "Now is not the time to make a scene, Grafton. You are an earl, and this is your first ball. You need to make an impression that doesn't include beating a viscount bloody on the dance floor."

Just because Miles was right didn't mean that Anthony wasn't tempted. "I will be a perfect gentleman as long as he is. I'll not have her upset by that ass."

Miles's gaze changed as the crowd murmured. "Before you worry about Miss Dowder's past, you had better take care of your own." He nodded toward the garden doors.

His last affair, Mrs. Minny Minot, had walked in with the Earl of Bancroft. She was an actress with the most stunning figure. She could lure in devil and saint alike with her assets. Anthony crossed to the pair, forcing his expression to remain bland. "Mrs. Minot, I was not expecting you tonight."

"No. I suppose not. It has been two months since you came to see me, and his lordship has been a most entertaining replacement." She rubbed her ample chest along Bancroft's arm.

She smiled smugly, and Bancroft wore an apology across his face. Anthony should have been irate, but he didn't care. He'd stopped seeing her because the thought of any woman always led him back to Sylvia. He must have been blind not to see it before. "Mrs. Minot, I wish you well. Enjoy your evening. I believe it will be one to remember."

Opening her mouth, she paused, and then closed it again.

Bancroft laughed. "Come, Minny, the music is about to start, and I want a glass of wine before we become parched."

Whatever Minny mumbled, Anthony couldn't quite hear as he made his way across to Sylvia.

Sophia must have seen March enter too, as his sister had rallied around Sylvia for support.

Anthony bowed. "Miss Sylvia Dowder, it would be my honor if you would open the dancing with me tonight."

She looked around her at the people watching. He'd given her no choice without making a scene. "I…I would be delighted, my lord."

The first strains of the minuet sounded. Perhaps he should feel guilty for trapping her, but he was too happy at having her on his arm as they walked to the dance floor and he stood in line across from her.

The master of ceremonies was a chubby fellow with a yellow waistcoat and a shock of gray hair that fell over his eyes. His breeches were too tight, and his shoes shined to perfection. He was like a farcical drawing from the paper.

Anthony gave him a nod, and he turned to the musicians, who began the set. He made his turn, as did a lady at the far end of the line. It was several turns before Sylvia was beside him.

"You should have asked someone else to dance, my lord." She had spoken quickly and was too far away for him to reply.

Another few stanzas, and they came together at the center. "I did not wish to dance with anyone else."

It was fun to make a statement and have the other person unable to respond. Perhaps it would give her time to think about what he'd said.

"I don't see why that would be. There are many lovely ladies here." She was gone a moment later, and he noted a leer from March as they passed.

It was torture to wait for the next time she was beside him. "I don't think you should look for some secret meaning. Only that you are the only woman I wanted to dance with."

By the time they stood across from each other again, the dance ended, and the dancers stepped away for refreshments.

Anthony crossed to her and offered his arm. "Shall I escort you back to your sister?"

She took his arm. "Why are you acting this way?"

"What way?"

"Like we are courting."

"Miss Sylvia?" March bolted across the room.

Sylvia made a curtsy but did not smile or give any indication as to her emotions. She watched him until it was clear he would say no more. "Hello, Lord March. How are you?"

"You look very lovely tonight. May I ask if you will save the next dance for me?"

"No." She'd whispered, but there was no mistaking her reply.

Anthony wanted to jump for joy and punch March in that stupid nose of his.

Mouth hanging open, March stepped back. "No? You will not dance with me?"

"Why on earth would you think I would? You should count yourself lucky that I don't make a scene right here in the ballroom. You can rest assured that the only reason I have not is because I respect Lord Grafton too much to do so."

His eyes grew round and rather puppylike. It was disgusting. "But Sylvia, I have missed you."

"Who is the lovely young lady I saw you enter with?" A coldness settled over Sylvia that Anthony had not seen before. It was an eerie calmness, which didn't bode well for March.

"Miss Melony Smyth. She is the granddaughter of an earl." His smugness was enough to make one run screaming from the room, perhaps the country. As if either of them would care about his connections.

"How long have you been courting her?" She raised her eyebrows and leaned in a fraction of an inch.

"Almost four months." He was too stupid to notice her clipped tone or see she was baiting him.

"Have you proposed?"

His smile was slow and sickeningly sweet. "Are you jealous, Sylvia?"

"Don't be absurd. Have you proposed?" She crossed her arms. It was the first sign she'd grown annoyed.

"Miss Smyth accepted my proposal of marriage last week." At least he had the good sense to look embarrassed finally.

"Will you toss over that poor girl for me, now, or were you planning to have me as a mistress? Whichever it is, you are the worst specimen of a man, and I sincerely hope that girl realizes what an ass you are before she gets to the church." She turned and walked out on the veranda.

"I—she—the nerve. That woman has no right to speak to me with so little respect. I was good to her. It's not my fault I became a viscount."

The gentleman in Anthony knew he should walk away and say nothing, but the American in him couldn't make himself do it. "It seems to me Miss Dowder was as polite as you deserved. Your behavior was completely ungentlemanly, and you should have been thrashed. I'm sure, had she had a brother, he would have called you out for such poor treatment. However, as it is, you have gotten away with your disgraceful behavior and should count yourself lucky that she managed to keep her voice down."

Wide-eyed, March gaped. "You would have a viscount marry a girl of little consequence and without connections? I would have done my family and title a disservice."

Anthony's fisted fingers bit into his palms. It would have been far worse if March had done the right thing, as then he would never have gotten to know his Everton lady. "I would have you be a gentleman and not just play at one. Good evening."

Whatever March might have responded, it was lost in the din of the crowd as Anthony made his way out of the ballroom, down the hall, through his office and out to the veranda. It wouldn't do to have half of London see him go after her. His surreptitious route took him in the other direction.

As bravely as she had set March down, she appeared hurt and small standing in the corner of the rose garden.

Easing down the steps, he watched as the guests enjoying the cool night walked back inside for the next dance. "Should I have thrashed him and tossed him from the house, Sylvie?"

Her arms were crossed, and she gripped her elbows. A long sigh brought her slim shoulders up and down. "As wonderful as that sounds, no. He would not learn anything from it, and you would come to regret it. I'm not selfish enough to want you to beat him soundly just for my benefit."

"I'm pretty sure I would not regret it. His nose needs breaking." Anthony's fists itched to do just that.

She released her arms and chuckled. "It would be a glorious thing, and I thank you, Tony, but we'll have to let it live in our imaginations."

"Too bad." Closing the gap between them, he let the floral scent of her envelop him. No rose garden could compete with her.

Eyes bright, she looked at him. "How do you think the ball is going?"

"Everyone is drinking and dancing. I'd say that's a success." If everyone inside would suddenly disappear, it would suit Anthony just fine. He wanted to have her to himself and explain his feelings and why it took him so long to recognize them. He had no idea how he would do that. His heart sank.

The clouds had cleared, and her torches were lit, giving the garden the look of a fairy tale, and she the queen of the fairies. "You will be the toast of London in the morning. Everyone will be impressed."

"What about you?"

"Me?"

"Yes, will you be impressed?"

She cocked her head. "It's not important what I think, Tony."

But it was the most important opinion. "Did I tell you how beautiful you look tonight? If I didn't, I am an imbecile. You are by far the loveliest woman at the ball."

Wide eyes narrowed. "Are you drunk?"

"Not yet." He laughed.

"You know that there is no need to compliment me. I work for you and can do nothing but write gossip for your reputation. Actually, I'm thinking of giving that up." She kicked the ground with the tip of her slipper.

Catching a glimpse of her slim ankle, he longed to see more of her, all of her. Lord, he was losing his mind over a bit of leg. "I'm only stating the truth. Why give up the column?"

"I may have gone too far by defending myself. People will begin to figure out that Miss Tattler and I are the same person."

He couldn't argue with that. "Perhaps just take some time off and return with a new nom de plume. I hate to think of you giving up on something you love."

"You don't think readers would recognize the writing style?"

He scoffed more harshly than he'd intended. "People rarely see what is right in front of them, let alone notice someone may or may not have a similar pen. If you want to give it up, then that's different, but if you do it to keep peace, Sylvie, I say do what makes you happy."

"I will give it some thought. Thank you, Tony. You had better get back to your guests and return the same way you came, or there will be more gossip than either of us can tolerate by morning, and all this work to keep you single would be for naught."

Frustration warred inside Anthony. He'd told her to do what she wanted, but his own desires were kept at bay. Just because she was right didn't mean he had to like it. "I will sneak back into my own home if you will promise to allow me to escort you in to dinner."

"You should escort your mother to the table, or your mother and aunt."

A growl he'd been holding in made its way up from deep in his chest. "All these rules will make me a madman. Let's just break them all."

Hearing her laughter was worth all his frustration. "No. I will find my own way in, and you will make a good impression for society. It's better that way."

The joy in her voice drew him closer. "Won't you ask me for that kiss? In that dress, with high color in your cheeks, you look delectable, Sylvie."

"I… No, Tony. I will not ask for a kiss again. It's for the best." Skirting him, she ran up the steps, across the veranda and into the ballroom.

Anthony walked the torch-lit path that wound through his garden.

Daniel, Earl of Marlton, stepped out of the shadows, smoking a cigar. "I'm sorry to intrude on your privacy. I thought it better to keep to the shadows until the lady had gone."

"Did you hear all of that?" He was horrified that he might have made a fool of himself.

"No, you both spoke too low, but it seemed like a serious conversation." He walked along with Anthony.

"I suppose it was more so to me than to the lady. You could have made yourself known, Dan." The air grew heavy. His heart lay just as heavy with no idea how he would win Sylvia.

"I think it will rain again."

Anthony walked farther into the garden. "It will, but not for a little while, I think."

Keeping pace with him, Daniel said, "You know, if you want her, there is nothing stopping you."

"Only the lady herself."

"I see. If she does not like you, then you might have to accept that you cannot have her." Daniel puffed on his cigar, but it had gone out. Sighing, he tossed the stub away.

"She likes me, but she has ideas of what is an appropriate match, and Lord March's treatment of her has sullied her opinion of men with titles."

"I see."

"This is my problem, Dan. No need to sound so grave. I didn't want to marry, so having the woman I want thwart me will not change the outcome of my life."

Daniel stopped and observed the sky. The first drop fell and hit the path between them. "Best if we return before we get soaked."

They rushed back toward the house and onto the abandoned veranda.

Stopping before the French doors to the ballroom, Daniel turned to Anthony. "A broken heart can change a life forever. I hope you will make an effort to change the lady's mind. She is a fine girl. Don't let her lack of title or connections turn you into a fool."

In the ballroom, the dancing was at its height and the colorful guests were like confections moving around the floor. If Anthony hadn't been so frustrated with his situation, he would have enjoyed the sight more. As it was, he wished they would all go home, and he could have Sylvia to himself.

Chapter 11

Sylvia had to find a way to make Anthony see that his pity was not needed or warranted. She would be fine, and his attention would do neither of them any good. How she was going to convince him, she didn't know. Perhaps he would just lose interest or one of the ladies who distracted him in the past would come forward.

Still pondering Anthony's behavior, she missed the approach of her mother until Felicia was standing directly in front of her.

With her lips pursed in typical disappointment, and her hands perched on her hips, Mother said, "Please tell me that you did not insult a viscount."

It grated on Sylvia that Mother felt she could still badger her, even after she'd moved out of the house and was supporting herself. "To what are you referring, Mother?"

"You know exactly what I am referring to. Did you thwart an attempt to make amends by Lord March?"

Serena and Lord Stansfield inched closer until they flanked Sylvia.

Meanwhile, Sir Henry Parker stood just over Mother's shoulder.

"If you are asking if I refused to dance with a man who publicly humiliated me, then the answer is yes. I have no intention of accepting any kind of amends from Hunter Gautier. I would rather be flogged in the town square."

Lord Stansfield covered a laugh.

Sir Henry frowned. "You would do well to get into Lord March's good graces again. He is a peer and has many friends. Besides, if you married him, even after all the gossip, all would be forgiven."

Mother nodded. "At least someone sees my point."

Taking a deep breath, Sylvia stayed her gathering temper. "Mother, I love and respect you, but your point is moot. I will never marry that miserable sod. In his social climbing efforts, he recently engaged himself to Miss Smyth. So you see, his intentions toward me are not honorable in the least."

Serena gasped. "Mother, you have to admit, Lord March behaved very badly in the past. You cannot blame Sylvia for holding a grudge against him. His transgressions would be impossible for anyone to forgive."

"He's a viscount, Serena. I would think your sister could forgive him if he is willing to renew his interest." Felicia stomped her foot.

"He is engaged, Mother. Are you proposing I become his mistress?" Sylvia's temper could not hold on much longer.

Lord Stansfield cleared his throat and placed a hand on Serena's arm for only an instant. His voice was soft but deep and firm. "I know that I am an outsider, ladies, but this conversation is drawing attention from the crowd. Perhaps you might continue it another time in private."

Looking around, Sylvia noted several people had turned to watch the altercation. "Thank you, my lord. You are correct. This is not the time or the place for such talk. Mother, I will see you at tea on Tuesday, and you may berate me to your heart's content at that time."

Serena followed Sylvia to the hallway and into Anthony's office. Once the door was closed, she sighed. "You did the right thing, Sylvie. He's a horrible man, and I would hate it if you married him."

"Thank you. At least someone is on my side."

Serena took her hands. "I will always be on your side. I should have been stronger with Mother when you first left home, but I was so used to agreeing with her. I hope you can forgive me."

Hugging her twin, Sylvia said, "There is nothing to forgive. You had to stay and live with her. Enough about Mother. I quite like your Lord Stansfield. Not only does he have a sense of humor, but he handled Mother wonderfully."

Blushing, Serena got a dreamy look in her eyes. "He is rather wonderful." She frowned. "I am liking Sir Henry less and less. In fact, the more Mother likes him, the less I do."

"Do you think Lord Stansfield will offer?" Sylvia would love for Serena to find someone to make her happy.

She shrugged. "I think he likes me, but there is a shyness about him. It could take him a while to offer, and I fear Mother and Sir Henry are still conspiring."

"I have seated you next to his lordship for dinner. Perhaps you might use all of your charm."

They both laughed.

"Thank you, Sylvie. You are my best champion. I wish I could be as strong as you."

"You are as strong. You just need to find your voice. Not to worry, though. Until you do, I shall speak up for both of us." Sylvia wished their mother cared more about her daughters' happiness and less about marrying them off as soon as possible to a rich man.

Serena ran her fingers along the back of the chair behind Anthony's desk. "You know, Sylvie, he seems quite taken with you."

"Who, Lord Stansfield? Don't be absurd. He only rallied behind me for your sake."

"No, silly, Lord Grafton. Anthony Braighton rarely takes his gaze away from you. He made a point to open the ball with you, and I assume he ran after you when you escaped the ballroom. Though, he was discreet. He returned with the Earl of Marlton, and that will keep the gossips quiet."

"We are friends, nothing more. Any further regard Anthony feels for me is only out of some warped sense of duty. He has a notion that he's ruined my reputation with his regard at the Rochester ball." Sylvia really had to make sure Anthony saw he need not worry over her. If Serena noticed, soon others would as well. That could lead to a real disaster.

"Are you sure it's not more? He looks like a man smitten to me."

It was too ridiculous to even hope for such a thing. Besides, she was not good for Anthony. They fought much of the time, and he could do far better than a woman thrown over by a prominent viscount. No. She would go back to Everton's, and Anthony would find a mistress to amuse him until he decided to marry.

It was easy to think such things, but her heart contracted with visions of Anthony with random women.

"Anthony Braighton would no sooner want a woman like me than he would marry one of his actress friends."

Serena's mouth dropped open. "You cannot compare yourself to one of those women. You are a lady, Sylvia. Your situation is completely different. You could still marry, and marry well, if you wanted to. I think if Mother would have been kinder, you would be enjoying a normal season with me this year."

"Perhaps, but I'm glad you have suitors, and it sounds as though you really like Lord Stansfield." It was time to deflect the conversation away from herself.

"I suppose I had better go back out there. Will you be all right?" Serena patted her curls and brushed out her ivory gown before tugging her gloves into place.

"I'm fine. I will check on dinner service and be up before everyone enters." Serena kissed her cheek and bounced from the room.

Hoping for something to keep her away from the ballroom, Sylvia was disappointed and pleased to find the kitchen was in perfect order and the staff prepared for service.

Back in the ballroom, she watched as Anthony escorted both his mother and his aunt into the dining room.

"May I have your arm, Miss Dowder." Miles Hallsmith stood next to her, holding out his arm.

She placed her hand on his arm. "I would be grateful, and I happen to know we are seated beside each other."

"Are you flirting with me?" His voice lilted with silliness.

"Not at all." She used the same tone. "How dare you assume such a thing."

As neither of them were titled, they entered late, and Sylvia avoided Anthony's glare. The table shined with crystal and china, and the food was glorious. Silver candelabras placed along the center of the table cast a romantic glow. It was so artful, it would be a shame to devour the sumptuous fare.

Sylvia forced herself to smile at Sir Henry Parker, seated to her left. "I hope you will enjoy the food, Sir Henry."

"I suppose you are responsible for the seating, Miss Sylvia." His haughty tone sent an unpleasant chill down her back.

"In my position as a lady of the Everton Domestic Society, I am referred to as Miss Dowder now. However, I did think it might be nice to get to know each other."

He pursed his lips and narrowed his gaze. "If you think you can win me over for yourself, I can tell you I would never court any woman in service. You may cease and desist."

"Good lord, Parker, you're just as bad mannered as you were in school. The lady was only being polite, so that she might know the man intent on marrying her twin sister. Must you twist everything to a hateful result?" Miles was like a beacon of light when it seemed the walls were crashing in.

Henry sat back and put a blank stare on his face. "I was only being certain we understood each other."

"Most kind," Sylvia said before turning her attention to Miles. "Are you always so forward?"

He shrugged. "I've known Henry all my life." He leaned closer. "I sincerely hope your sister does not become Mrs. Henry Parker."

"I shall tell her you said so."

Serena's giggle drifted across the table. Something Lord Stansfield had said amused her and she blushed.

"Mr. Hallsmith, do you know Lord Stansfield's first name?" It was terrible, but Sylvia couldn't remember it, or perhaps she'd never known it.

"If I'm not mistaken, it is Rutledge. Rutledge Haversham, Earl of Stansfield. He's terribly wealthy and has an enormous farm somewhere in the west, though I don't know where. I do know that he rarely gambles, drinks in moderation, and can be quite amusing once he gets to know a person. His only flaw is that he is not easy with strangers and often misjudged because of his stoic tendencies. I think your sister could do far worse."

Sylvia recalled the name and the moment she'd heard it before. Her face heated. Having just been thoroughly kissed by Anthony, she must have been addlebrained to have forgotten.

Lady Collington sat to Anthony's left but spoke loudly enough for the entire party to hear her. "The table is the most beautiful I have ever seen, my boy. Even my dear son never put on a fare such as this. You have done right by the family and elevated the Grafton title to new heights. I'm prodigiously proud of you."

Since Anthony spoke in a normal tone, they couldn't hear his response. His gaze fixed on Sylvia, and she tingled with his regard from her head to her toes.

His favor for her would only lead to disaster. Hers for him, in heartbreak. It had to be stopped. Looking away, she tried to decide what to do. She had a job to do, so she couldn't stop seeing him.

"Miss Dowder, are you all right?" Concern formed in small creases around Miles's eyes.

Perhaps the answer was right in front of her. She leaned an inch closer to him and smiled. "Thank you, Mr. Hallsmith. I assure you I am fine."

He studied her. "I can't decide if you're flirting with me or trying to make Anthony jealous."

Was she that obvious? "I am most certainly not trying to make anyone jealous."

A lazy smile spread across his handsome face. In the candlelight, his red hair shone warm with shades of red, bronze and gold. He was pleasant and intelligent, so why didn't he stir the same feelings in Sylvia as the unsuitable Earl of Grafton. "Then I shall assume you are flirting with me. How delightful."

"Are you teasing me?" She forced a sharp bite into her voice, but he was too charming to garner any real anger.

"Of course. What else is there to do when you are the last person I would ever expect to flirt with me?" He glanced over her shoulder.

Sylvia refused to look at Anthony even though she could feel him staring at her. "Why do you say that? I am as apt to flirt as the next lady."

He leaned his elbow on the edge of the table, his chin on his hand, and made green doe eyes at her. "Not true, but let's get back to the flirting."

Unable to help herself, she giggled. "You really are the most charming man."

Lady Pemberhamble cleared her throat from across the table. She gave Miles a sour look, though it was hard to tell, as her regular expression was rather bitter.

Sitting back, Miles gave her a nod then turned back to Sylvia. "I am all charm and no substance, and I'm sure you recognize that."

"What I see is a man who would have everyone think that is true, but you are observant and thoughtful. Your sister was with the Everton Domestic Society, was she not?"

Taking a bite of game pie, he closed his eyes with appreciation. "Delicious. Yes, Phoebe was very successful at the Society before her marriage to the Viscount of Devonrose. She enjoyed the work very much. I wonder if you enjoy it, Miss Dowder."

She hadn't really until she started her assignment with Anthony. Perhaps she should ask Lady Jane for more of the same type of assignments. "I find the work occupies the day well enough. I am useful and not under anyone's control. I like that quite a lot."

"And you feel marrying would put you under your husband's thumb?" He finished his pie so quickly one might think he'd not eaten in a week.

Sylvia tasted it and had to agree the tender bits of meat were well cooked and spiced to perfection. "As I'm sure you know, I nearly made it to the altar, and thus my experience with men is less than complimentary."

Nodding, he signaled for the footman to refill his wineglass. "No one will complain about the food or wine tonight. You have done an excellent job here."

"Thank you, but the cook and Lord Grafton are responsible for those items. I only assigned the menu. I did not cook it."

"You don't give yourself enough credit, Miss Dowder. However, before we get too far off topic, let me say that your experience is skewed by one man's thoughtless act. We are not all cads, you know." The lamb was served, and he dug in with enthusiasm.

"You may be right, but it is all I have to go by. Men think of themselves first, and so I must consider my own needs without regard to them."

After he sipped his wine, he stopped and held it in the air a moment before carefully placing it on the table. "I disagree. Take my friend Anthony Braighton as an example, if you would?"

"You have lost me, sir." Her heart pounded, and surely everyone around her could hear it. It drummed in her ears like a military march.

"Anthony thinks of everyone before himself. He worries about his mother, his sister, the servants, and his new tenants. I'll admit he has enjoyed some aspects of his new title and salary, but it has come to him at a cost. If you watch him now, you will see he has not taken the first bite of his sumptuous meal. Instead he asks the people seated near him how each course is and how they are enjoying it. He also watches you quite a lot." Miles shoveled in a piece of lamb and chewed.

Sylvia chanced a glance at Anthony. He spoke to Lady Collington, who told him the lamb was exquisite.

Anthony's head snapped up and he met her gaze, smiled, and raised an eyebrow in question.

Unable to help herself, she smiled back before turning away. "Yet even Lord Grafton takes his own pleasure where he can find it. He's become a notorious rake these last six months."

Miles shook his head. "I would say that was true until a couple of months ago when he stopped seeing any of his previous 'friends' and began to pay exclusive attention to a certain Everton lady."

"Don't be absurd. I work for him, nothing more." Her heartbeat tripled. Much more of this conversation, and she would faint in her pudding.

"Yes. I can see by your charming blush that it is nothing more."

She took a deep breath and calmed her nerves. "You may think what you like, but his lordship is not the right man for me, as there is no right man. I am an Everton lady, and that will not change. If he has any regard for me, he will shuck such nonsense when our association is finished. In fact, I predict that in a month's time when we meet for his house party, he will have found a nice widow or opera singer to attach himself to."

Frowning seemed out of place for Miles, but there it was. He whispered, "You think of him too meanly, Sylvia. He is a man of deep feelings."

Serena called to her and diverted her attention with delight over the sweets, and for that Sylvia was grateful.

Dinner broke up and the partygoers made their way back to the drawing room and ballroom.

Overhearing a dozen compliments about the dinner, Sylvia smiled. Anthony would be the talk of London just as they'd planned. His mother would leave him to his cavorting, and he would be happy. An ache started deep inside her. It was what she wanted. She just had to convince her heart of that fact.

The music resumed, and she danced with Miles then Mr. Tucker before retreating to the corner and watching the revelers. Serena danced once with Sir Henry, but it was cool and polite, if her expression was to be believed. She accepted two more dances with Lord Stansfield and appeared far more engaged and happier. Mother might think herself disappointed, but once Serena was happily a countess, she'd be delighted. It was just a matter of having Stansfield propose before Sir Henry.

Between dances, she found Serena and pulled her to the outskirts of the ballroom, where they could speak in private. "I have an idea."

Serena clapped her hands. "What is it?"

"I think we need to keep you away from Sir Henry until Lord Stansfield works up his nerve to ask for your hand. Let's get Mother to agree to a short vacation at the country house. Then you and I will go to Lord Grafton's house party. Mrs. Horthorn can chaperon both of us unless Mother is determined to go. Either way, I will make sure you and Stansfield have time together, and hopefully he will propose before we return to London."

Serena's eyes misted. "Do you really think so? He is nice, and I like him so much more than Sir Henry, but he is not terribly loquacious. How will I ever win him?"

"Serena, he must win you, not the other way around. If you like him, he will ask." Sylvia pulled her in for a quick hug. "All will be well. You just tell Mother that you are tired and would like a fortnight in the country, and insist I come too. I will tell Lady Jane that I will be away. The house party is all prepared, and the final items, I can take care of before we leave or when we arrive at Riverdale."

With her head tilted, she put her finger to her chin. "I would prefer to avoid Sir Henry. I will do as you say, and we shall hope for the best at your earl's estate."

"He is not my earl."

Serena smiled with a wicked glint. "Oh, I think he very much is."

* * * *

The last of the guests left, and Sophia found her staring out the veranda doors to the dark garden. The torches had all gone out hours before.

Sophia took a deep breath. "It was a lovely ball. You've made my brother look every bit the earl he aspires to be. You should be very proud of yourself."

"Thank you, my lady. I think it went well. Are you and his lordship leaving now?"

"Yes. Mother went to bed, and Anthony has disappeared. Would you like us to take you home?"

A pang of regret shot through Sylvia as she thought of what woman Anthony might have disappeared with. "Thank you, but the Everton carriage is waiting for me, as is Mrs. Horthorn. I am well protected."

Sophia's smile was warm as she leaned in for a sisterly hug. "Then I bid you good night. I look forward to seeing you at Riverdale."

"I have a wonderful week planned," Sylvia said.

"I'm certain you do."

"Sophia, are you ready?" Lord Marlton called from the door. He held her light blue wrap over his arm.

"Yes, Daniel." She walked to her husband, and he waved good night to Sylvia.

Once the front door closed and she was alone, she knew she should find Mrs. Horthorn and go home, but she stepped into the cool night air.

She felt him before he spoke. "I thought they would never leave."

"Didn't you enjoy the ball?" Maybe she had gone overboard with the food and drink, but everyone had a good time and his next invitation would be coveted.

The guttering light from the ballroom cast him in romantic shadows. "It was all perfect. I couldn't have asked for anything more except to have you alone. And here you are."

"I will be leaving shortly."

"But not yet." He ran his fingers along her upper arm.

A chill filled with promise and delight flowed through her from everywhere his skin met hers. "What are you doing, Tony?"

"Wishing I hadn't been such a fool where you are concerned. Praying it's not too late." His breath tickled her cheek.

"Too late for what? We are friends. You are my employer. There is nothing more between us."

More of the candles in the ballroom chandeliers guttered out, until they were left in darkness. "I should have noticed how beautiful you are sooner. Well, I noticed, but I told myself it didn't matter that you are stunning, smart and funny. I was sure I never wanted what other people covet."

Stepping away, she stumbled in the dark. He caught her elbow and righted her, causing her chest to press against his. "I saw you talking to your actress and assumed you would leave tonight with her or invite her to stay."

"I have not spent time with her since you became my Everton lady, Sylvie. I have given up my rakish ways with no regrets." His lips pressed to her forehead.

She knew she should pull away, but her body betrayed her, and she leaned into the kiss, letting the warm sensuality of meeting in the darkness wash over her. "Miles told me you had stopped seeing her, but I thought he just didn't know who you've begun seeing since."

Moving back enough to put space between them, but keeping one hand on her arm, he said, "You spent a lot of time with Miles Hallsmith tonight."

"Yes. He is very charming." It was the truth.

"Is Miles my competition?" Anger bit into his words.

"Are we part of a horse race? If so, I want no part of it." She pulled away from his reach. "I will be going to the country with my family for two weeks. I will drive directly to Riverdale from my family's home. You shouldn't worry, all is in order and Serena and I will arrive a day or two earlier than the other guests."

"You didn't answer my question. Is Hallsmith courting you?" As his voice lifted and the fire in his eyes shone in the moonlight, there was no doubt about his anger.

It should be easy to lie and say yes. It would be the best thing to do. Once he came to his senses, Anthony would be glad she'd released him. "I don't need your worry or your pity, Tony. You can rest easy in the knowledge that my reputation is secure. Miles is a good companion, and we enjoy each other's company. He has not made any formal overtures, but I see no reason to discourage him."

"But you see reason to discourage me." If this went on much longer, he would be in a full rant.

"You are the Earl of Grafton. You should consider that in everything you do. Now that the ball is behind you, you will find your opportunities within the ton will increase. Your businesses will prosper from connections you make. You have to think about that, and not some warped sense of duty because hateful people like to gossip."

If she hadn't heard him breathing, she might have thought herself alone on the veranda. His silence unnerved her to the point where she backed toward the open door. Her heart lodged in her throat, and she was ready to bolt for the foyer where Mrs. Horthorn would be waiting by now.

"Is my guilt the only possible motivation I might have to court you?" Danger rang in every word.

Another step, and she was inside the ballroom.

His shoes sounded against the wooden floor as he followed her in. The only light was a sliver shining through from the foyer. "Could it be that I have developed feelings for you?"

"No. I must go, my lord. You will see that by the time we meet again, I was right. I appreciate your concern, but anything more is unnecessary and unwanted. I will not ruin you for London nor stop you from your pursuit of happiness abroad." Sylvia ran for the light without looking back. Her lie had been a kindness to them both. If Hunter could hurt her, then Anthony could destroy her. She couldn't take that chance.

Pulling the door open, she masked any expression before she entered the foyer.

Mrs. Horthorn waited by the door. "There you are. Is everything in order?"

"Yes. Thank you. I'm sorry to keep you waiting. Shall we go?" Sylvia half expected Anthony to burst from the ballroom demanding she stay and talk to him, but the threshold remained empty, and she hurried out to the waiting carriage.

Wells handed her up. "A fine ball, Miss Dowder."

"Thank you. I'm glad it all turned out well. I doubt I'll be back at Collington House, Wells. I will tell you goodbye now."

He bowed. "Take care, miss."

She thought she caught the hint of a smile from the stoic butler as the carriage rolled down Grosvenor Street.

Chapter 12

Brooding day and night wouldn't do. Anthony had to do something to find out why Sylvia preferred Miles Hallsmith to him. What had Miles done or not done that secured the lady's affections?

When they kissed, his world contracted, and it was impossible she could counterfeit that kind of longing. Her desire had been so raw and intense, it had crashed through him. There was no way he could have been mistaken.

Miles had no title, and that seemed important to her. March had made her skittish against titled men, and rightfully so.

The clock in the hall chimed eight times. Miles was the man with answers, and sitting behind his desk wouldn't bring Anthony any closer to getting them.

Tugging on his coat, he called into the hallway, "Wells!"

Wells appeared, expressionless in the doorway. "Yes, my lord?"

"Have the carriage brought round. I'll be going to White's this evening after all. Please give Cook my apologies and have the staff enjoy whatever she prepared. I'll dine at the club." He made a note to devise a plan to win Sylvia, and the first item on his list was Miles Hallsmith.

While Wells didn't reply directly, he excused himself and returned a few minutes later. "The carriage will be ready in ten minutes, my lord."

"Too long. I'll catch a hack." Anthony rushed to the door.

"But, my lord. You have a perfectly good carriage. Three of them. You must only wait for the driver to get the horses harnessed and bring them around. By the time you find a hack at this hour, you will have wasted twice that time."

It was hard to argue with the butler's stoic logic. "You're right. I'll wait for Jonas to bring the carriage."

"Very good, my lord." With a bow, Wells exited.

By the time the carriage was ready, Anthony was tapping his foot on the front steps and looking like some rabble rather than the earl who owned the house. "White's, Jonas," Anthony said while jumping up without the benefit of the step or driver.

He would get to the bottom of it and gauge Miles's interest. Even if he could not have Sylvia, he wouldn't allow her to be hurt by yet another man. Between March and himself, she had been through enough.

It was the longest drive to St. James of his life. Jonas must have traversed half the city before he finally pulled up to the well-to-do gentleman's club. Without waiting for the driver, Anthony opened the door and jumped down. The wet street greeted him with a puddle, but he didn't care. Up the steps and he was admitted. He searched the gaming tables, but no sight of Miles.

"I hope you don't intend to join a game, Grafton," Thomas Wheel called from a cluster of chairs where he was drinking brandy alone.

Anthony joined him. "No. I'm looking for Miles Hallsmith."

Thomas downed his brandy, put the glass on the table and leaned forward until his elbows rested on his knees. "You have a quarrel? I thought the two of you were friends."

"We are. No. It's nothing like that." Maybe he'd lost his mind.

"You forget, Anthony, everything you think is written on your face just like your sister."

Trying to hide his distress, Anthony changed the subject. "Speaking of the ladies, why aren't you at home with your lovely wife? You rarely come to White's since your marriage."

"Dory is having a lady's gathering with your sister, Sophia, and Elinor Rollins. Her Grace is in town for a few days without that brood of children, so they are taking advantage." Thomas was a far better bluffer than Anthony, and while he sounded annoyed, Anthony knew better. Not only did he love that brood, as he called it, he admired the women occupying his wife's time for the evening.

"A nice night for you to get out of the house. Why isn't Daniel with you? I can't imagine my brother-in-law is at home chatting with those three when they've been apart for so long."

Thomas made a horrified face. "Perish the thought. They will be on about children and husbands and who knows what else. No. Daniel went to see his mother, as she too is in town this week. Now, what do you want with Hallsmith?"

The footman came over and offered him a brandy.

Anthony sipped the drink and closed his eyes. "It's nothing, Tom. I just wanted to ask him some questions."

"It's about a woman." Thomas laughed but kept his voice down.

"How do you know we're not in discussions about me using some of his brother's land to graze my cattle?"

Thomas grinned and sipped his refilled drink. "For a number of reasons. First, Ford Hallsmith is an ass who refuses to let anyone graze his land. I have tried on several occasions, and Miles cannot talk him into it. I think he'd buried gold under the grass and is afraid some cow will unearth his fortune. Second, the look on your face when you entered was far too intense for cattle. And third, while we have been away for a few weeks, I did hear the rumor about you and a certain lady. In fact, she is a lady who I have met on many occasions. Miss Sylvia Dowder, I believe is the lady in question."

Sure that his annoyance was plainly written on his face, Anthony rolled his eyes. "Sometimes I forget you were a spy in the war, Tom. Remind me not to sit with you when I'm trying to keep something to myself."

Thomas shrugged. "What I want to know is what does it have to do with Miles Hallsmith."

"It really is none of your business what I need to talk to Hallsmith about."

"Did I hear my name?" Miles approached from behind Anthony.

Frowning at Thomas, who obviously saw him walk in, Anthony said, "I was looking for you."

"I didn't touch her, Tony." Miles held up his hands in self-defense.

"I know that. I just want to know why she prefers you over me?" It sounded like the question of a petulant child or a jealous lover. Dear God, what had happened to him? A funny, smart slip of a girl had gotten under his skin and invaded his heart. That's what happened.

Miles sat down and called for a drink. "I don't believe she does, though I wouldn't mind the attention. I like her. She's funny and not hard to look at."

"She told me she preferred you."

Puffing up like a pigeon, Miles grinned from ear to ear. "Really? Well, isn't that a nice change? A lady who would rather be courted by a third son than an earl. Still, it seems to me she was far more interested in me when the conversation was about you."

Thomas cleared his throat. "Grafton, what exactly did the lady say?"

The entire conversation was a nightmare. "She told me that Hallsmith here is a good companion and she liked his company. I think she also said she wouldn't discourage him, but I was so furious by then my hearing was muffled by the blood flowing through my ears."

"What did she say about your desire to court her." Thomas was too direct even for Anthony when it came to such an embarrassing subject.

"I don't know. Something about me being an earl and how I should think about my title and how I was acting out of pity. I can assure you both, I do not pity Sylvia." Anthony drained his brandy.

"Maybe she just prefers me." Miles's grin was too big, and Anthony's fist itched to punch him in it.

"Maybe." It came out like a growl.

Thomas grinned, too, and both men were starting to try Anthony's patience. "It is possible that your title is the issue. We all know what happened when the last man she trusted was elevated in title."

Why did it always come back to March? Anthony had been so happy with the way she'd reacted to March's overtures at the ball. Then his jealousy had turned toward Miles. "Well, I suppose I could give up my title, but it hardly seems practical. Besides it's a bit prejudicial to hate me because I'm an earl."

Miles said, "I like her, but it was obvious to me that her heart lay elsewhere. I assumed it was with you. She seemed extremely interested in the fact that you had given up Mrs. Minot. I'm not sure she believed me. However, her attention was riveted, and she couldn't take her eyes off you. I was actually sorry I had said anything about you, since before that the flirting had been very pleasant."

Anthony ran his fingers through his hair. "I'm a fool who is doomed to get exactly what I asked for."

Both Miles and Thomas laughed at that.

Thomas said, "I suggest you fire the lady then make a fool of yourself. She might be more receptive to your groveling if she is no longer in your employ."

"I did fire her once, or maybe she quit me. I can't remember. We argued, and I asked for another lady." The same misery plagued him as it had the week he'd lost his Everton lady.

"You know what I think?" Miles stood. "I think we should go back to your very stately home and get stupidly drunk on your very fine Italian wine."

Thomas stood and slapped Miles on the back. "An excellent idea."

The idea did have merit. At least if he were drunk, he might be able to think of nothing, instead of his constant thoughts of blue eyes and soft brown hair attached to a woman with a quick wit. "Let's go. I've had a new shipment from my cousin, and it's the finest bottle yet."

Three hours and five bottles later, Thomas stumbled to his carriage and headed home.

Miles put his glass down on the low table and lay back on the divan. "I have had enough. All this talk of women and wine is fun, but now I'm drunk and there is no woman in sight."

Laughing, Anthony had to agree. Yet the only woman he wanted was out of reach both literally and figuratively. "I think I've ruined everything, Miles."

"I doubt it. You'll just have to win her over and prove you won't betray her the way March did. You may be sure you won't have any competition from me. Well, unless you want some."

Head spinning, Anthony didn't know what the right answer was. A rock the size of his fist settled in his chest. "I want her to be happy. If you are the one who can make that happen, I think I would step aside, Miles. I love her, but if she doesn't have those feelings for me, then I'll learn to live without her as long as she's happy."

Miles sat up, but then held his head for a long time opening and closing his eyes. "This is more than an infatuation, isn't it? You're serious."

Anthony contemplated the dark burgundy liquid rolling around in his glass. "My sister hates wine. Isn't that funny? We come from a mother whose family is known for their wine, and my sister has never liked it. We had wine on the table at lunch and dinner every day growing up. I was having a taste from the time I was twelve and telling Mother what was good or bad about the wine. Sophie just spit it out saying it was terrible. To me wine is like life, the very nectar that pumps my heart. I usually have a glass every night with my meal. I savor it like it was the fruit of the gods. But if you gave me a choice between wine and Sylvia, I would not hesitate to smash every bottle in my cellar. I would die for her, but I'd like to live for her. I think she is the only woman who can make me happy, and I know she is the only one who I want to try to please every day for the rest of my life."

Mouth hanging open, Miles leaned back but kept his feet on the floor. "You, my friend, are in trouble."

* * * *

When the carriage rolled up to the front door of Riverdale, Anthony's heart pounded with excitement over seeing Sylvia after three long weeks, and he knew Miles was right.

Flowers bloomed around the front of the picturesque home. It was simple but beautiful, and that, too, reminded him of Sylvia. He sighed and breathed deep the floral scents.

The front door opened. He prayed that his Sylvia couldn't wait any longer to see him and had arrived early.

Mrs. Horthorn and the Riverdale butler, Kravitz, exited, sending Anthony's hopes into a miserable spiral. If he'd thought about it sooner, he would have known her journey from the country would take her longer.

He plastered a pleasant smile on his face and jumped from the carriage. "Mrs. Horthorn, how good to see you. You are early."

"Indeed. I apologize for my hasty arrival, but I have two wards this week, and it wouldn't do to be tardy." She curtsied and smiled in that bland way she had.

His excitement ramped up again, but he was careful to mask his emotions. It would be exhausting to keep his feelings from his face all week, but he couldn't have everyone know he was in love the second they saw him. No. That wouldn't do at all. "Are your charges arriving today, madam?"

"Yes, my lord. Miss Dowder wrote to tell me she would be a day early to see that everything was in order." Mrs. Horthorn glanced at Kravitz, who'd stayed a few steps back.

A million questions rolled through his head, and he stifled each one in turn. Asking for the minutest detail of Sylvia's arrival would certainly alert her chaperon to his emotional state. Anthony turned to his butler instead. "And, Kravitz, will the lady find everything is in order?"

"I sincerely hope so, my lord. We have prepared the house, garden, an area by the lake and several other items just as Miss Dowder requested in her letters. In my humble opinion, we are ready for your party to arrive." Kravitz bowed then pushed his shock of brown hair into place. His impassive expression never wavered.

Oh, what Anthony wouldn't give to be able to show so little emotion. "Very well." He offered Mrs. Horthorn his arm. "Shall we tour the garden while we wait for the ladies Dowder?"

Taking his arm, she blushed. Finally, someone besides him showed something in this stoic country. "How many will be in the party, my lord?"

They walked around the house and left Anthony's luggage to the staff. "This will be a small group. I hope the week will be fun but a relaxing break from London. There will be only nine of us: your two charges, my sister, her husband, Miles Hallsmith, Lord Stansfield, and I assume, the good mother of the Dowder sisters."

"Oh no, my lord. Mrs. Dowder will not be attending. Something keeps her at their country estate. That is why I was called into action."

Joyous news! Sylvia would not have to deal with Felicia during their relaxing week. "The party shall miss her, but we will soldier on."

Mrs. Horthorn giggled. "Indeed."

The gardens were on the wild side for English taste, but the meandering path, overgrown grasses, and clusters of wildflowers suited Anthony. "If I may ask, what brought you to the Everton Domestic Society, madam?"

"Boredom."

"I beg your pardon?"

She nodded then stopped to admire a yellow daisy. "I was bored. My husband had died a few years earlier and left me a pile of money. I love to sew and knit, but really that's not enough to make a life of. Since I'm not titled, the invitations dwindled and I was left sitting home alone every evening. I know I'm not young, but it was terribly tiresome."

"I can see how that might be so." He'd never thought about what widows do with their time. Frankly, he had no idea what young women did on the day to day.

"One morning while breaking my fast, I read an advertisement in the newspaper for the Everton Domestic Society. It said they help families in need, and when necessary a dowager chaperon would be provided. I got to wondering about it and paid Lady Jane a call. She hired me on the spot. That was two and a half years ago, and I'm so happy I joined Everton's."

"You're content there then?"

"Where else can a woman of my years get out and meet people and do interesting things. The Everton ladies are all extraordinary, each in her own way. Every assignment is different. I live at Everton House because I have constant company there and it affords me whatever I need, which isn't much."

If it was so perfect, he would be hard pressed to talk Sylvia out of her position there. "It sounds ideal."

She shrugged. "Interestingly, it is a last resort for the young women and a second chance for we dowagers."

Offering his arm, he smiled. "I am glad to know you, Mrs. Horthorn. The Dowder ladies are in good hands this week."

She placed her hand in the crook of his elbow. "You can be quite charming when you put your mind to it, my lord. I will be keeping my eye on you."

They both laughed as a footman dashed across a small lawn toward them. He was out of breath and skidded to a stop before them. "A carriage has arrived, my lord."

"Jack, there is no need to do yourself harm, but thank you. We will go directly and greet the ladies." Quite proud of how calm he'd sounded, Anthony wanted to run about like a fool and arrive at the front drive as randy as a schoolboy. It was probably best that he was charged with escorting Mrs. Horthorn, and they kept a stately pace back to where Sylvia and Serena were being handed down from the Dowder carriage.

Serena looked around with wide eyes. "My lord, this is a stunning home and so close to town. I've never seen anything like it. It's heavenly."

He bowed over Serena's hand. "Thank you, Miss Dowder. I'm glad you like it and am honored you're able to be here this week."

Sylvia's smile was more practiced and staid. "Good to see you again, my lord. I hope you found the house in order."

With his back facing the other two ladies, he gave Sylvia the same attention he had her sister. However, this time he allowed his lips to touch her knuckles.

A tiny gasp escaped, giving him hope that she had experienced the same delight he had from the contact.

Easing back, he met her gaze. "The pleasure is mine, Miss Dowder. I am thrilled to have you back at Riverdale. Mrs. Horthorn and I were taking a turn in the garden, but Kravitz tells me all has been readied for a wonderful week."

"Your staff has been very helpful and all via written correspondence, which was quite convenient." Stepping back, she avoided making further eye contact.

"I understand your good mother will not be joining us this week." He attempted to sound disappointed by the fact.

Serena said, "It was the strangest thing. Mother had every intention of traveling with us, but an old friend of hers arrived just days before our departure. Lady Honoria Chervil and Mother have known each other for many years, and the two will spend the week catching up on old times."

Biting her bottom lip, Sylvia hid a smile, though not from him. "Yes, it was a surprise. In any event, Mother is happy to see her friend, and we have come to Riverdale with the knowledge that Mrs. Horthorn will chaperon us to the best of her ability."

"I'm glad everyone is happy." Mostly, he was glad Sylvia would not have to contend with her mother's disapproval. He didn't know if he could tolerate an entire week of her obvious favoritism without speaking out. "Shall we go inside and get you settled?"

He had a small study that he retreated to once he'd seen the ladies to their rooms. It had a poky little fireplace, a barely adequate writing desk and chair, and three comfortable chairs surrounding a coffee table.

Sylvia had been adamant that she and Serena could and would share a room. He couldn't think of any reason not to grant her demand, so the young ladies were in the large guest room that had two beds. It had belonged to his two great-uncles many years before but had been redecorated by his cousin to suit guests.

Sylvia cleared her throat and knocked at the same time. "My lord, I wanted to check and see if there was anything you'd like to add to the week's activities. I have planned something for each day, but there will be time for whatever you choose."

He stood to greet her. Her stiff delivery troubled him. His behavior had put a divide between them and it wouldn't do. "Perhaps some hunting with Daniel, Miles and Stansfield if he's interested, but that would be an early morning activity and shouldn't interfere with whatever you've planned."

"Very good. Do you have any special food requests? Cook has the menus planned but asked if you'd like something special." Still standing in the doorway, she clutched her hands in front of her.

"Sylvie, please come in and sit down. This calling to each other across the room is too cold for friends." Holding his breath until she stepped inside, he finally let it out. "Thank you." He sat. "I have no reason to change the menu. The food here has always been very good. I'm sure we will all be well pleased."

Staring just over his left shoulder, she said, "Very good. Tomorrow I have set time aside for the guests to rest after they arrive. You have a lovely back parlor that I thought we might use for cards after dinner. Your gardener has offered to take us all on a tour of the gardens. I have scheduled that for day after tomorrow just before luncheon. He is a bit of a genius about plants and wildlife if Kravitz is to be believed. I hope you will join the tour."

"Sylvie?"

Finally, she looked at him. "Yes?"

"Are you upset with me?"

"No."

"Then why should two friends have a conversation that sounds as if we've only just met?" Heart pounding, he waited for an answer that could break his heart.

She searched the room. "I suppose I feel awkward after our last encounter. You said some things that should not have been said. I might have been insensitive and hurt your feelings. I came here intent on putting all of that in the past. You have probably already left this behind us, and I shall do the same. I will finish this assignment; then, friends or not, we shall likely never see each other again."

The notion of never seeing his Sylvia again sent pain into his heart and gut until he thought he might double over from the agony. "I am certain you are wrong."

The most adorable crease formed between her eyes. "About what?"

"Everything you just said." He held up a hand to stop her from responding. "However, you may believe whatever you like."

She stood. "I have upset you. I apologize."

Rising with her, he kept his expression staid. "Not at all. You have done a fine job just as I knew you would, and we are still friends, Sylvie. I will see you at dinner unless you have more plans to discuss."

Worry etched around her eyes, and she bit her lower lip. "You understand, Tony, I am protecting us both. We have nothing in common, and you plan to leave the country."

Checking the open doorway over her shoulder and finding it empty, he rounded his desk and strode forward until he towered over her. "I say, what we have is passion and not at all unpleasant. You want me to believe we are not suited. I understand your position, Sylvie. I will not lie to you. I plan to convince you that we are the only people suited to one another."

Wide-eyed, she licked her lips. "I don't know what to say."

Those lips called for his with an ear-piercing ring. "Say nothing then."

Kravitz spoke to a footman in the parlor next door.

Anthony stepped back. "You should check on dinner. I assume the other ladies are resting but will be up and about very soon."

Her deep breath lifted her breasts in the most mouth-watering way. "I will see to it."

"I will see you at dinner then." He had rattled her, and that was the point, but she had unsettled him as well.

Rushing from the room, she lifted the hem of her skirt and disappeared behind the door.

This was going to be harder than he thought. Impressed with his own control, he closed his eyes to keep from running after her. Yearning to grab her and tell her he would have no other, he knew she had to come to him on her own terms. Sylvia's strength and intelligence should not be discounted. She was no shrinking violet. It was part of what he loved about her, maybe most of what he loved.

"Are you unwell, sir?" Kravitz said from the threshold.

Anthony loved Riverdale, but its smaller size meant that there were few places to hide. "I am fine. Is all in order for the guests arriving tomorrow?"

"The rooms have all been cleaned and readied, my lord. Mrs. Long will cut fresh flowers in the morning and place a vase in each room. Is there anything else you would like us to do?"

Standing, Anthony shook off the effects of being close to Sylvia and cleared his head. "I sent several cases of wine last week. I assume they arrived."

"They have been placed in the cellar."

"Bring up two bottles for tonight and decant some brandy in the parlor facing the garden. Miss Dowder favors that room for the evening gatherings." Anthony liked the idea of doing something because Sylvia liked the room or opening a bottle of wine with the hope of enjoying it with her.

"Yes, my lord." Kravitz tugged his coat into place and rushed out to do Anthony's bidding.

It was time he went up and dressed for dinner. Perhaps a bath to cleanse away his doubt. He had one week to make her see the truth or for her to refuse him and leave him tattered.

Chapter 13

Sylvia and Serena dressed for dinner. Despite her determination to keep Anthony away, she let Jenny help her into a rust gown that looked pretty on her. The dark orange hue complemented her hair and made her eyes look darker. It pushed her breasts up and showed more figure than she should as an employee. A gray serviceable dress would have been more in line with her plans to repel his attention.

Serena let Jenny tighten her corset. "I don't understand, Sylvie. Why don't you want to encourage his lordship?"

"We are not suited. He is an earl and I am an Everton lady. There is no future for us, and when he realizes that, he will break my heart." Anthony had his own hopes and dreams, which didn't include her, but she wouldn't tell her sister his secret.

"But if he loves you…"

Sylvia lifted a hand to stop whatever drivel her sister was going to say. "He does not love me, and I do not love him. It is merely our proximity. The moment I am out of his life for good, he will forget all about me."

Corset tied, she stepped into her dress and waited while it was buttoned at the back. "Will you also forget?"

"It is best for girls like me to have short memories, Serena. Wanting the impossible only lands one in trouble. I will go back to my world, and he will stay in his, and all will be well."

Serena frowned. "It sounds to me like a terrible way to go on. You will regret him, and if he's smart, he will always regret you. But perhaps it is as you say, and his feelings are not deep. An infatuation can be forgotten easily enough."

It was a good thing dinner would be served soon or Sylvia was going to be sick right there in front of her sister. If that happened there would be no hiding her feelings, which were becoming more and more dangerous.

Checking herself in the glass, she said, "I'm going down to see if anything needs doing before dinner. Will you be all right?"

Serena studied her for a long moment, cocked her head, then said, "I'm fine. I'll be down when Jenny finishes my hair."

If Sylvia hadn't known better, she would think her sister was up to something, but Serena was never devious. She said and did exactly what was expected of a young lady and daughter of a gentleman.

Kravitz met her at the bottom of the stairs. "Miss Dowder?"

The poor butler wasn't sure which Miss Dowder she was. Sylvia and Serena had often teased people by posing as each other when they were young. It was tempting now, but she couldn't do it. "I am Sylvia Dowder, Kravitz. How can I help you?"

He bowed. "There seems to be some question of seating. Will Mrs. Horthorn be dining with you every night or just tonight?"

Following him into the dining room, she admired the simple white setting and the informal glassware. Everything was exactly as a country home should be. This one was just close to London and set in the most beautiful piece of property God ever created. For an instant, she let herself love Riverdale and imagined herself the mistress of such a heavenly place.

Shaking off the stupid notion, she moved Mrs. Horthorn to Anthony's left and herself beside her chaperon. "It is entirely up to her, but I would guess she will dine with us nightly. My sister will sit to his lordship's right then move down the table when titled guests arrive tomorrow. You may always place me at the farthest end from his lordship."

His calm facade slipped, leaving a deep frown. "As you wish, miss."

Sylvia loved the house more than she should. Even the dining room, with its wood wainscoting broken up by papered walls, painted with tiny roses. Large windows faced south and let in the most beautiful light during the day. The sun was setting, and soon the silver candelabras would be lit before dinner was served. The first evening would be rather casual, but the rest of the week elegance and opulence would be the theme.

No one would ever doubt that the Earl of Grafton was less than the perfect aristocrat, regardless of where he was born. At least she had seen to that.

Once she was on to another assignment, it would be up to Anthony to maintain his status. There was nothing out of the ordinary about it, but she wanted to cry.

Voices from the small parlor next door alerted her that crying would not do. She drew a deep breath and put on her practiced smile before joining the others.

"Good evening, Miss Dowder." Anthony bowed. "I was just telling your sister and Mrs. Horthorn how you transformed my London house. It's interesting that it now resembles the decor here at Riverdale despite you having only had a glance of this house prior to the changes."

"I suppose that is true. Though the London house is more elegant." She loved Riverdale's light cozy feel. It was exactly what she'd tried to give Collington House. It suited her more than it should since it was meant only to suit Anthony.

Mrs. Horthorn nodded and examined the furnishings. "It's uncanny, Miss Dowder. You have captured his lordship's taste perfectly."

"Thank you. I did my best." Heat rose in her cheeks, but she turned away and hoped no one noticed.

Anthony held an uncorked bottle of wine, which he had plucked from the side table. "I thought we might have a glass of wine. This is from my cousin's private label. He doesn't sell this, only keeps it for family. I rarely bring it out, but tonight is a special occasion."

Accepting a glass, Serena smiled. "What occasion is it we're celebrating, my lord?"

Surprise widened his eyes and stood him up straighter. "You ladies being here and the start to a wonderful week. I cannot think of anything grander than a few good friends and a fine bottle of wine."

Serena's smile broadened. "What a lovely thing to say. Thank you. I can't wait to try it."

Once he'd given Mrs. Horthorn and Sylvia each a glass, Anthony lifted his. "A toast. To good friends and to beginnings."

They all repeated the toast and sipped the wine.

Sylvia let the full, fruity flavor wash over her lips and tongue. Notes of spices and mushrooms made their way into the experience. Closing her eyes, she reveled in the blossoming flavors of the cool wine. When she opened her eyes, Anthony was staring at her, his expression warm and filled with emotions she refused to name.

"Dinner is served in the dining room whenever you are ready," Kravitz announced from the doorway.

Anthony sighed. "Shall we go in, ladies?"

Sylvia wanted to believe Anthony was being so perfectly cordial because he was the only man amongst ladies. She talked herself into it and even speculated that he might be trying to charm Serena. When they walked into the dining room and he saw that she had moved herself down a seat, his frown told a different story. Perhaps she should go back to her previous notion of pursuing Miles Hallsmith. At least when that fell apart, she wouldn't be devastated. Anthony's betrayal would destroy her, and she couldn't let herself be vulnerable to it.

"My lord, Sylvia tells me that you have been to Italy. What was that like?" Serena's enthusiasm was contagious.

Anthony put his fork down and finished his bite of goose. "Italy is beautiful and exotic. My family has a large vineyard in Tuscany. It is mountainous and green. The cities were trampled by Roman soldiers. Some of the greatest minds made discoveries. Tuscany is small, and each country has its own ruler. Umbria is lovely. In the south, they grow the most amazing lemons. Life is slow, and wine is life. Unlike the English, Italians argue in public over the smallest thing. They are filled with passion." He glanced at Sylvia.

Serena sighed. "Is it like America? Americans always seem filled with life and excitement."

He peered out the window. The sun was nearly down. "America is wild and new. Tuscany is old. My cousins will talk about anything. Things that even as an American I find unsuitable for casual conversation. It is a refreshing change, but lately, I have begun to prefer England."

"Then you don't plan to return to America?" Mrs. Horthorn asked.

Again, he glanced at Sylvia.

She didn't want to care what he answered. Why should she care whether he chose to live in Italy, America, or England? Eventually he would marry some wealthy, proper twit, and she would read about it in the newspaper. Her own thoughts were making her ill.

"I have no intention of ever living in Philadelphia again. I have a partner who runs my business from that end. I like England, and now that I have a title, there are many people who depend on me here. Besides, I have people whom I care about and would not wish to leave behind." His gaze roved over Sylvia, and he sipped his wine.

The room was closing in on Sylvia. The little she had eaten was churning in her gut. "Will you all excuse me? I'm not feeling well."

Anthony stood. His forehead creased, and he rounded the table to help her up. "Can I do anything for you? Shall I call a doctor?"

Stepping back, she put quick distance between them. "No. No. I'll be fine. I need some air is all. I'll go to the garden for a few minutes then rest for the night."

"Are you certain?" He stepped closer, looking like he intended to sweep her up and carry her away.

"I'm fine. It's been a long day and I feel a bit flushed. That is all." She ran from the dining room, down the hall, and out the rear door to the garden.

The cool night air eased her nausea. She had no idea how she was going to get through the week if she couldn't be in the same room with Anthony without falling into a pit of despair. She would have to harness these feelings and put them aside before they ruined her. An Everton lady did not lose her head over a client. She did her job and moved on to the next assignment, and that was what Sylvia was determined to do.

In the dark garden, only the moon lit her way. It was not quite full but gave enough light for her to find the path. Still she wouldn't go far for fear of losing herself in the little wilderness at night.

Roses scented the light breeze, and her skin prickled with the dropping temperatures. Clutching her arms around her waist, she closed her eyes and breathed deep the night.

As she was thinking it a pity it was too cool to remain in the garden, the soft wool of a shawl settled around her shoulders.

"I thought you might be cold." Anthony's breath tickled the back of her ear.

She clutched the shawl and wished his arms came with the fabric to hold her and keep her warm. "You shouldn't be out here with me. What will my sister and Mrs. Horthorn think?"

Still dressed for dinner, he was striking in the moonlight. His dark hair glowed, and he faded into the night, but those piercing eyes captured her heart. "You have been away from the table long enough that dinner ended. The other ladies were tired from their day and retired early."

"Then we are truly alone." Her voice broke and trembled.

He brushed his knuckles along her jaw. "Are you afraid of me, Sylvie?"

"No. I could never fear you, Tony."

"I should hope not. I would never hurt you. Never." He was too close, too handsome and too delectable.

She stepped back. "All men say such things, when they have no idea what hurts a woman."

Shaking his head, he offered his arm. "It's late. Can I escort you back to the house?"

"I can find my own way." The bite in her voice was too sharp, but she had to get away from him and make him see how awful they were for each other.

"Are you cross with me now?" His golden eyes flashed like a lion's.

Tugging the edges of the shawl around her, she stomped her foot. "We don't all of us need a man to tell us what to do or carry us back to the house. I am independent. I am an Everton lady." Her voice cracked again.

"What does that have to do with a gentleman offering escort? You English made these rules. I'm just trying to follow them. If you want to return on your own, then go ahead." He threw his hands up in the air.

It was too hard to be near him and want him, but know it was wrong. "I want you to leave me alone. If I ever want something from a man, it will not be a man like you. I'll pick a mister, not a lord."

"Is that what this is all about? A stupid title. I can give it up if that's what it would take to convince you. I will tell the king I don't want his stupid title and give it all back. What more can I do?" In his excitement, he'd begun waving both hands around.

Men and their solutions were ridiculous. "You all think you can have whatever you want. I don't want you. Can't you understand that?"

The air seemed to suck out of the world. Sylvia couldn't breathe or speak. She wanted to take it back, but she couldn't do that either.

Anthony's eyes widened, grew cold then sad. "If that's true, then I owe you an apology. I should have realized my interest was not reciprocated. Forgive me and my foolishness. If it's a mister you want, I'm sure Miles Hallsmith will be happy to court a lady such as yourself. You've made quite an impression on him. Again, I'm sorry to have misunderstood."

Before she could call out to him, he'd disappeared into the dark garden. She knew she'd done the right thing, but the sorrow in his expression would haunt her for the rest of her life. A tear rolled down her cheek, and she dashed it away before the next came. Soon too many followed, and she went in the house, up the steps, and to her room. She wished she'd not insisted on having Serena in the same room, but her sister was there with open arms and it felt good to have someone care about her distress.

She cried until no more tears would come.

Serena petted her hair. "Do you want to tell me what happened?"

"No. I want to be stronger and not want things I cannot have." She swallowed down another round of misery and buried her face in her pillow.

Sitting on the edge of Sylvia's bed, Serena asked, "What is it you cannot have?"

"What every girl wants. What I wanted before Hunter ruined everything. A husband, children, and a home."

"Oh, Sylvie, you are a fool. You can have all those things if you want them. I suspect you could have them with a very rich, handsome, and charming lord, who is under this roof right now. The question is why don't you want those things? Is it just fear, or do you have a good reason?"

"Fear is a good reason."

"You are the bravest person I know, Sylvie. You can stand up for anyone and help them accomplish anything. You are funny in a wicked and wonderful way, and I hate that you've lost some of that. But you have let fear run your life for the past year. You should have thanked your lucky stars that you didn't marry Hunter and live the rest of your life with a man who would do such a terrible thing. He did you a favor, and you should be the first one to recognize it. If you love Anthony Braighton, you should allow yourself to be happy."

"I don't. He doesn't. We aren't." More tears and several handkerchiefs later, exhaustion won, and Sylvia slept.

* * * *

Her head pounded when she woke up the following morning. She rang for Jenny, who rushed in with a pot of coffee and a blue day dress slung over one arm.

"Where is Serena?"

Jenny placed the dress on the end of the bed and poured the coffee. "She was up early and is walking in the garden. This is the latest I've ever known you to sleep, Miss Sylvia. Are you feeling all right?"

"I'm fine. Perhaps too much wine last night," she lied and wondered when it had become so easy to do so.

"Mrs. Long asked me to remind you that you said you would help arrange flowers for the guest rooms."

Sylvia drank the bitter coffee down in two long gulps. "I did say that. Help me dress, Jenny. I have a lot to do before the other guests arrive."

If she stayed busy, she could avoid Anthony for the entire day. She would see him at meals, but it would be easy enough to ignore him, and surely after her behavior in the garden, he'd not speak to her again.

More tears pressed against the back of her eyes, but she fought them down. She had to keep her wits about her or she'd be made a fool, and that wouldn't do. Being a member of the Society was all she had. If she became a laughingstock and the object of even more gossip, she'd never work again.

Once dressed and her hair pulled back in a sensible bun, she pushed her distress down and pulled her shoulders back. "Jenny, I'll be on the servants' level if my sister should need me. I have a long list of things to do before luncheon."

"Can I help you with anything, miss?" Jenny's offer was genuine and kind.

Sylvia hugged her. "You've done more than enough. It's been wonderful to have you take care of me these last few weeks. However, you are Serena's maid, not mine. A girl like me can't afford to become spoiled when I'll be back in service without a lady's maid by the week's end."

It was the proper thing to think, if only she could remember her place and be happy with her choices. She hustled down two levels.

Wildflowers filled the kitchen table, and the heavenly scent mixed with yeasty bread and biscuits filled all of Sylvia's senses to overflowing. "This is wonderful."

Yellow, white, lavender, and green, all in full bloom and various sizes. Mrs. Long had two maids helping her cut stems to six inches and place the flowers in groups by type. "Isn't it lovely, miss? The last earl didn't care for the wildflowers of the area. Rest his soul, but he only liked hothouse flowers. None of these happy blossoms ever came in the house unless his mother visited. The dowager loves flowers in every room and particularly these yellow daisies in her room. I hope we shall see her again. Some say she's stern, but she was always kind to the staff."

Sylvia plucked a daisy from the table and ran the soft petals under her nose. "I think his lordship will have his aunt to visit. They seem quite close."

Cook was a tiny woman with wispy blond hair that poked out from the edge of her cap. "It would be nice to see her ladyship again. She rarely visited when her son was here. He preferred the Devonshire country house with all its grandeur. Riverdale was too plain for his taste. A good master, but not here much at all."

"Perhaps it will be different with his lordship. He seems taken with this house." Mrs. Long put the last flower in its place.

Sylvia could stay among the flowers for the entire day and not be a bit sorry. "What shall we arrange them in?"

"We have vases." Mrs. Long shooed the maids in the direction of a cupboard in the room across the hall.

They returned with two trays filled with small vases of various shapes and colors. Blue, pink, and cream porcelain, all painted with birds and flowers.

"How lovely." Sylvia took a cream oval-shaped vase. She accepted the pitcher of water from Mrs. Long and filled the vase halfway before placing flowers in it. The white and yellow made for a fresh bouquet, but the bits of lavender were charming.

"Oh, miss, you are good at this." Mrs. Long clutched her hands together under her chin. "I shall try to imitate your work."

In a short time, all the vases were filled, and springtime had invaded the kitchen. It was perfection. The flowers at Everton House were beautiful, and each day fresh flowers were put on tables. Still, they weren't as vibrant as these picked here at Riverdale. She could be happy arranging flowers in the morning.

She shook off the notion. Getting lost in such thoughts wasn't good for her, yet she couldn't seem to help it.

"This is a lovely sight," Anthony said from the bottom of the kitchen stairs.

All four servants stiffened, and Mrs. Long cleared her throat. "My lord, can I help you with something?"

He shook his head. "I wanted a word with Miss Dowder."

Holding her breath, Sylvia swallowed her jumble of emotions. "Thank you, ladies. The flowers look stunning. Can you see that they are placed in the guests' rooms?"

"Of course, miss," Mrs. Long said with a quick curtsy.

Sylvia proceeded Anthony up the stairs. At the top, she waited until he was beside her. "What can I do for you, my lord?"

"Tony."

"We are not alone." She had to put some distance between them before she lost herself in those eyes.

Glancing around, he huffed. "I don't see anyone."

"You know what I mean."

Capturing her gaze with his, he said, "Unfortunately, I know exactly what you mean, Sylvie."

"What is it you need, my lord?"

"My sister and her husband have arrived. I want you to come to the small parlor and say hello. Sophia, in particular, was eager to see you again."

"I would be pleased to see them." Sylvia strode down the hall to the parlor. Riverdale had two parlors, and this one was only called small because the other was so grand. The room had light blue and wood walls. The wood had been kept light and clean, and the ceiling was painted a lighter blue.

Lord and Lady Marlton sat in one of three groupings of chairs. They faced the side garden where Cook had vegetables and herbs growing hip tall.

Lord Marlton stood. "Miss Dowder, how wonderful to see you again."

"My lord, the pleasure is mine." She curtsied.

His frown was daunting. "The first thing we must do is get you to stop calling me my lord and start calling me Daniel."

Her cheeks were on fire. "I will try, my—I mean, Daniel."

Sophia's smile showed lovely white teeth against her warm skin tone. "Sylvia, you've done a wonderful job making my brother seem like a real earl."

It was a sisterly jibe, but Anthony bristled. "I am a real earl."

"Of course, you are, but to have the rest of London agree that an American can be a real earl is quite a feat. Yet, your Everton lady managed it beautifully. The ball was such a success, they are still gossiping about it in town."

Sylvia wanted to jump for joy. However, she forced herself to only smile politely. "I'm so pleased it all worked out. Of course, I had a lot of help from the Everton Domestic Society and the servants. It was my pleasure to be a part of his lordship finding a proper place amongst his peers."

Daniel offered his arm to escort Sylvia to where they had been sitting. Once she took it, he said, "You will have to learn that we are a very informal bunch when not in public, Sylvia. I can't have you calling me Daniel and Tony his lordship. I shall feel awkward. Can we make a pact that within our group, Christian names are a habit?"

"You are very kind, Daniel, but by the end of this party I shall exit this group and likely only see you in public, then only briefly." Part of her died and the rest wanted to follow when the truth blurted from her lips.

He handed her into a yellow, embroidered, overstuffed chair and sat on the divan next to his wife. "I have a suspicion we shall meet more often than you think."

Before Sylvia could ask him what he'd meant, Sophia cleared her throat. "What fun things have you planned for us this week?"

"I thought since everyone will arrive today and be a bit tired, we might just play cards after dinner tonight. Tomorrow we can tour the gardens, and in the evening my sister has agreed to play for us. She is quite talented."

Sophia raised her eyebrows. "And perhaps Lord Stansfield might be delighted by her talents as well."

There was little sense being coy. "I had hoped as much."

"I have met him several times, and while he is a tad reticent, when he does speak, he is intelligent and thoughtful. A good match for a sweet lady like Serena." Sophia spoke as directly as her brother, and her American accent made it sound like fact rather than the subterfuge often laced in English conversation.

"Thank you, Sophia. I would very much like to see my sister happy."

Daniel's brows drew down in a frown. "And what of you, Sylvia. Are you happy as an Everton lady?"

It was impertinent for him to ask. Perhaps being married to an American caused his forthrightness. Sylvia hated the question and lied. "Of course. I come and go as I please. I have my own money. I am bound only by the rules of the *Everton Companion*, and those are easy enough to follow." That lie might have gone too far.

Sophia sat forward. "Daniel doesn't mean to be rude. It is only that when we were all together at the ball, your mother…well, she made us all quite angry with her dismissal of you in favor of Serena." She held up her hand to stop Sylvia from interrupting. "We adore Serena and she should have all good things and be happy in whatever life she chooses, but so should you. Your mother is a good woman, but she did not show herself well that night, and we have been concerned for you ever since."

It was perhaps the sweetest thing anyone had said to her in over a year. Here she thought no one cared what happened to on-the-shelf Sylvia, and there was an entire family, not her own, who were worried. "Mother has been through a lot because of the termination of my engagement to Lord March. She does not know how to fix the problem, and since I have made choices that she disapproves of, it has made it even harder on her. On that particular night, Lord March intimated to my mother that he might be interested in rekindling our romantic attachment."

"The nerve!" Sophia fisted her hands, and her nostrils flared.

A low growl sounded from behind Sylvia. She turned and saw the lion awaken in Anthony's eyes. It could be a very safe net to have these two Braighton siblings on one's side.

Daniel took hold of one of Sophia's hands and pried her fingers open. "You'll have to forgive them. Once they like someone as they like you, they are very protective. March does deserve a sound thrashing. Please finish what you were saying."

Caught between delight and terror, Sylvia took a moment to remember what she'd been saying. "Um, I told Mother I would never entertain any offer from Lord March, and she was extremely put out. She wants me to be married."

"But not happy?" Sophia asked.

Sylvia sighed. "Happiness is a luxury that a twenty-four-year-old, untitled lady can little afford, in Mother's opinion. Frankly, it is the opinion of most of society. Only the Society gives me another option. To her, it would be a miraculous recovery if Hunter and I married as planned. Right now, she feels as if she's wasted over five years on me that might have been spent finding Serena a husband. From her prospective, I am a complete disappointment and Serena the only glimmer of hope that she hasn't completely failed as a mother."

"And does being an Everton lady make you happy?" Sophia's lips thinned into a line.

"I am honored by your concern. Truly, I am, but you need not worry about me. I live in a nice home where I have friends and I'm safe. Most importantly, I'm not married to a man I detest."

Sophia sighed. "I suppose that is true. I have enjoyed our time together, and I'm not happy this is the final week of your contract with my brother. Perhaps you might visit us in the country in a month when we return there."

When she disobeyed her parents and left home, all her friends had abandoned her. Even Serena had stayed away for a short time. Knowing that she now had friends who cared to see her clogged her throat with joy. All of this because of Anthony. How would she ever repay him? "I…I don't know what to say. That would be lovely."

Slapping her hand down on the cushion, Sophia smiled. "It's settled then. I will write you with the dates, and Daniel will send a carriage to convey you."

Sylvia wanted to hug someone. She stood and so did Sophia. It seemed the countess needed a hug too. The embrace was genuine and warm. Sylvia was about to dissolve into a puddle of tears over having a friend who would not abandon her.

Pulling away, Sylvia swallowed the lump in her throat. "I have to check on a few things for this evening. If you will excuse me?"

Chapter 14

Anthony watched Sylvia run from the room. "That was very kind of you, Sophie."

"I like her, and more importantly, you like her." Sophia dabbed a tear from her eye with her gloved hand.

"It's good that you like her, since I intend to ask her to marry me."

Sophia's mouth opened and closed several times. "I had no idea you had come to your senses, Tony. When can we begin the celebrations?"

"As soon as I convince the lady she wishes to marry me, too. She has told me I am not a proper match for her. Miles seems to be my competition, though he claims it is not the case. It's all quite confusing. I may have to accept that she does not like me." Vomiting was not out of the question, since his stomach rolled at the idea of losing Sylvia.

Daniel laughed. "I would hazard a guess that it is not that she doesn't like you, Tony. She can't look at you without blushing. In my experience, if you make enough of a fool of yourself over a woman, she'll come around."

Sophia smacked his arm. "You nearly got yourself killed. I didn't ask for that."

"No. That was more than any of us bargained for. However, you are worth it, my love." He kissed the tip of her nose.

Anthony groaned. "I'll leave you two lovebirds alone. The other guests will arrive any moment, so don't get too cozy in the parlor."

Sophia giggled as Anthony stepped into the hall.

* * * *

The day proceeded exactly as Sylvia said it would. She'd planned every detail to make his guests comfortable and happy. Dinner had been lively, and afterward, the card tables were filled with laughter for a few hours before the company broke up and went to bed.

Glancing up the stairs, Anthony caught sight of Mrs. Horthorn and Serena, but there was no sign of Sylvia. Perhaps she had gone to bed earlier. After all, she had worked to make everyone else's night pleasant, she must be tired.

In the foyer, Kravitz bowed. "My lord, I think all have gone to their beds."

"Very good. I suggest you do the same. We have a busy day tomorrow."

"Thank you, my lord." Kravitz slid the bolt on the front door and strode toward the servants' stairs.

The window in his study was open, and a cool breeze blew in. Anthony stood looking into the darkness.

The shrubbery under the window rustled.

Anthony stepped forward and pushed the glass farther open. "Is someone there?"

"It's me, Tony." Sylvia pushed through the dense foliage. A leaf stuck in her hair and she had a smudge of dirt on her cheek.

"What on earth are you doing out there?" He was torn between laughing and worry.

"I took a walk and got locked out. I didn't realize I'd been out so long, and the staff must have thought I'd gone to bed." Her teeth chattered.

The window stood four feet above ground, so only her head and shoulders were above the sill. He put out his arms. "Shall I pull you in?"

"I should tell you to go and open the door, but honestly, I cannot go back through these bushes to get out of here." Lifting her arms up to him, she blushed the most stunning pink.

Anthony braced his knees against the wall, leaned out and wrapped his arms around her under her arms. Heaven would not be as wonderful as holding her, regardless of the reason.

Her hands came around his neck and her cheek settled alongside his, soft and cool from the night.

Her slight weight made it nothing to draw her inside, but he held her as he backed away from the window. Since she made no effort to disengage from him, he held on to her. "I wouldn't mind staying just like this a while, Sylvie."

In a long breath against his chest, her breasts lifted and fell. "You are very warm, Tony."

"Ask me for that kiss." He breathed in her floral scent and wanted more than anything to do so every day for the rest of his life.

"It's not a good idea."

"Ask me anyway?" It was a plea, and he didn't care if he sounded desperate. He needed her.

"Kiss me, Tony?" A whispered breath was all it took.

Cupping her cheeks, and then threading his fingers through her hair, he kissed her bottom lip, then the top.

She answered each small caress with the same. "I'm never going to be your mistress."

"I know that." He deepened the kiss.

Her sweet tongue danced with his.

His body burned to know every inch of hers and make her his own.

"We have nothing in common."

He silenced her with another kiss that took his breath away.

Tiny moans sounded from deep in her chest, and she ran her hands down his back, to his waist, then up his abdomen to his chest.

Lord, how he wanted to feel those soft hands against his bare skin. He nibbled the flesh behind her ear and down her neck to her shoulder. "We have a lot in common."

"You said you didn't want a wife. You came to the Everton Domestic Society with the single notion of not marrying. You told me you would run away to Italy as soon as you could." She kissed his throat just above his cravat.

Tearing at the knot, he pulled open the neck cloth. "I say a lot of things that are stupid. You will get used to it."

Taking advantage of his newly exposed skin, she kissed his Adam's apple and below. "I don't want..."

He froze. "What don't you want, Sylvie?"

Heaving breaths, she was as desperate for air as he was. He longed to kiss her throat, chest, and lower until he knew every inch of Sylvia Dowder.

He wanted to taste every part of her and give her more pleasure than she could stand. The growing need was impossible.

Where her eyes had been filled with passion, suddenly confusion and fear clouded them. "I don't want you. I'm sorry, Tony. This is all my fault. I will be more careful in the future. You'll not have to drag me in windows again. You will find the right woman now that you're open to marriage. I am not the one. I am no one's perfect match."

Then it happened, his heart broke in two. Everything he wanted was right in front of him. She'd asked him to kiss her. She'd wanted him as he wanted her. What had happened? "Why are you saying this?"

"Young men all reach a point when they are ready to marry. The woman is not consequential. You will find the right one." She ran to the door.

"Sylvie!"

She stopped and pressed her forehead against the wood with her hand gripping the doorknob. "I don't want you, Tony. Can't you understand that?"

"Please, Sylvie, don't say things that will hurt us both, then run from the room." She might as well have flayed him open with a dagger and twisted the blade. Nothing could hurt this much and not kill him.

"I'm sorry." She fled the room, and her soft footsteps sounded on the stairs until they too were gone.

He sat in the chair nearest to him. It was a short-legged thing he hated, as it forced his knees up and made him look like he was sitting on a child's chair. It reminded him of when he got too big for the chairs in the nursery.

It was insane. She loved him; he knew she did. No one could kiss him so tenderly and hold him with so much intensity and feel nothing. Sylvia was not cold and never calculating, so the only answer was that she loved him.

Closing his eyes, he forced his emotions into check. Running up the stairs and banging on her door until she told him what was wrong with him would not be smart, no matter how tempting.

He was going to need help.

* * * *

Anthony walked along with the group as his gardener talked of this flower, plant, and tree or that. If he'd not been so distracted, he might have cared about the dissertation.

The problem with finding someone to help him was he didn't want to embarrass Sylvia in any way. He couldn't tell his sister about the kiss, and she would certainly want to know how he could be so sure that Sylvia loved him. He would have to find some other way.

Miles slapped him on the back. "You might want to put on that bland mask you've been working on."

Knowing he was right, Anthony hid whatever emotions were crossing his face. "I must work on that."

They slowed their pace and put some distance between the others and them. Miles asked, "She still hasn't fallen into rapturous love with you?"

"If she has, she's far better at hiding it than I am." He wouldn't tell Miles anything about his encounters with Sylvia any more than he would tell Sophia.

"You might try her sister."

"Have you lost your mind? They're not interchangeable like pawns on a chessboard. I could no more court Serena Dowder than I could court Mrs. Horthorn or my own sister." The notion of hurting Sylvia in such a way was completely abhorrent. She might not ever admit to loving him, but he loved her and was nearly certain she had some feelings for him too.

"Your sister is married, and Mrs. Horthorn a bit old for you. Serena Dowder is pretty in a way you seem to enjoy, and she is available for the moment. You could do worse. But it looks as though you won't have much time. Stansfield looks about ready to propose. You might want to move quickly." It was all so matter-of-fact to Miles and his English sense of order.

"Miles, if you want to court Serena, you should. If Sylvia loves you, I would relish her happiness despite my own misery. But I will never court her sister. You English have no heart to think one woman is as good as the next."

"These two look exactly the same. I don't see what you're so upset about. It's not unusual to marry another sister when the first is not available or is unwilling."

True or not, the idea was repulsive. Miles had clearly never been in love. "I appreciate your advice, but from now on, you may keep it to yourself."

Laughing, Miles jogged to catch up with the others.

Sylvia wore lavender. He'd noticed it was a color she favored during the day. Her cap became caught in the rosebush, and she laughed as Sophia tried to pull her free. Rather than continue to be attached to the bush, Sylvia pulled the bow at her chin and released the hat. Her hair tumbled loose around her shoulders while Daniel rescued her hat.

Seeing her with his family, enjoying the day, everything was as it should be. If only she would talk to him and tell him what fear kept her away from him. How could he prove himself if he didn't know where the battle was to be fought?

Stansfield and Serena walked apart from the party, talking softly together. There was little doubt of their regard. Her mother favored Sir Henry, a man of lesser title and poor character. None of the Dowder women made any sense. Well, except Serena. She preferred Stansfield and had asked for help to gain his proposal over Sir Henry's.

Perhaps Serena was the Dowder twin he needed to speak to after all.

* * * *

After the evening's musical entertainment, the party broke up and many of the guest went out into the torch-lit garden. Anthony had liked the torches from the ball so much he had ordered them placed each night in the gardens of Riverdale.

The grand parlor overlooked the garden. Sophia and Daniel walked arm in arm into the shadows. The moon was almost full once again. Time slipped by him more quickly, and he wondered if he was too late to get what he wanted.

"Tony?" Sylvia whispered. She'd managed to creep up behind him without him hearing her.

Turning, he caught sight of her, and his heart swelled. She changed into a shimmering blue gown for dinner. When she'd first come downstairs, he'd been bewitched. If he were honest, he still was under her spell. "Yes, Sylvie."

"Was everything to your liking today? I have a picnic planned for tomorrow afternoon, but I can change it if you wish." Tense and tentative, she had none of the fire she'd displayed when they argued or kissed.

"Today was perfect. Everyone had a good time and still had time to rest. The gentlemen and I are going hunting at first light, but a picnic sounds lovely for the afternoon. I assume you have arranged everything with the staff." Not kissing her full bottom lip was becoming harder and harder.

"Yes. I'm glad they enjoyed it. And you? Did you have a good day?" Her cheeks pinked.

"Are you making small talk? There is no need. We are friends still. You have made it clear that you would prefer if I quelled my desire for you, and I will comply until you change your mind."

She blinked several times, and her mouth opened and closed like a fish out of water. "I will not change my mind."

He bowed. "As you say. Then why do you seem out of sorts?"

Chewing her bottom lip, she clasped her hands together. "I think you must hate me now, and we still have five more days before we are separated. I suppose I'm embarrassed."

Like the magnetic force of the sun, he was drawn to her. He stopped when he was close enough to reach out and touch her, but he resisted the temptation. "Sylvie, I can say with absolute certainty, I could not and will not ever hate you. I'll not lie, I am disappointed, but my feelings for you remain unchanged."

She shifted from foot to foot and gnawed on her lip, which drove him mad. "Your sister must surely hate me."

"I'm sure that is not so. I have not shared our private conversations with Sophia. Besides, your friendship with her is not reliant on ours." He longed to wrap her in his arms and ease all her worries, but it was too soon. Even with time running out, there was still enough to change her mind.

A tear slipped down her cheek. "Thank you, Tony. You cannot know what it means to me."

Unable to resist, he thumbed her tear away and rubbed the moisture between his fingers, letting her joy and sorrow seep into his skin. "I do know because I know you, Sylvie."

"You and Sophia are so close, I thought for certain you would have told her."

He could get lost in those eyes. "I will never do anything that will hurt you. Including discussing our falling out with my sister. Though, I don't think that would change how she feels about you. Still, I would not risk it, and I know it would make you feel self-conscious."

She swallowed several times. Tears welled up in her eyes, making them the bluest pools. With a quick curtsy, she turned and rushed away.

In the hall, she said, "Serena, are you going up to bed?"

"Yes, will you join me?" The sisters' voices were very similar.

Soft footsteps followed and disappeared.

* * * *

Unable to sleep, Anthony had wandered the house as long as he could stand it. Guests and servants alike had gone to bed. The moon shone through the glass doors, and he followed it out into the garden.

A hint of blue near the veranda caught his attention, and he quickened his step before he lost sight of her.

Leaning on the stone wall without the benefit of gloves, Sylvia was watching the garden.

"Are you all right, Sylvie?" He climbed the five steps up to the veranda and walked toward her.

Straightening, she turned to face him.

It was Sylvia's dress, but this was Serena. "Tony, what are you doing here?"

"I did not realize that we were on first-name terms, Miss Dowder." Whatever she was up to, he wouldn't let her get away with it.

She stomped her foot. "How did you know it was me?"

"I know what Sylvia looks like."

"We are identical." She crossed her arms and pouted.

"Not to me."

She leaned back against the railing and frowned. "Well, that is something. Our parents can't even tell us apart. I thought if I put on Sylvia's dress, and mind you I had to wait a long time for her to fall asleep, I could find something out."

"So, you wanted me to believe you were Sylvia. For what purpose?" Perhaps he had misjudged Serena. Maybe she was more like her mother than he'd thought.

One arm around her waist, she bit the thumbnail of her other hand. She watched him under hooded eyes. "I don't know if I can trust you or not."

He held his arms out. "We are alone in the garden by your design. Though I don't know what you would have done if I didn't come out here tonight. You must trust me enough to risk your reputation. What I want to know is, what are you after?"

Dropping her hands to her sides, she stood up straight. "I have noticed you have an interest in my sister. You pay her special attention and call her by her pet name. I also know my sister, and she seems out of sorts around you, which is unusual. Tonight, I overheard your conversation."

"Overheard?"

She huffed. "All right, I was eavesdropping, but I don't usually do so. I just wanted some information."

Anger and curiosity took hold of Anthony. Being spied on didn't sit well with him, but he was curious about Serena's reasons. "And did you get what you wanted?"

Shrugging, she lifted her palms. "I heard enough to know that you are in love with my sister. I don't think any man would protect someone who thwarted him if he was not in love. Am I right?"

The eagerness in her voice spoke of hope rather than malice. "Why would I tell you anything when you already know I have kept other things to myself to keep her safe?"

"Because I can help you. I know Sylvia better than anyone. I can tell you if she returns your feelings. If you are in earnest, I'd be willing to help you."

"Let me see if I understand you correctly, Miss Dowder. You listened at my study door to find out what my relationship with your sister was. Then you waited until Sylvia was asleep and took her gown, put it on, then came down here to deceive me and pretend to be her. You claim this was to gain more information, but how do I know you weren't going to ruin her or embarrass me?" He towered over her and did his best to look threatening.

It must not have been a very good job, as she did not appear the least bit intimidated. She tapped her lower lip with her index finger. "It does sound more like I'm a nit. I don't suppose you have much reason to believe me. Though I am risking my reputation, and whatever chance I have with Lord Stansfield, to meet with you."

"You risk Sylvia's reputation, not your own. If we were seen, it would be she people would talk about."

Horror flashed in Serena's eyes, and she searched the garden for prying eyes. "You're right. This was a foolish venture."

He had to agree. Still, it was hard to find any ill will in Serena's misguided actions. "If you really want to help me, and I'm not convinced you do, tell me how I win your sister."

"The thing is, I believe Sylvia loves you already." She wouldn't make eye contact with him. Her gaze shifted to the stone beneath her feet like she'd said something terrible.

However, hearing it made his heart swell and his nerves twitch all at once. He wanted to jump around and yell it from the rooftop. "Isn't that good news?"

She shrugged. "One would think so, but she told me you and she don't suit. Now, when she said that, I assumed you weren't interested, but I watched you and could easily tell that wasn't the case. So, if she loves you, and you love her, what could the problem be?"

"I thought you were going to help me with that." He hoped his light comment would ease his pain, but it only tightened the noose.

A long sigh, much like the ones he adored coming from Sylvia, lifted Serena's shoulders. It was strange how they could be so alike and yet so different in his mind. She met his gaze. "She must believe you will hurt her, like Lord March, and if you did that, it would destroy her because her feelings are much stronger."

March again. His entire life revolved around a man who had no connection with him. His fingers ached to choke March's skinny neck. "I am getting rather tired of hearing about that ne'er-do-well viscount."

"But you must see the similarities."

Rage snapped the words from his lips. "Between me and that pig, I most certainly do not."

Lowering her voice, she stepped closer. "I do not mean you any insult, my lord. I agree that he is the worst of men, and I hope you are quite a bit better for my sister. Try to look at it from her perspective. Hunter Gautier was a second son of a viscount, and he courted and proposed to Sylvia. She was only a month from her wedding day when his older brother died, and he became a viscount. Mother was ecstatic that her daughter would marry a viscount. It was rather disconcerting how happy our mother was over a man's death, and Sylvia struggled to be content with the situation.

Then one week later, just three weeks before a day planned for all her life, he came and said she was not good enough for him." Serena wiped a tear from her cheek.

"That must have been very hard for her." Killing March was out of the question, but perhaps he could ruin him financially. He would ponder that later.

"Mother was inconsolable. She cried and carried on for days. Took to her bed and wouldn't come out." Serena folded her arms and rolled her eyes.

Anthony didn't understand. "What did Sylvia do? Did she cry?"

"If she did, I never saw it. First, she fainted, but I think that was just from shock. After that, Sylvia was too angry to cry. She attempted to console our mother, but when Mother finally recovered, she was cruelly disappointed in Sylvia. That was when Sylvia left home in favor of the Everton Domestic Society."

He sat on the stone railing and wished he'd been there to comfort her when she needed a friend. "Miss Dowder, I appreciate all you've told me, but what does it have to do with me? I have not mistreated Sylvia in any way, nor would I."

"You are a young man who was elevated to a title unexpectedly. She doesn't think she is good enough for you."

"What?" He knew her hesitance was because of what March had done, but he assumed it was him she disapproved of. The idea that she could think herself unworthy of him was ridiculous. Impossible. "You must be mistaken. She is far too good for me in every way."

A slow smile spread across Serena's face, and she giggled. "I'm pleased you think so, my lord. Do you know why Mother prefers Sir Henry to Lord Stansfield?"

"I can't imagine. Stansfield is a fine man with land, title, and funds, while Henry is a vainglorious ass. Pardon my language."

Serena covered her chuckle. "All true. So, don't you think it odd that Mother prefers Henry?"

"I assume you will tell me why."

Nodding, she narrowed her gaze. "She prefers him because he has less rank, and therefore, has less chance of betraying me, while the Earl of Stansfield might well change his mind at any moment. Henry needs my dowry. He will offer for me, if I give him a chance. Rutledge needs nothing, but I do think he likes me. Maybe more than likes." Her voice took on a dreamy quality.

"Your mother is willing to let you marry an ass, rather than have another scandal."

She shook off her happy daze. "Mother would do anything to secure a husband for me and be able to say she did not fail. I wish I could tell you it wasn't so, but there you have it."

"Somehow my brilliant Sylvia has begun to believe the rhetoric your mother sells?" Another bout of anger welled up inside Anthony. Felicia Dowder was worse than March, but he'd said he would try to think kindlier toward her, and he would try. It would not be easy.

"My sister can run your house and fix all your problems, but mostly she is avoiding her own. She was very strong when Lord March betrayed her, but I think that was because she didn't love him. She agreed to marry him because it was what we were raised to do, and no one else had asked." She stared him down, suddenly a fierce tigress. "However, she loves you, and your betrayal would not be so easily dealt with."

"I will not betray her." This was impossible. He was shouldering the blame for an act he would never commit.

Serena grinned and gave him a jaunty shrug. "All you have to do is convince Sylvia of that, and that she is good enough for you."

"Any thoughts on how I go about doing that?"

"You'll have to be patient and consistent."

"What if I just drag her up to Gretna Green, and we get married. Wouldn't that convince her of my earnestness?" It was a good plan and required action. He could get what he wanted and start their life together while proving himself.

Blinking, Serena gawked. "It would only solve half of the problem. She would not feel worthy and might think you had only married her out of a sense of duty because of the bit of gossip that began in London."

It wouldn't do to have her think he'd married her out of pity. "I could go to her and profess my love."

"Why have you not already done so?" Her knowing gaze was annoying.

"Because she won't let me. Any time I've tried, she tells me we have nothing in common and in a few days will never see each other again."

"Sylvia told me that your sister invited her to the country next month."

He didn't like where this was going. "You want me to wait another month? What if she accepts another proposal? What if she marries Miles Hallsmith next week?"

Serena paced the veranda then stopped to think. "Do you think that is likely?"

"I don't know, but I'm not willing to risk it." He sounded like an idiot and he felt like one. Standing in the moonlight, whispering a plan for something that should have been easy for two people in love. It seemed his life was never as easy as it should be. He was willing to make a fool of himself for Sylvia, but he didn't know it meant doing so in front of her sister too.

"Then you had better stay underfoot between now and then and make sure she has no suitors who might ruin your plans. You may call on me to assist you should the need arise." She touched his arm. "I think you are the perfect man for my sister, Anthony, even if she doesn't know it yet."

"Thank you, Serena. And, should the need arise, I shall take you up on the offer to help."

She walked toward the house. "I suggest you arrange a few meetings where you'll behave yourself, but make sure she knows how you feel."

He bowed. "I will be at her beck and call."

Giggling, Serena went inside and out of sight.

Not sure if he'd just gained an ally, or if a devil had conned him, he laughed to himself. If Sylvia was smart, Serena was cunning. Where Sylvia could solve any problem through hard work and good sense, Serena would manipulate the situation to suit herself. They were the same, but so different, and he was relieved to have Serena for him, rather than against him. At least he hoped she was.

Chapter 15

With the men all gone hunting, Sylvia found the house too quiet. She told herself the men left the rooms feeling empty, but if she were honest, it was only Anthony she was thinking about. He filled the house with his energy and kindness. Just look what he had done for Serena by inviting Lord Stansfield.

She sat on a bench she'd found the day before hidden under the canopy of an oak tree in the wild garden. Her life had changed so much in the last year, and now she was stable. Still, she would miss Riverdale when she left at the end of the week. The estate's owner was another level, and she would grieve his loss.

"I've been looking everywhere for you." Serena pushed aside a branch and joined her in the small clearing.

"You have found me."

"This is lovely." Serena sat next to her.

"Yes. It's quite perfect."

Sighing as she did when she was bored, Serena asked, "When will the men return from hunting?"

It was getting close to midday. "Soon, I imagine. His lordship knows we have a picnic planned. He won't be late. However, if they should be delayed, we will begin without them."

"Perhaps you should get a dog, Sylvie."

"Why on earth would I want a dog?" Her sister could come out with the most unexpected statements.

"To keep you company. You refuse to entertain the idea of getting married. You'll need company." Serena tugged on a loose thread on her glove.

Somehow, hearing someone else say it made her uncomfortable. It was one thing to think of the next few years alone, but the rest of her life was a long time. "That's not true. If I met the right man, I would consider marriage."

"It seems to me he's already here, and yet, you will not give him a chance."

"Why are you saying this, Serena? Can you not just be happy that Lord Stansfield is clearly smitten with you? Why must you make me feel bad about my situation?"

Turning on the bench, Serena opened her eyes wide. "I do not wish to make you feel bad. I want you to be happy. If you tell me you will be happy in five years with no one to sit with on a winter's night and no children to raise, I will drop the subject."

Serena's direct regard as she waited for Sylvia to declare her contentedness was enough to start a rumble in her stomach. "I think I'm going to be sick."

"I'm going to take that as your answer, and you should really reconsider your position with regard to Anthony Braighton."

She didn't know which was worse, the idea of being alone or risking her heart with Anthony. "I have no designs of becoming a countess. I will leave that to you, Serena."

"Then you are a fool, and I never thought I would say such a thing about my brilliant sister." Serena stood, pushed the branch aside, and stormed off toward the house.

Before coming to Riverdale, Sylvia could have counted on one hand the number of times she had cried, yet in the last two days, she'd been near tears almost constantly. Getting through the week would be difficult, but once she was away from him and the things that reminded her of him, her life would go back to normal. Brushing aside the escaped tears, she took a breath and walked back to the house.

Tall grasses, bushes, and wildflowers flanked the winding path. Staring at them, she nearly bumped into Miles. "I beg your pardon, Mr. Hallsmith."

His easy smile made any situation less grave. "Not at all. I was sent to find you. The party is going out to the lake for the picnic."

"I didn't intend to hold everyone back. You should have gone without me." She quickened her step.

Miles took her elbow and slowed her pace. "They will wait because you are part of the group, and your company is wanted. You may think of yourself as an employee, but the party, myself included, thinks of you as an equal who completes our happy group."

"That is kind of you to say." She knew her place, and no number of generous words would change the fact that she was an Everton lady in the employ of the Earl of Grafton.

He bowed. "It is the truth."

The carriages were loaded with food and happy guests by the time they arrived in front of the house. It was a short ride to the lake, but they would take the carriages nonetheless.

Miles handed her up into an open carriage and sat next to her with Daniel and Sophia facing them.

Sophia took her hand. "It is a perfect day for a picnic. I can't wait to taste everything Cook has packed for us. Well, except the wine."

It was too wonderful to have a friend again. "I have arranged tea and lemonade as well as wine. I know you do not care for wine and thought others might not wish to drink so early in the day."

Daniel declared, "I have been up since before the sun and bagged several fowl for the table. I am entitled to some of the family's fine wine."

Laughing, Sylvia felt like family. "And you shall have it."

The carriages stopped where Sylvia had arranged for a bit of lawn to be flattened for the picnic. They spread the blankets, and servants arranged the food. Meats, cheese and bread, all cold and perfectly suited to a picnic.

At some point in the last few days, Sylvia's appetite had left her, and she didn't find any of the sumptuous treats appealing. She took several sips of wine, but then abandoned her glass.

Mrs. Horthorn leaned against the tree and worked on her sewing.

They played word games, and a light breeze made the day delightful.

It wasn't easy, but Sylvia managed to stay far away from Anthony until the group went for a walk along the edge of the lake. She'd let everyone go ahead when he stepped beside her.

"You have arranged a perfect day, Sylvie." He kept his hands clasped behind his back.

Somehow his keeping those hands to himself made her even more aware of how wonderful they felt wrapped around her. "I had no part in the weather or the setting. But it did turn out nicely."

"You chose the spot and arranged everything." He sighed, his gaze drifting over the landscape. "Someday, children, maybe our children, will play in this field and swim in the lake." His voice was far away.

Swallowing emotions she couldn't pretend to understand or accept, she turned toward him. "Why must you say such things?"

"I can't deny what I wish for. However, if it upsets you, as I see it does, I will try to keep my desires to myself. I may not always succeed, but I will try, Sylvie."

The tree where Mrs. Horthorn sat was out of sight, and the party had gone into a stand of trees at the far end of the lake.

She was alone with the one man she should never be left alone with. "Your sister and I will go to Marlton in four weeks. She is so sweet to invite me. Then this morning she confirmed the date. I thought surely she would wait until we were back in town then forget about the invitation."

"Sophia is not like your friends of the past. You will have to get used to that. When she says she will do something, you may count on it happening."

"I would truly love to believe that people are honest and good, but my experience tells a different story."

He stopped and peered out over the lake and hillside beyond. Green hills rolled on for miles on the clear day, and a light breeze rippled the lake. "It is a shame that is so. Perhaps it will be a Braighton mission to show you a different kind of people."

Head and stomach aching, she couldn't take his sweetness or her own desire for the impossible. "I think I will go back to the house if you don't mind."

He touched her cheek, his expression taut with concern. "Are you ill?"

"Just a little tired." Her shoulders ached.

"I will take you back."

"No. You stay with your guests. I will be fine." Without waiting for a reply, Sylvia ran toward the carriage. "Jonas, please take me back to the house."

The driver helped her in then jumped up and did as she asked.

Once inside, she dragged herself up to her room. Her head pounded, and she collapsed onto her bed.

"Wake up, Sylvie," Serena commanded in a whisper.

Groggy and confused, Sylvia did as she was told and blinked herself to a sitting position. A full march of a thousand troops trudged through her head. "I have the most terrible headache, Serena."

"Yes, his lordship said you weren't feeling well. Mrs. Horthorn and I followed you back. It took me scolding him for Anthony to stay with his guests by the lake. He is very worried about you."

The room spun but then settled into position. "I shouldn't have drank that wine."

Standing beside the bed, Serena placed her fists on her hips. "When was the last time you ate something?"

"We just came from a picnic." Sylvia wasn't used to her sister reprimanding her. She had always been the twin who took charge.

"Where you ate nothing and fell ill. Yes, I know. When was the last time you actually ate a meal? You put coddled eggs on your plate this morning, took one bite of toast and a sip of coffee. Then you excused yourself and disappeared into the garden for hours. I did not sit near you at dinner last night, but I suspect you neglected your meal then as well."

Trying to remember the last full meal she had eaten took her back to the night before they had arrived at Riverdale. Since then, she had eaten a bite or two, but her appetite had flagged. "I suppose I have neglected my meals."

"You suppose." Serena shook her head. "Mrs. Horthorn has gone to the kitchen to fetch some soup. I am going to sit here until you have finished an entire bowl and some bread as well."

"Oh, Serena, I don't know if I can manage an entire bowl."

A scratch sounded at the door before Jenny and Mrs. Horthorn walked in. Jenny carried a tray with a steaming bowl that filled the room with the aroma of herbs and chicken.

Sylvia's stomach lurched.

"I should have been paying better attention." Mrs. Horthorn came to the edge of the bed and brushed Sylvia's hair out of her face. "Had I realized you were neglecting yourself, I would have insisted you eat something sooner."

"I am fine." If only the racket thrashing around in her head would ease, she would be all right.

Serena stomped her slippered foot. "You are not. Jenny, you may leave the tray. Will you help me get Sylvie into a nightdress?"

"Oh no, I'm not staying in bed. I have work to do." She pushed her hands into the mattress, but the room spun, and she collapsed.

Jenny reached out and steadied her. "Miss Sylvia, your sister is right. You need to take care of yourself."

Pulling herself to her full height, Mrs. Horthorn stuck out her chin and pulled back her shoulders. "I can handle your responsibilities this evening. Rest and eat. You have already taken care of everything to the last detail. No one will want for anything, and by tomorrow, you will be back on your feet."

"I cannot ask you to do that." Failure washed over her. She was an Everton lady. She had to do her job.

"You did not ask. I am an Everton dowager, and it is my duty to help when you are in need." She softened her tone. "Don't worry. It will all be fine. I have run many a dinner party in my time, and this one is ordered down to the last detail." With a pat on the cheek, Mrs. Horthorn strode from the room and closed the door behind her.

Jenny helped her out of her dress and into a nightgown.

Too weak to get up from the bed without help, she allowed them to prop her up with pillows. "This is ridiculous. I am not an invalid."

"Do not be a bad patient, Sylvie. Eat and drink, and I will tell you all about my day." With Jenny's help, she moved a chair near the edge of the bed and sat.

Once she checked to see that there was nothing else to do, Jenny excused herself, leaving the twins alone.

Sylvia spooned a sip of soup into her mouth. Her stomach roiled, but the soup was light and flavorful. "I'm not sure I can eat this, Serena."

"Go slow, but you will eat it."

"And if I am sick?" she challenged.

Serena leaned down and revealed a pan. "Then you will be sick, I will call Jenny back, and you will still eat tonight. I suggest you try to keep your food down."

"When did you become so bossy?"

Serena put the pan back on the floor and leaned forward with an intensity in her eyes that Sylvia had never seen before. "When my sister, who I love more than anyone in the world, stopped taking care of herself. I don't know why you torture yourself like this."

"I merely became distracted. I will eat." She took another spoon of soup as proof.

"You may lie to me if you wish, Sylvie, but lying to yourself is not healthy."

The world loomed off kilter with Serena being the reasonable voice. Sylvia didn't like it. She took several more sips of the soup, which was more palatable. "Tell me about your time with Lord Stansfield."

A warm smile eased the worry in Serena's eyes. "He has a large farm in the northwest and is very keen on preserving the land. I like that he is passionate about things. Nothing about him is superficial, as he cares deeply for everything he involves himself in."

Half the soup was gone. "Including you?"

Serena blushed. "Perhaps. He is attentive and solicitous. I want to believe he likes me, maybe even loves me."

Tearing off a bit of bread, she asked, "And do you love him?"

"What does it feel like to be in love, Sylvie? I miss him when he's gone, but not in a lonely way. It's more like if something happens, I want to tell him about it. I long to know what his day is like and if he is happy."

Sylvia's body tingled with all those same desires whenever she thought of Anthony. Her headache had calmed to a dull ache as she finished her soup. "I think you must love him."

"He kissed me yesterday." Serena blushed bright red.

Joy for her sister washed through Sylvia. "Did you kiss him back?"

Nearly purple with embarrassment, Serena nodded. "It was more wonderful than I could have imagined. Mother said all men are brutes, but Rutledge is kind, thoughtful and tender. Do you think Mother intentionally lied to keep us from liking our husbands?"

Feeling much more herself, Sylvia popped a morsel of bread in her mouth. "I think Mother's advice is colored by her own experiences and fear. Father is not brutal, but he is stern, and I see no love in their marriage. Perhaps she wanted to protect us the way she protects herself."

"Well, I am glad it didn't work. I quite enjoy being in love." Serena folded her hands in her lap and closed her eyes. Her expression filled with warmth and delight.

"I'm happy for you." Sylvia wasn't certain her mother hadn't been at least partially successful. The idea of love made her sick and might have been what caused her current condition. "I think I will rest now, Serena."

Inspecting her empty bowl and half-eaten bread, Serena nodded and took the tray away to the table near the window. "Get some sleep. I'll dress in another room then go down to dinner."

Alone, she couldn't get Anthony out of her mind. Not that he had left her for a moment in the last few months. His kisses fueled her soul and haunted her nights. She wanted more of them and him, but he would break her in two when he betrayed her, and she couldn't risk it. No. It was for the best to go their separate ways.

Still the dread of a lifetime on her own nagged at her. She didn't love Miles Hallsmith, but he was nice, she liked him, and he seemed to like her. Perhaps what started as a way to dissuade Anthony might be a viable option.

She would think about it in the morning. Weighted eyelids kept her from continuing her internal debate. Snuggling into the mattress, she let sleep take her.

* * * *

When she woke, it was dark outside. The room was no longer empty, but it wasn't Serena come to bed as Sylvia would have expected.

Anthony's woodsy scent warmed her from the inside out.

"Tony?"

"I was worried about you, Sylvie." He sat next to the bed, his hands on the coverlet and his forehead on his hands.

She ran her fingers through his thick, soft hair. "I'm fine."

Capturing the hand, he pulled it into his and kissed each finger. "You must promise you will always take care of yourself and never do such a stupid thing again."

The kisses shot desire from her fingers through her body and settled deliciously between her legs. "I promise. I never meant to harm myself. I'm sorry to have worried everyone."

He gazed at her with hooded eyes filled with pain and anxiety. "I don't know what I would do if anything happened to you. And if it was my fault, I could not live with myself."

Moving herself down the bed until she was face-to-face with him, she cupped his cheeks. "You were not to blame. I just got distracted and missed a few meals, then the wine today went to my head. It was not your fault, and you're right, it was stupid of me."

His lips pressed to hers, soft and long.

The weight of the kiss filled her to the brim with love and longing. It might be wrong, and it would certainly not last, but it was too wonderful to force an end. She would never know passion like it again, so she drank it in by the gallons and let it overtake her every bone and muscle. Even her eyelids tingled with his touch.

Easing out of the kiss, he pressed his forehead to hers. "I love you, Sylvie. I shall always love you. I know you don't want me, and I respect your decision. But it will not change my love for you and my need to see you safe."

It should have been a perfect moment, but Sylvia heard her mother's warning about men with high titles using girls and tossing them out like bad water. Felicia's voice rang in her head about how men of worth, or any man, thought of their wives as property, nothing more. Difficult as it was to place Anthony in the bin with men in general, it was impossible to ignore that voice in her head. Besides, he had told her he wanted other things, and she allowed his secret to play over in her head and rattle around with Mother's tenacious noise. "You should not say such things."

"I cannot lie." His breath mingled with hers in the dark bedroom.

"My sister will find us. You must go now, Tony."

Sighing, he lifted his head, kissed her nose then her forehead. "I would not object to being found and having you marry me as a result."

"And come to resent me in a year or two for trapping you into marriage and keeping you from your dreams." It came out more harshly than she'd intended.

He shook his head. "My dreams have changed, and no matter where they take me, you will always be in the center of them. You have very little faith in me. I will endeavor to change that. You should rest now. The guests are playing cards and think I have gone to write a letter. I should rejoin the party. I will see you in the morning, my sweet Everton lady."

Watching the door long after he'd gone, she cried herself back to sleep. Coward was the last thing she thought about herself.

* * * *

Usually up with the dawn, it was strange for Sylvia to be blinded by the sun coursing through the window. She shielded her eyes. "Good Lord, what time is it?"

"Nearly ten, miss. I'm sorry to wake you, but I think you need to eat something." Jenny fussed with a breakfast tray at the table, placing a plate, cup, and saucer out for Sylvia.

"You should not have gone to the trouble for me, Jenny. I could have gone down to break my fast." Stretching the long, still hours from her muscles was at once delight and agony. Her stomach growled at the scent of fresh bread and coddled eggs. "But I'm starved, so I thank you."

Jenny chuckled. "I'm glad to see your appetite has returned. You were always a good eater as a baby. Far better than your sister. At least from what I remember."

Jenny was only a few years older than she and Serena, but her mother had been their nanny from the cradle until she passed a year earlier.

Sylvia sat and breathed deep the wonderful scents. She tore a piece of bread and smeared it with jam before popping it in her mouth and washing it down with the best sip of coffee. She closed her eyes. "Was your mother with our family long before we were born?"

"Oh, yes." Jenny straightened Serena's empty bed. "She was your mother's lady's maid, but when your mother married, she took a lower position to stay with her. When you girls were born, your mother promoted her."

Stopping her trouncing of the poor eggs, Sylvia asked, "Are you saying your mother followed mine from her childhood home?"

"She was her lady's maid, but your father didn't find her high-minded enough for his wife's lady's maid, so he hired another." She fluffed the pillows and folded the coverlet.

Food pushed aside, she focused on Jenny. "Jenny, did your mother ever say why mine is so adamantly against men? I mean to say, why she thinks them all bad?"

Jenny frowned. "I don't know if it's right me telling you such a thing, miss."

"I need to know if she's right."

There must have been enough desperation in Sylvia's voice. Jenny sat on the other chair at the table. "Before your father proposed, there was a great love, a duke if the story is to be believed, who proposed to your mother. They were engaged in secret."

"Why would it be a secret?" Such matches were usually very public affairs.

Jenny's brown eyes tightened, and her hands fisted. "He was only playing a young girl, and once he had what he wanted, he left her flat. Terrified she would be found out and ruined for all society, she married the first man she danced with at her next ball, your father. She didn't even wait to find out if she liked him."

"She doesn't. Oh, Jenny, I am a fool. My entire life is clouded over by the act of one terrible man, well two."

Jenny stood and walked to Sylvia's bed. She tugged the covers into place. "You are far better off not married to that Lord March. I think he might have been of the same cloth as your mother's duke."

"Perhaps, but I was not as foolish." Panicked, Sylvia pushed the food aside and rose. "Can you help me get dressed, Jenny? I need to speak to his lordship right away."

"Of course, but he's not here, Miss Sylvia."

"What? Where is he?"

She shrugged. "London by now. I heard the groom say there was an emergency at the dock and he left before dawn."

"What of the rest of the party?"

"They are still here. Her ladyship is playing hostess until you wake. Pall-mall is set up on the lawn, and they all sounded excited about it this morning. They all raved about the picnic yesterday…"

Jenny kept talking while straightening the room, but Sylvia stopped listening. She had ruined everything with her fears, and now Anthony was gone before she could tell him what a fool she was.

Chapter 16

London might not be burning, but Anthony's ship was smoldering and sinking. Thousands of dollars' worth of textiles in her hull, and he could save them before she went down. He'd found a way through to the hold despite an explosion that partially collapsed the deck. He'd dragged six armloads of his cargo out and handed each over to his captain and crew.

Captain Blake McCormick grabbed an armload. His ruddy skin was black with dirt and soot. "It's enough, milord. No sense risking your neck for some bits of cloth."

"I can get one more load out, and that will be the bulk of it."

McCormick shook his head. "We got the men and much of the cargo, milord. Let her go before we're burying you at sea."

"One more load." Anthony ran back across the buckled deck to where it had collapsed. He climbed under the mast and through a hole and into the hold. It was a maze of wood, and he was calf-deep in water.

The ship creaked with strain, and the acrid stench of tarred wood burning filled his lungs, forcing painful coughing. He reached the bundled bolts of cloth that had only arrived in London hours before. Lavender cloth from India. He'd written a letter to his friend and supplier in India asking for as much fabric in lavender as he could find. He longed to gift it to Sylvia when she agreed to be his bride. It seemed that would never be, but he couldn't let the cloth go down as tragically as his love for one stubborn Everton lady.

A loud pop and crack jerked the ship starboard. The mast dropped through the deck, and wood crashed around Anthony. Half the crow's nest smacked against his body between his neck and shoulder. Pain shot through him as his body cracked in half. Unable to lift his right arm, he abandoned the cloth and dragged himself agonizingly toward the surface. He used the same object that had nearly crushed him to haul himself forward, dragging his body up the main mast.

Agony rocked him from his collarbone, which he was sure was broken. Daylight shone just above him. If he could get to what was left of the deck, he'd be able to ask for help.

Sylvia's sweet face burned into his mind, he defied the pain and pushed upward.

"Milord, grab my hand!" McCormick called, but Anthony saw no hand.

He reached into the smoky darkness, and meaty fingers closed around his.

The mast snapped and tossed him to the side. Pain shot up his leg.

Captain McCormick hauled him to the light. His body scraped against the ragged edge of the destroyed deck, tearing shirt and flesh as he went.

"Fetch a surgeon," someone yelled.

McCormick and two other men carried him to a cargo carriage and laid him in the back. Pain was all that stood between him and oblivion. Staying alive to see Sylvia again was his only salvation. Every rut on the ride to his townhouse brought a new level of misery.

Anthony closed his eyes and let the memory of that last kiss in the darkness of her bedroom soothe his battered body. He'd told her he loved her at least, and in his heart, he knew she loved him too, even if she was too afraid to say the words.

Wells's voice cut into his dream. "My God, did you send for a surgeon?"

"Yes, he's coming directly." The voices grew fainter.

"Help me get him upstairs. Be easy with him." Wells sounded near panic.

Anthony wished he had the energy to tease his stoic butler, but he was barely staying conscious. "Contact her."

"I will send word to your mother immediately, my lord." They put him on a bed. "You men can go. The footmen will assist me from here. If only you had a valet, he would be very helpful now, my lord."

Pain ebbed and flowed with his level of lucidity. He wanted to tell him to contact Sylvia, but perhaps it was better she not see him in his weakness. All that lavender cloth that would have looked so lovely on his sweet Sylvia.

* * * *

He woke in a haze. The room refused to come into view. "What?"

A soft hand touched his forehead. "You are fine. A broken leg and collarbone along with some cuts and bruises, but you will heal." Her Italian accent a balm, Momma caressed his cheek.

In a harsher voice, Aunt Daphne added, "You could have been killed."

"But you were not," Momma insisted.

His vision cleared. "I'm having trouble seeing you."

"It's the laudanum, for the pain."

It was worse to not quite be in the world. To drink one's self blind on occasion was one thing, but this he hated. "Don't give me any more of it."

Aunt Daphne huffed. "You say that now, but the pain will change your mind."

An attempt to move his right arm was agony, so he took his mother's hand with his left. "No more, Momma."

"As you wish, *piccolo amore*. But if you change your mind, do not be too proud to ask for help."

"Do you think you can take some soup?" Aunt Daphne sounded stern, but he heard her worry. She had lost so much, and this had likely been an ordeal for both women.

"I will try, Aunt. I'm sorry to have caused you worry." He tried to push himself to sitting, but pain shot through him from both his collarbone and his leg.

"Do not injure yourself," Momma scolded. "I will get Wells, and Daphne will call for something to eat."

They left him alone, staring at the ceiling. Sylvia had picked the bed curtains and the new bedding. She was all around him, but not with him. His body hurt, but his heart ached worse.

Mother returned with Wells.

"I shall have to pull you up from the waist so as not to re-injure you, my lord. Will you put your left arm around my neck and apply what pressure you can in assistance?" Wells said it all as flatly as he might have described an afternoon caller on a Tuesday.

"This is quite embarrassing, Wells, but I thank you." He did as he was told, and with minimal pain, they got him to a sitting position while Mother propped pillows behind him.

"It is temporary, sir, and I am glad to be of service." With a bow, Wells left the room.

"Momma, what day is it?"

She sat on the edge of the bed. "It is Friday. You have been incoherent for two days. What were you thinking, going into that burning boat?

Captain McCormick came by yesterday and told us all about it. Once you got all the men to safety, why not let the cargo sink?"

"What would Papa have done?" He adjusted his position using his left arm and managed to find a more comfortable seat.

She huffed. "Gotten himself killed most likely. I have written your sister. She should be back at Marlton tomorrow, but I sent the letter to Riverdale yesterday. I didn't want to send word until we knew your condition. You had me quite terrified."

Hating to worry her or make her sad, he took her hand. "I'm sorry."

She shrugged. "You are the one who will pay the price. The surgeon set both bones and said you are to stay in bed for a week before you try to get up. The leg should not have weight on it for six weeks. He will bring you crutches when he returns, but that collarbone will make it difficult to use them."

Daphne returned with Lila, a kitchen maid, who carried a tray with tea and soup.

"Thank you, Lila."

Her dark blond curls bounced as she curtsied and ran back out the door.

It was more difficult than expected to spoon soup with his left hand, but he did his best. "Aunt Daphne, the staff at Riverdale misses you. Perhaps a visit soon is in order."

"I always loved that house. We can talk about it when you are better. For now, I need to rest. I've taken up residence in Sophia's old room. Very comfortable." Cane in hand, she ambled out the door and down the hall.

The small amount of soup exhausted him. "I think I need to rest too, Momma."

She took the tray away and put it on the table. "We will bring you more when you wake."

On the third day of being awake and in bed, he couldn't take it anymore. Swinging his legs over the side of the bed, he waited for the pain to ease before gripping the crutches. He couldn't put much pressure on his right leg but managed to hobble around the room and get himself seated in the chair. He rang the bell for Wells.

Moments later the door opened. "I see you have relocated. Very good, my lord. How can I assist you?"

"There is a pile of paperwork on my desk downstairs and I'm sure a mountain of mail. Will you bring it to me here? I must do something besides sit and moan all day long."

Wells stared for a long beat. "Is that wise, my lord? You are barely out of bed."

Despite his butler's stoic demeanor, the man cared about him, and it warmed Anthony to know it. "I don't know how much I can do, but if I get through one scrap of paper a day, at least it's better than nothing."

"Indeed. Is there anything else?"

"I would like to see Captain McCormick. Can you send word to the docks and see if you can locate him?"

Wells frowned. "I will do my best, my lord."

The mail appeared less daunting than the pile of papers. He sorted through it and found one small envelope with Sylvia's familiar hand. Heart pounding, he broke the seal.

My Dear Tony,

I hope you are recovering quickly. Please believe that when you hurt, I hurt in equal measure.

I came to see you, as your good sister informed me of your injuries. However, I was told you were in no state to see anyone and could think of no way to explain our relationship to your mother and aunt. In fact, I have no explanation for it myself.

Not hearing from you in London, I thought perhaps your feelings for me had changed, which would be completely within your rights. I do not deserve your regard. It was then I received Sophia's letter telling me you had been injured.

Worrying about you has become my only comfort, and I would dearly appreciate some word about your progress. That said, I am extremely vexed with you for risking your life so nonchalantly. Can you know how precious you are to so many people, and still have done something so reckless? I'm certain your mother and aunt have already scolded you, so I will let that be the end of my reproach.

I imagine you are not able to get around, and perhaps you would like to hear about how the rest of your house party went. You may be assured the guests all had a grand time, but without their host, they left two days early. We did play pall-mall as planned on the day you received the missive that drove you to London.

Sophia and Daniel stayed to the end of the week, but Serena, Mrs. Horthorn, and I returned to London. It appears as if Lord Stansfield will offer for Serena any day, and we have had a long talk with Mother. She is amenable if not enthusiastic. It is thanks to you that we will celebrate Serena's happiness. My gratitude is immeasurable.

On the morning you left Riverdale, I learned something about my mother and about myself. If ever we meet again, perhaps I can share that revelation with you.

I thought you might be interested to know that I have decided against giving up my secondary employment. I enjoy it, and against the advice of a well-respected friend, I shall continue to take pleasure from the process. Though, a name change might be in order, a suggestion from another good friend. You may keep an eye out for juicy tidbits.

I'm sure you have had quite enough of my ramblings. Please know that I wish you a quick recovery and pray for your health daily.

Affectionately,
Your Sylvie

She was in his house. She had come to see him. Heart pounding harder than it did when he'd run into the sinking ship, Anthony read the letter again. Could it be that her worry over his regard meant that her feelings had changed? Hope blossomed inside him as he read her closing over and over.

He rang for help and a footman.

Sean arrived. "I'm sorry, my lord, Wells was unavailable. Can I help you?"

"Will you ask my mother to come in?" It would be awkward, but he could barely lift his right arm, let alone try to write a letter.

"Mrs. Braighton went out for a while. Her ladyship is reading in the study, shall I get her?"

Anthony groaned. Perhaps he should wait for another alternative. "Did my mother say when she would return?"

"I cannot say for certain, but she said something about tea with an old friend."

"Please ask my aunt if she would be so kind as to help me pen a letter."

Deciding what to write in response to Sylvia's letter, that would be appropriate for his aunt to know about, was impossible.

The door opened, and Aunt Daphne came in preceded by her cane, which she waved in the air. "I have come to write your letter. To whom are we communicating?"

Sean brought a tray with parchment, ink, and pen, then moved a small desk and chair closer to where Anthony sat. "Will there be anything else, my lord?"

"No, Sean. Thank you."

Once the door was closed, Daphne sat at the desk and dipped the pen before looking up at Anthony for instruction. "So, what is your salutation?"

Good Lord, this was punishment because the agony of two broken bones was not enough. "The letter is to Miss Sylvia Dowder."

One curved eyebrow lifted high on her forehead. "The girl from Everton's?"

"Yes."

"Are you planning on hiring her again?"

His internal groan made its way to the surface. Maybe he should wait for his mother or contact Miles. A terrible idea. None of his options were good ones, and no matter who helped him, the embarrassment would be severe. "Aunt, this is difficult enough. Might I ask that you write the letter and not ask me too many questions?"

She harrumphed. "Shall I begin with 'Miss Sylvia'?"

"Dearest Sylvie."

"That is completely inappropriate, and a lady of virtue would be highly insulted. She deserves more respect. Just because she is in service of a kind does not give you leave to lose your manners." Daphne put the pen down and watched him.

He closed his eyes. This was never going to work out the way he intended. He would have to answer, but not in the way he had hoped.

Daphne picked the pen up and dipped it in ink. "You might try, 'My Dear Lady.' That would be appropriate."

He struggled not to roll his eyes. "I see your point. My Dear Lady. Thank you for your letter. It came at just the right time to occupy my mind as I recover from my injuries. Please be assured your worry is unwarranted. I am fine and will make a full recovery."

Daphne scribbled the last word. "I shall sign it 'Grafton' and post it immediately. It was kind of her to write regarding your health. I have always liked that girl, good head on her shoulders, not too much of a nitwit."

"I like her too." Anthony wanted to tear up the letter and wished he had the energy to do so.

"Perhaps you should offer for her. She is not titled, and there would be no money from the family, but you are rich enough. Of course, there is that mother of hers, but all women become idiots when they are trying to marry off a daughter. It stands to reason that a woman with twin girls would become twice as idiotic when they come out into society." Daphne stood with the help of her cane.

"I may do so. Thank you for your thoughts." It was easier to agree without personal commentary. His pain increased the longer he sat up, and every move became agony.

"I'm going to send Wells up to help you back to bed. You're pale as a sheet." She strode from the room, leaving the door open.

Grasping his crutches, he pulled himself to the edge of the chair and stood on one foot, found his balance, and hobbled to his bed.

Wells ran in. "My lord, you should wait for help. If you fall, it will be disastrous."

"All this mollycoddling is driving me to Bedlam. If you will take the crutches, I will get myself into the bed."

Taking the crutches, Wells said, "I understand, my lord. However, if you need help, I hope you will ask for it."

Painfully, he pushed himself with one leg and one arm into his bed and closed his eyes. "I will. It must be time for me to rest, Wells. See that I'm not disturbed for an hour or two."

"Yes, sir."

"Oh, and, Wells, see if you can find me a copy of the most recent *Weekly Whisper* newspaper."

Both the butler's eyebrows rose. "I'll see what I can do."

It was not the same as seeing her, but even a little slice of Sylvia was better than none.

* * * *

Anthony had never begged for anything in his entire life, but four weeks after his injuries, he pleaded to be allowed to go downstairs. He was an earl but felt more like a six-year-old boy. "If you don't let me out of this room, Mother, my next stop will really be the madhouse. I have stared at these four walls for weeks."

Mother bristled. "You could fall. Then all this time healing will be for nothing."

"Wells!" Anthony's holler shook the walls.

Stern as always, Wells stepped inside Anthony's prison. "My lord?"

"You will help me down the steps. I will use the railing and your shoulder for stability." He handed Wells his crutches.

Daniel walked in. "I will help you, Tony."

Smiling like a woman coming into a ballroom rather than an argument between mother and son, Sophia said, "Then Daniel will help you into our carriage."

"Sophia!" Mother gasped.

"You cannot keep him cooped up here forever, Momma. He needs to get out of this room and this house. Daniel and I will take Tony to the country, where we will care for him, and he will get some fresh air and finish his healing. We have a fine doctor near Marlton, and I have already contacted him with regards to Tony's well-being."

Anthony had never loved his sister more than he did at that moment. "Bless you, Sophie. Wells, pack my trunk. Get Sean to help you. We will leave within the hour."

"You will be in agony bounced around in a carriage for two days." Mother might have been right, but it would be worth it.

He hopped across the room, stopped next to his mother, and kissed her cheek. "Thank you for taking care of me. You have been a perfect nurse. You and Aunt Daphne are angels, but now it's time for me to go."

Daniel steadied Anthony when he wobbled on one leg. "I have had the carriage re-sprung and added pillows, so the ride should be better for you, Tony. We will wait on your trunk and be ready to leave."

Wells was already hard at work packing his master's clothes and personal items. Sean brought everything over. Anthony was happy to have won the argument regarding dressing that morning. His casted lower leg looked ridiculous next to his other, and he could only wear one boot, but the cast would come off soon. "Wells, be sure to pack my other boot. I will need it before we return."

"That's the spirit," Daniel said. "Let's get you out of this room."

Putting his hand on his brother-in-law's shoulder, Anthony wished there were words to convey the magnitude of his gratefulness. "Thank you."

Daniel grinned. "I can imagine this has been trying. We would have come sooner, but little Adel had a cold then passed it on to Charlie. We canceled all our plans and stayed at home until they were well."

"You are here now, and I was in too much pain to be moved earlier. Your timing is excellent."

"You might tell your sister that. She has been fretting for weeks."

One step at a time, they hobbled and hopped down the curved stairs until they reached the marble foyer. Anthony sucked in long breaths. "Perhaps a rest and a small meal before we depart."

Helping him to the parlor on the left, Daniel nodded. "I'll see what the cook can put together on short notice."

Sophia sat next to him and hugged him. "You didn't answer my letters."

Struggling to lift his right arm, he managed to raise it almost to his chest. "I have been unable to write much and used what I could do for business matters. It's getting better. Another few weeks and I can respond to all my mail."

"Did Sylvia write or come to see you?"

"Why do you ask? Have you spoken to her?"

"I thought she would contact you once I told her about your injuries. I have only had a minimum correspondence with her. When the children were ill, I had to postpone her visit, so she took a new assignment. Also, she is helping her mother and sister plan a ball to announce the engagement."

"She did come, but Momma sent her away. She wrote, but I had to filter my answer through Aunt Daphne, of all people." It came out with more bite than he would have liked, but he was at the end of his wits from both his separation from Sylvia and his confinement as an invalid.

Smiling, Sophia clapped and hugged him gently. "I'm sure that was quite a letter. It will all turn out fine, Tony. We'll get you away from here, and if you like, I'll help you write to Sylvia."

After eating, he kissed his teary mother goodbye and managed to get himself into the carriage by jumping up one step at a time. It had been so long since he'd been outside, the sun hurt his eyes, and it warmed him to the bone.

Daniel laughed. "You look as if you just escaped purgatory."

"As wonderful as Momma and Aunt Daphne are, I have never been happier to leave home in my life."

Sophia sighed. "Even with the new springs and cushions, this ride will be hard on you, Tony."

"I don't care, Sophie. I will grin and bear it."

Nodding, she leaned into Daniel's shoulder. "The children will be happy to see you. Charlie is particularly excited to see his uncle. He danced around the parlor when we told him we were going to pick you up."

"Adel is not happy I am coming?" Anthony closed his eyes.

Daniel said, "Adel is more reserved but equally happy to have you visit."

"It will be perfect. I couldn't bear another day in that room." The dry roads meant there were ruts, but they didn't get stuck along the way. It would likely take him days to recover from the journey, but it was worth it.

Chapter 17

Sylvia checked the ballroom one last time before heading up the steps to see if Serena needed any help. The musicians were already there and setting up their instruments under the very specific instruction of the master of ceremonies. He gave Sylvia a haughty nod, and she made a curtsy.

The wooden floor shone, and soon the chandeliers would be lit. The Dowder townhouse was smaller than most, but they had a large parlor that was easily converted for a ball. The meal would be served buffet style, and refreshments were already being set out.

"You are quite adept at all of this preparation and organizing." Mother stood in the doorway, hands clasped in front of her.

"Thank you, Mother."

Mother glared with little expression. "Your father wishes to see you before you go upstairs."

It might have been the first time Father had requested her presence. "I will go to him immediately."

She was just outside the double doors when Mother called out, "Oh, I meant to tell you, I had a note from your Earl of Grafton last week."

Sylvia's heart stopped beating and she had to blink several times to keep her head. "And what did it say?"

"That he was delighted to hear of Serena's engagement, but that his recent accident and injuries would keep him away from the ball. He wished the entire family well. I thought it quite nice of him to bother with a note at all. He must regard you very highly." Felicia watched her with narrowed eyes.

Nothing of the truth would be the right thing for Sylvia to say. "I would think the note is a tribute to you or Serena. It certainly has nothing to do with me."

Felicia's stance relaxed, and she gave one nod.

Father's study was the one room the women of the house rarely entered. He kept himself locked up in there for hours at a time and rarely interacted with the household. Sylvia knocked.

"Enter." His deep voice came through the door.

The masculine room was filled with books and a stale cigar smell, which Sylvia had always hated. The desk was crowded with open books of various texts about history, botany, horsemanship, fishing, and a few other subjects. Father was always off on some learning tangent. If he had been willing to share his interests, it might have been fascinating, and maybe even fun, to learn along with him. However, he'd always kept his hobby to himself.

"Good evening, Father. You wanted to see me?" She waited near the door in case Mother had been mistaken.

He looked up and pulled his spectacles from his face. "Sylvia, come in. I had a letter with regard to you today, and I thought we might discuss it."

She sat in the window seat, as there were no other chairs besides Father's. It was necessary to stack several books and put them aside to make room for herself. "May I ask who the letter was from?"

Scanning his desk, he riffled through several papers before he picked up one, plucked his spectacles back on his nose, and studied it. "A Mr. Miles Hallsmith."

Sylvia's heart sank. It was not a question of liking or not liking Miles. He was a fine gentleman who had been very kind to her. Still, she had a vain hope of Anthony forgiving her and reiterating his desire to marry her. "I see."

"I didn't know you were acquainted with Mr. Hallsmith." He gazed at her over the lenses.

"During my work with the Everton Domestic Society, I have had a few occasions to be in his company. What does Mr. Hallsmith want?"

"He asks for permission to court you. He has a good living, despite being a third son, and he appears to have a good head on his shoulders."

Crying was not an option. Father hated tears more than any other feminine habit or trait. "He is a good man."

Father pushed away his spectacles and the letter, folded his hands on the desk, and leaned toward her. "Is there some reason I should deny him permission, Sylvia?"

"None that I can think of."

He leaned back in his chair but kept his hands folded, resting them on the slight bulge of his stomach. "I have always thought of you as a sensible girl. Do you like this young man?"

Swallowing all the emotion rocketing to the top of her tolerance, she said, "I do not dislike him."

A deep frown creased his mouth and around his eyes. "Despite what you may think and what your mother has displayed over the last few years, I do care about your happiness, Sylvia. Perhaps you might give Mr. Hallsmith some thought before I respond."

"I will think about it. Thank you, Father."

He returned his attention to a book on dog breeding. "Go on and get ready for this fiasco."

Sylvia ran from the room and up the stairs to her sister's room.

"Sylvie, you look like you've seen a ghost. What has happened?" Serena was a vision in a yellow gown, her hair up in a dozen curls with a string of pearls winding through her chestnut-brown tresses.

"Miles Hallsmith has asked Father's permission to court me."

Frowning, Serena asked Jenny to leave them. She took Sylvia's hand, and they sat on the edge of the bed. "But you are in love with Anthony?"

"Miles is a good man with much to offer a girl like me." Sensible Sylvia, that was who she was. Miles was a good match.

"Sylvie, you're being a dope."

It was more Serena's sharp tone than what she said that shook Sylvia out of her dazedness. "I am a dope? Miles is a nice man with a good living who clearly likes me. Why shouldn't I welcome his attention?"

"Everything you said is true, but where is your heart, Sylvie? Anthony loves you, and you love him."

She hiccupped but kept her emotions deep down in her gut. "How would you know his feelings?"

Serena blushed. "He told me. I think I caught him at a weak moment when he needed someone to talk to, and he asked for my help in winning you. I planned to help him too, but then he was called away from the house party and injured."

Bewildered by the idea that Anthony would have shared his feelings with her sister, she didn't know what to say. "Did he think you were me? Why would he tell you how he feels?"

Taking her hands, Serena whispered, "That's the amazing thing, Sylvie. I actually took your dress and pretended to be you, but the moment he saw my face, he knew who I was."

"How?" Few people could tell them apart.

Serena sighed. "I think because he loves you so much that love doesn't shine when he looks at me. It's the only explanation."

It was becoming harder to not cry. "I think his feelings have cooled."

"Why would you think that? Have you heard from him since his accident?"

Having carried his missive around since it arrived weeks ago, Sylvia used the cool reply as a reminder of what her life was and how foolish it was to consider another. She pulled the parchment out of her reticule and handed it to Serena. "I wrote to him. I couldn't say all I felt in a letter, but it was filled with emotion and the hope he would understand. This is the reply I received."

Serena opened the page and read it. "This is a very feminine hand, Sylvie. Are you sure he wrote this? And 'My Dear Lady' doesn't sound anything like the Anthony Braighton I met. The entire note is far more formal than I have ever heard from him. Perhaps someone wrote it for him because he was incapacitated."

"It is not in his hand, but if his mother helped him pen the note, it still may reflect his lack of emotions."

Folding the letter, Serena shook her head. "You were looking for an escape, and you found one in that letter, which is clearly not from Anthony. If you want to run away from love, you should at least be honest about it. If you want to marry Miles Hallsmith because he is safe and can't hurt you, then do so with open eyes. You may lie to me if you like, Sylvie, but don't lie to yourself."

She handed the letter back, and Sylvia took it. She wanted to bristle and posture, denying everything her sister said. The problem was it was all true. The idea of loving Anthony still terrified her even though she knew her mother's poisonous ideas had colored her own. At the first sign of trouble, she had jumped ship and clung to that note like a lifeline. "You're right. I will write to him again in the morning."

"Good. Now, do you like my dress?" Serena stood and admired herself in the glass.

Wrapping her arms around her from behind, Sylvia giggled. "You are stunning and will be the most beautiful bride. I'm so happy for you."

The clock in the foyer chimed eight o'clock. "Oh, my, we had better get downstairs. The guests will be arriving."

"I need just a few minutes."

"Of course, I will see you downstairs, but don't take too long or you'll miss the announcement." Serena bounced with glee.

"I won't. I promise."

Once Serena had left the room, Sylvia gazed into the glass with a long look. How had she become the cowardly sister more worried about her virtue than her happiness? If only she could see Anthony and explain it all to him.

Taking a deep breath, she smoothed her skirt and strode out the door.

Guests arrived, and the din rang at an uncomfortable level. When the music began, Serena and Rutledge took the floor. Both smiled; the world was a perfect place and them perfect in it. At least one thing had gone right this year, and Serena's happiness was well worth any price.

"Should I not have sent that letter to your father?" Miles smiled, but trepidation shone in his green eyes.

Her admiration for Miles was never in question. He was everything a young man should be: kind and lighthearted. "It was lovely of you to think of me, Mr. Hallsmith."

"Would you be scandalized if I asked you to dance the second with me? I understand it will be a waltz." His grin was infectious.

"I would be delighted."

"Good. Your sister looks well pleased, and so does Stansfield. You should be proud of your matchmaking skills, and your ability to make Anthony Braighton the perfect Earl of Grafton."

It should have meant nothing, but the mention of his name gave her gooseflesh, and she longed to see him more than she wanted to take her next breath.

"I see I've lost you." He still smiled, but it didn't reach his eyes.

Sylvia pulled herself together. "I only arranged a few parties and played hostess. His lordship did the rest."

The music ended, and the dancers left the floor in search of refreshment.

Father appealed to the master of ceremonies to address the ballroom. Mother stood by his side, the most unnatural smile on her face.

Miles stood by her side, and she appreciated his friendship. Perhaps marrying a man who would be a friend without passion was not as cowardly as Serena seemed to think. Yet, the notion ripped the joy out of her soul.

In formal attire, Edwin Dowder struck a fine figure as he cleared his throat and asked the room for their attention. "Welcome to our home. We are delighted to announce the engagement of our eldest daughter—though only by a few minutes—to Rutledge Haversham, the Earl of Stansfield. We are elated and wish the happy couple great joy."

Everyone applauded, and several ladies they'd grown up with ran to find Serena, where they became a gaggle of giggling girls.

Sylvia backed away until she was pressed into the corner and out of sight while Miles was busy laughing at the excited young ladies.

Something hard poked her in the ribs. "What?"

Lady Daphne Collington frowned at her and pointed with her cane. "You will not make your mark on society from the darkened corners of ballrooms, Miss Sylvia Dowder."

"I do not wish to detract from my sister's excitement, my lady."

Over the last few years, time had caught up with her ladyship. She'd developed a slight hunch in her back, and of course the cane was now required. Still, her frown was daunting. "Are not those same silly girls your friends?"

Sylvia tipped her chin up. "A friendship with an Everton lady is frowned upon. Therefore, if I entered the fray, I would cause all of them to scatter. Since Serena would support me, she would be left to celebrate with only me. This way she can enjoy her moment with those silly girls, as you called them."

Her frown in place, she nodded. "You have chosen a hard road, Miss Dowder. But you must know that a true friend would not abandon you in your hour of need. I would guess your sister knows that as well."

At that moment, Serena searched the ballroom until her gaze fell on Sylvia. She cocked her head.

Sylvia smiled and nodded, letting her know she was fine and not to worry.

"Take my great-nephew for instance. Anthony must think quite a lot of you. He was barely out of bed and unable to write, but rather than allow your letter to go unanswered, he asked me to write for him."

Unable to draw a breath, Sylvia opened her mouth, closed it, opened it again. She tried again and managed a gasping breath. "You wrote that letter?"

"I just said as much. He must be very fond of you. His concern that you would worry over him was acute. Of course, I tamed any notions he might have of embarrassing you with his American style of writing."

How could she have been so stupid? His aunt wrote the note. The note that made her think he didn't love her anymore was washed out by her sense of propriety. What he must have suffered to ask her to write it at all. "Thank you, my lady. It was most kind and well written."

"Perhaps you might write to him again now that he is better able to respond, though he stills struggles with his right arm."

If it were any other night, she would run upstairs and pen a letter immediately. "I will send a missive to Collington House in the morning."

"You won't find him there. He has disobeyed his mother and left London." It was hard to tell if Daphne was proud or annoyed with Anthony for making his own decisions.

"He's not alone at Riverdale I hope." It was a moment of panic that he might be in need of help, and here she was enjoying a ball. Well, not really enjoying it, but she was in attendance.

"No. Lord and Lady Marlton came for him and took him to the country to finish his recovery. I believe Angelica's mothering was quite too much for him. Sophia will make sure he is walking in no time. You may contact him there. Now you should make yourself seen before you are labeled a wallflower. Or worse, a dowager." Daphne waved her cane and walked away.

Sylvia laughed, but she was already calculating what she should do.

The music started, and Miles came to collect her. "I believe this is our dance, Miss Dowder."

Taking his arm, she walked to the dance floor. As the music lifted, he guided her around the floor. "You dance very well, Mr. Hallsmith."

"How else is one to woo ladies?"

"Is that what you're doing?" She chuckled.

"Well, I would if I didn't see that look in your eyes." Expertly, he maneuvered them out of the path of another couple who were not as adept at the waltz.

"What look is that?"

He pulled her in closer. "The look of a woman who is in love with someone else."

"Oh. I'm sorry." She wished she hid her emotions better. Harming Miles in any way was the last thing she wanted.

He shrugged and spun them adeptly along the outside of the floor. "It's all right, Miss Dowder. Tell your father you do not wish to court me. I will survive. I'm not sure Tony will, but you should not worry about me."

"What do you mean? He is healing well. I just spoke to his aunt, and she told me he is doing well and recovering at Marlton." Maybe Daphne hadn't been told everything due to her age. Lord, what would she do if anything happened to Anthony?

"Relax, he will recover from his stupidity, but I don't know if he will ever get over you."

"Why did you ask my father if you could court me when you are such good friends with Tony?" It made no sense.

A wicked smile followed a long dramatic sigh, and he bowed at the end of the dance. "For two reasons, Miss Dowder. Because I like you, and if you liked me, we might suit. But I admit I suspected your feelings for Tony, and I already knew his depth of emotion where you are concerned. I thought to test a theory. If you agreed to court me, you would not have been the right woman for my friend. Since you did not agree, perhaps you might consider another offer I have for you."

"You are rather devious, Mr. Hallsmith. What offer could you possibly make me?" Charming as he was, she was slightly confused.

"The offer of a gentleman to convey you to Marlton. I leave in the morning and will stay a fortnight."

"I cannot travel two days with you, Mr. Hallsmith." Even as she said it, she was scheming some way to make it work.

"Is there not some friend at the Society who might come with you?" His gaze passed over her shoulder.

Sylvia turned to see the direction of his gaze. Roberta Fletcher was walking toward them, her smile bright, and the pink gown she wore a perfect complement to her constant blush. "I will see if I can arrange a chaperon. If you are willing to make a late morning departure."

His gaze never strayed from Roberta. "I will be glad for the company, and Tony will owe me a big favor."

Roberta reached them and threw herself against Sylvia in a hug. "I am so glad to see you, Miss Dowder. I do not know a soul at this ball and made a terrible mistake in thinking your sister was you."

Laughing, Sylvia kissed her cheek. "It happens all the time. Don't trouble yourself."

"That is exactly what your sister said. She was very sweet."

Miles cleared his throat. "Will you introduce me to your friend, Miss Dowder?"

"Of course. Miss Roberta Fletcher, may I introduce my friend, Mr. Miles Hallsmith?"

He bowed. "A pleasure to meet you, Miss Fletcher."

"Likewise, Mr. Hallsmith."

"Miss Dowder, I will call for you in the morning. If you cannot make appropriate arrangements, send me a note. Miss Fletcher, do you have any space on your dance card for me?"

Roberta stuttered her first word then took a deep breath. "I am available for the next dance, sir."

Grinning like he'd won some rare jewel, Miles bowed. "I shall count the seconds."

Once he'd excused himself, Roberta lowered her head. "Is he a nice man?"

"He is a very nice man."

"Oh, no, is he courting you, Miss Dowder? I would never interfere." Her blush deepened, and she squeezed her fingers together until her knuckles whitened.

Sylvia took hold of Roberta's hands. "I am not interested in Mr. Hallsmith. He is a very kind and smart man who is conveying me to the country if I can find a chaperon by tomorrow morning. He is a friend."

"He is very handsome." Pink as a ripe peach, she peeked across the ballroom at Miles.

"Indeed, now stop staring before you make a fool of yourself." Sylvia laughed.

* * * *

"Miss Dowder, I have traveled to the country on extremely short notice twice in as many months on your account. That is a first for me," Lady Honoria Chervil announced as they turned onto the drive to the Marlton estate.

"I appreciate you making the journey. Mrs. Horthorn was otherwise engaged." Sylvia's heart pounded so loudly she was sure they all could hear.

Miles grinned. "It has been a most entertaining journey with you two ladies. I can't remember enjoying two days on the road more."

"You are a charmer, Mr. Hallsmith. It is no wonder Miss Dowder thought it best not to travel alone with you."

Sylvia rolled her eyes. There was no point in saying anything. The two of them had been teasing her since they'd left London. It seemed Lady Chervil was the reckless aunt Miles had always wanted and they hit it off immediately.

"Miss Dowder, you will catch your first glimpse of Marlton when we round this bend." Miles spoke low, adding to the suspense.

It was nearly a castle, it was so big. A large pond reflected the massive house in perfect detail. Even from that distance, it was clear the family was outside to the left of the house. Two children ran across the field while someone was chasing them. A woman, likely Sophia, sat on a blanket near the tree. In a chair near the woman, a tall man was watching the antics.

Sylvia's breath caught at the idea of how close he was. He might reject her. It was foolish to take Miles up on his offer without giving notice of her coming. They would all think her impertinent at least. But her foolish heart demanded she risk everything, even her virtue, to know if he still loved her.

The carriage rounded the final bend and headed straight on toward the house.

Daniel stopped playing with the children, and the nanny ran to collect them while he strode toward the drive with Sophia.

Anthony followed them at a slower pace.

Leaning back so as not to be seen, Sylvia gasped for breath.

Honoria patted her knee. "You've come this far, my dear. Don't lose your nerve now."

When the carriage stopped, Miles jumped down and greeted Daniel and Sophia. "Tony, I've come to cheer you, and to ensure my efforts would be successful, I brought you a gift."

Lady Honoria Chervil popped down from the carriage.

Sophia oohed and aahed over the unexpected guest.

"It is good to see you, my lady," Anthony said. His voice was closer, but Sylvia was too much of a coward to look out the window.

"Are you going to come out?" Miles asked.

Taking a deep breath, Sylvia poked her head out. "I hope I am not intruding."

Anthony was thinner than when she'd last seen him. He stood leaning on a cane, and his right arm lay in a sling around his neck. Staring, perhaps afraid she would fade away if he blinked, he opened his mouth. "I—you are a welcome surprise."

The footman waited and handed her down.

Sophia ran over and wrapped her in a hug. "I'm so happy you are here. I would have sent for you next week after everything calmed down from your sister's ball. And of course, we have all been helping Tony to recover from his injuries."

Whatever she was about to say, she thought better of it. Maybe it was because they were not in private, or because she thought a man with a cane wouldn't appeal to Sylvia.

"Mr. Hallsmith was kind enough to inform me that he had room in his carriage. I apologize for not having time to write before barging in."

Daniel bowed over her hand. "Don't be silly. We are thrilled to have you and Lady Chervil here. Sophie, we should alert the staff to have two more rooms prepared and settings for dinner."

It was impossible to take her gaze from Anthony's golden stare. He might be more ferocious as an injured lion.

"I'll arrange for tea. You must be famished." Sophia took Daniel's hand, and they rushed up the steps.

The nanny scurried up behind them with both children in tow.

Miles chuckled and offered Honoria his arm. "My lady, may I escort you inside?"

"I would be delighted. Why is it you are not married? You are indeed handsome and charming," Honoria gushed.

"Alas, I am a third son, and more to the point, my friends have married up all the best ladies." His voice faded as they walked up the stairs and into the house.

Anthony stepped forward. "I never dreamed you would come. Well, I dreamed it, but thought it only a wish."

"You don't mind then?" If her heart beat any faster, she would faint like some waif in an opera.

"Your letter gave me some hope, but then my injuries prevented me from further investigation, and all this time passed with no word." He took another step.

The carriage pulled away, leaving them alone in the yard.

A breeze rustled her skirts, and several birds flew as one out of the tree.

"Your letter was so abrupt, I thought you had lost interest." She closed the distance between them until she peered into those dangerous eyes. "Last night, your aunt informed me that she penned the note."

"When last we met, I wouldn't have thought it mattered to you if I lost interest. In fact, you seemed keen on me not loving you." He ran his knuckles along her jaw.

Even that light touch was a bit of heaven. "A lot has happened in the last six weeks. I hope you will give me a chance to tell you all about it."

"It doesn't matter."

Sylvia's heart sank. Tears pressed at the backs of her eyes. "I'm sorry to hear that, but I completely understand. It was foolish of me to think you would tolerate all my rejection and still want me."

One side of his full kissable mouth lifted, and joy lit his eyes. "Oh, Sylvie, the only foolish thing is that you would think I could stop loving you. What I mean is, you may tell me everything, and I want to know all of it, but I will love you no matter what. If you choose to keep your revelation to yourself, I will still love you. You are all I want…"

The happy scream of children at play filtered out from the window.

He leaned toward the lane. "Shall we walk? That window is the parlor, and I expect we have an audience."

"Can you? Walk, I mean?"

"The cast came off yesterday, but other than a bit of an ache, it's not bad." They followed the lane where it curved around the side of the house to a small garden.

"I should have demanded to see you when I came to the house." Shame dug a hole in her and gnawed at her gut.

"My momma can be very imposing, and what would you have told her? It was an uncomfortable situation. I wish I had been able to receive you, but you arrived before I knew the goings-on at the house. If I had known, I would have made certain you were allowed entry. Though, I'm not sure you would have liked what you saw." He made it to a bench in the rose garden and eased himself down.

"What were you thinking going into that sinking boat?" It came out sterner than she'd intended, and she sat next to him.

He cupped her cheek. "I was thinking that I had brought all that lavender fabric from India just for you, and I had to save it."

The kiss was gentle, pure, and filled with a lifetime of desire. He made love to her mouth, pulling her bottom lip between his, then the top. His tongue traced the line between her lips and she opened for him.

Carefully wrapping her arm around his neck, she toyed with the soft hair at the back of his neck. "I love you, Tony. I should have been brave enough to tell you before."

His eyes closed, and he pressed his forehead to hers. "Now is soon enough. I never thought I'd hear you say those words, my sweet Everton lady. I expected to pine for you for the rest of my life."

"You don't mind that there will be no dowry, and I'm surrounded by scandal?" It seemed only fair to give him a way out, even now after two days' travel.

"Marry me, Sylvie."

Joy and terror battled as one inside her. She'd never wanted to hear any words more. Yet, to say yes to another man then wait for him to change his mind— "I don't know what to say."

"If I thought I could get back up, I would go down on one knee, but I fear that is where you would find me until next week. Just say you'll marry me, and I'll kneel to you for the rest of our lives as the queen I do not deserve."

"I will marry you, Tony. I can't believe I'm saying it, but I can do nothing else." It was the truth. Her heart would have no other answer, and she'd chosen to push her fears aside when she got in Miles's carriage and trekked two days to see a man.

Chapter 18

He might be barely able to walk, but his heart lifted in flight. Anthony crept down the hall where he hoped his bride-to-be would grant him two wishes. It was past midnight, the house was asleep, and he was too excited to rest. Sylvia had said she would marry him despite her doubts. It had been the best day of his life.

The difficulty in using a cane quietly meant that the walk down the long hall took a great deal of time, but if he was discovered, it would ruin his plans.

Scratching on her bedroom door, he waited, hoping Sylvia was a light sleeper.

Sleepy-eyed, she opened the door. She was a vision in a voluminous white nightgown. It was so full it covered all but her neck, head and hands. "Tony? Is everything okay?"

He backed her inside, closed the door and threw the latch. The feminine room had lace covering every surface, and the moon shone in the window. It was odd how many times they met by moonlight. "If you're asking if I intend to break off our six-hour-old engagement, the answer is a definite no. I love you and I want to marry you."

The way her face lit up was the most beautiful thing he'd ever seen. "Why are you knocking on my bedroom door in the middle of the night then?"

"I want to make you a proposal, my sweet, beautiful fiancée." He took her hand and kissed each finger, careful not to let his cane make too much noise on the floor. If they were found out, Daniel might break the door down.

Even in the dim light from the moon, her eyes were bright with excitement. "Are you planning to deflower your bride before the wedding night?"

He loved her teasing tone and her wicked mind. All the things he loved about this quick-witted woman. "Well, I had hoped you might be amenable to making love tonight. Though, should you say no, I will not pressure you."

She pressed her lips to his and ran her hand down his chest to his waist, where she clutched the top of his breeches and pulled him close. "Yes."

Body trembling with need, he couldn't believe his ears. "Yes?"

"Make love to me, Tony." Keeping her hold, she pulled him toward the bed. "I have no idea what tomorrow will bring, but I know I love you and I want you tonight."

"I may have some difficulties due to my injuries." Lord, how he wished he'd left those textiles to sink so he could properly pleasure her.

"Can we not overcome them?" She raised her brows.

His rod demanded he not hesitate, and the rest of him was set on pleasing her too. "I know you are poking fun, but it would be my deepest wish that we try, Sylvie."

With a wide grin, she jumped up on the bed. "I am teasing, but I am not poking fun, Tony. I can't imagine you and I can't figure a way around your difficulties, as you called them."

Just as enthusiastic, but with less vigor, he placed his cane on the floor and eased himself next to her. He'd been sleeping on his back, as his arm and leg pain made any other position impossible. Frustration led him to inspiration. With an experienced woman, there would be no trepidation. "I'm not at all sure how much you know about this."

She leaned on his chest, her chin on her fist, and smiled. "I have never done it before, if that's what you're asking."

Trying to explain such things to a virgin left him tongue-tied. He shook his head. "At some point, we will have no trouble speaking of such intimate things. That being said, perhaps it is better to just be frank and blush our way through it. Usually, a man would be on top at least for this first time, but we may have to make a few adjustments."

As promised, she turned pink. It was adorable. Then her eyes narrowed while she was thinking. "I think I understand. Why don't you tell me what to do, and I'll try my best to comply?"

"I want more than compliance, my love. I want you to feel thoroughly ravished despite my condition. I want you to know this part of our marriage will get better and better. I want you to feel every delight."

Bright blue, her eyes glowed with desire. "Tell me what to do."

Here was the Sylvia he'd first met. A girl with spirit and curiosity. He pushed himself to sitting. "Would you help me remove my blouse?"

With the touch of an angel, she eased the linen over his head then his right side. She touched the dark bruise that still marred his collarbone. Like the wings of a butterfly, her hair tickled his cheek as she kissed his injury. "I hope you will be more careful in the future, Tony. I fear I will become a wretched wife should you risk your life like this again."

He kissed her cheek and down her neck to her throat. "I will not leave you, my love. Not that way and not for many years. I hope we shall have babies and grow gray before I should ever leave you."

"That is a lovely image." She ran her hands over his chest, exploring his body. "Shall I help you with your breeches, Tony?"

Lord, he'd not last five minutes at this rate. "I think we had better wait on that, but I would love to see all of you, Sylvie."

She bit her bottom lip. "I'm too skinny and don't have a full bosom."

"No. You are perfect in every way." He ran his hand from the frilly neck of her gown down to her stomach.

One at a time, she pulled the bows at her shoulders and neck then let the gown pool around her. Every inch of her porcelain skin glowed with warmth.

Leaning up on his good arm, he took one sweet nipple into his mouth and sucked it until she arched her back and gripped his head.

A low cry fell from her lips.

He sat facing her and wrapped his good leg around her bottom while his healing leg was safe to the side. He kissed and licked his way from those sweet breasts up to her neck and kissed behind her ear until she writhed against him.

"Absolutely perfect." He slid his hand between her legs and found her soft and wet.

"Tony?" She gripped his good shoulder. Even in her rapture, she was careful and thoughtful of his injuries.

"Let me show you. Let me give you pleasure."

Relaxing her grip, she allowed him to press his fingers inside her, gather her moisture and gently rub between her folds. She gasped and rocked against his hand.

As wonderful and maddening as seeing to her pleasure was, he longed to give her more and find his own pleasure too. Yet the way her face turned up to the moonlight and her mouth opened with a silent cry could have been enough. His fingers slid in and out of her with each rock of her hips. She set the pace.

As her gasps grew louder, he muffled them with his kisses, driving his tongue into her mouth in time with her gyrations until she tightened and soaked his hand with pleasure.

She collapsed against him, and he held her while the waves of pleasure wracked her body.

"How do I make you feel that way, Tony? I want to give you the same pleasure."

Try as he might to hold himself at bay, her words had his shaft at full attention. He untied the fall of his breeches, letting her see the effect her orgasm had on him.

Tentatively, she touched him, running one finger up his length.

He inhaled, and she repeated it with two fingers then her entire hand until she gripped him and slid up and down. It was sweet and sultry, driving him to the brink of eruption.

"Am I doing this right?" She leaned down and kissed the head of his cock.

"Dear God, Sylvie."

She sat up, eyes wide. "Have I done something wrong?"

He closed his eyes and controlled his body. "You are perfect, but that will have to wait for another time. I don't think this will last long if you kiss me there tonight."

"Then you like it when I kiss you there?"

"I like it very much." Just the conversation was so erotic, he was near to bursting.

She cocked her head. "And is there anywhere that I should not kiss you?"

Invalid or not, he pressed her back on the bed. "Nowhere. You have full reign of my body, my queen." He kissed her abdomen and dipped his tongue inside her bellybutton.

A tiny gasp escaped, and she arched her back.

He ran his tongue straight down and licked her bud, making her jump but open her thighs wider for him. He pulled that bud into his mouth and suckled then slid his tongue around and around before sucking again. Her body clenched, and he slipped his thumb inside her, reveling in the way her core tightened around his digit.

"Goodness, Tony. Is it always like this?" She leaned up on an elbow.

Leaning on his left elbow, he faced her. "For us it will be."

Dipping her head, she looked at him from hooded lids and was possibly the most adorable thing he'd ever seen. "Show me how to give you pleasure now."

He rolled to his back and with little pressure gave her leave to lie on top of him. "Straddle me, Sylvie."

Lifting her knees brought her center to the spot just above his shaft. She eased back, bringing his head to just breach her.

"It's easier if you go fast this first moment and get it over with. I promise there will never be pain again."

Her gaze met his, and she impaled herself on him. A tear bubbled over her bottom lid.

Cupping her head, he pulled her in and kissed her. "I'm sorry, my love. I promise, never again." He needed to move to relish the feel of her, but he held perfectly still with her soft, tight body wrapping him in delight.

"I'm all right. The pain has eased. I thought you had ripped me in two, but now the pain is gone." She rocked her hips and moaned.

The pleasure forced his own groan. He set a pace for her by gripping her hip. She rode him slowly, precisely and with agonizing beauty. Aching with a need for release, he held on and let the pleasure continue as long as she could stand it. When her body clenched, he could take no more and found his own ecstasy.

With her forehead pressed to his throat, and her hair spread out across his chest, he could be happy like this for the rest of his life. "If you roll over, I will go to the basin and get a cloth to clean you."

Raising her head, she smiled at him. "You can do that another time when you don't need a cane to make the journey."

Regret filled him when she climbed off him and went to clean herself. He should have kept his mouth closed and kept her with him longer.

She returned with the clean cloth and wiped the bit of blood from his shaft.

How could one person be so erotic and sweet at once? He grabbed her hand. "Come back to bed. I want to ask something of you."

"More?" She grinned but put the cloth back in the basin, dried her hands, and returned to bed, where she snuggled against him.

"I want to go to Scotland tomorrow."

She sat up, horror on her face. "You're leaving."

He grabbed her hands and kissed each palm, ignoring the pain the sharp movement caused in his collarbone. "No. Forgive me. I want to take you to Scotland tomorrow. Do you know the Duke and Duchess of Kerburghe?"

Eyes narrowed in confusion, she nodded. "I have known Elinor Burkenstock since we were children."

"They have a castle in Scotland, and it has become a bit of a strange tradition to marry in their small chapel." He held his breath.

"You want to run off to Scotland and get married? No banns, no article in the paper, and no special license?" Bewildered, she repeated herself. She grabbed her nightgown, pulled it over her head, and tied only the bows at the shoulders, so it hung loose around her neck.

Sitting up, he faced her and pulled her close. "I want to marry you, and I don't want you to spend the next six months worried about when I will come and tell you I have changed my mind. I will never change my mind, and to make sure you know that, I want to go to Scotland, where we can ignore all the silly English traditions."

Sylvia blinked and pushed her hair out of her face. "Yes."

"Yes?"

Finally, her gaze focused on him. "I love that you know me so well you know I will worry. I love that you have a plan to ease my concerns. I love that we will not go to Gretna Green, though I would have agreed to that as well. I will only regret that my sister will not be there. Yes, I will run away with you, to Scotland, Italy or the ends of the earth, Tony." She leaned in and kissed him so hard he had to clutch the bed to keep his precarious balance.

"And you don't mind marrying a cripple?" He'd wanted to be whole before he went to her. Had thought to give himself two more weeks before he stormed the doors of Everton House.

Smiling, she kissed the dark bruise again then leaned down and kissed his withered leg. It would take time to get his strength back. "Even if I thought it was permanent, which I'm sure it's not, I would marry my sweet, aggravating American."

"I'll never get any sleep tonight. You've made me very happy, Sylvie." Giddy as a boy just out of school for holiday, he tied his fall and gentled his blouse over his head.

"Nor I. Do you think we should send a message to His Grace and make sure he doesn't mind our coming?"

Michael Rollins was not the kind of duke who would mind friends showing up unannounced. "It will be fine."

* * * *

Lady Chervil was the last to arrive for breakfast. As soon as she had her plate, Anthony stood up. "Sylvia and I are going to Kerburghe and getting married."

Sylvia stared at her plate.

Four pair of eyes stared at him in silence.

Sophia was the first to recover. She slapped her hands down on the table, rattling the silver. "Not without me, you're not. If my brother is getting married, I'm going to be there."

"I'm going too." Lady Chervil held up her fork with a large piece of sausage attached to it. She grinned, ready for adventure.

Miles leaned back in his chair and nodded. "I hate to miss a good wedding. Besides, I'm not due back in London for two weeks, and returning to deal with my brother early does not appeal at all."

"I guess that's settled then, we're all going to Scotland for your elopement." Daniel stepped to the doorway and called for the butler. He instructed him to have three carriages readied.

Sitting, Anthony took Sylvia's hand. "I guess I had better send a messenger ahead after all."

Sophia cleared her throat. "Sylvia, are you in favor of this elopement? You are very quiet."

Lifting her head, she blushed and smiled just as a bride should. "I am very much in favor, Sophia."

Anthony let go the breath he'd been holding. She had agreed heartily last night, but had been so still this morning, he'd begun to worry that she'd changed her mind. "You should know me well enough, Sophie, to know I would never bully a woman into marriage."

"It never hurts to ask, Tony." She got up. "I need to inform the children, nanny, and my maid that we will be leaving this morning. You are lucky you didn't steal off in the night or I would have had to hunt you down with two children in tow. I would have been very aggravated."

"We are not running away. Just expediting our life together." He looked at Sylvia.

Taking a deep breath, she nodded. "And it cannot come soon enough. I do want to send a post to Lady Jane. It wouldn't do for her to hear of my marriage from another source."

* * * *

It was three days ride to Kerburghe in the borderlands of Scotland, and it was a very happy party with everyone moving from carriage to carriage with every stop. They slept two nights at inns where Anthony lay awake wishing he had Sylvia in his arms.

Sylvia grew quiet on the last day. "Will we marry as soon as we arrive?"

Lady Chervil was in the carriage with them, but she was either sleeping or pretending to sleep. He'd noticed her smile a few times when they spoke in low tones.

The trepidation in Sylvia's voice broke his heart. "No, we have to wait."

Where her shoulders had been tight, they relaxed. "Oh? Why?"

"Because I wrote to your family before we left England and asked them to come to Kerburghe for the wedding."

Eyes wide open now, Lady Chervil sat up. "You are full of surprises, my lord."

"Why would you do that? Father might prevent the wedding." Never had he met such a complicated woman. First, she was nervous about something he couldn't pinpoint, then happy that the wedding would be delayed, then afraid it might be stopped. He couldn't keep up.

"You said your only regret was not having your sister at your wedding. I don't want you to regret anything about our wedding day. Your father will not stop the wedding, and I doubt he'll want to."

"Of course, he won't. You're marrying an earl, and you're not under his roof anymore anyway. This entire thing is the most romantic event of my life." Honoria dabbed her eyes with a handkerchief.

Anthony thought he'd done the right thing, but she appeared so lost, he wasn't sure. "Have I made a mistake, Sylvie?"

She lurched across the carriage and hugged him. "Oh, Tony, you are the most wonderful man. How will I ever deserve you?"

Breathing for the first time in several minutes, Anthony relaxed. "If you will love me every day for the rest of our lives, that would do nicely."

"I will do my best." She sat down on the bench next to him as Kerburghe came into view. "Dear Lord, it really is a castle."

Hundred-foot walls loomed high over a moat with one wide bridge leading to the front gate. It was something out of a storybook but without the armed men walking the tops of the walls. "What did you think? I told you it was a castle."

"Yes, but this is quite foreboding." They crossed the bridge, went through the gate and into a wide yard.

The great doors opened, and Elinor ran out, followed by five small children. All six were waving madly while Michael Rollins, the Duke of Kerburghe, sauntered out and stood at the top of the steps.

The carriages pulled up, and Michael trotted down to open the first, where Sylvia and Anthony rode. He handed her down. "Welcome to Kerburghe Castle, Miss Dowder. I'm honored you would choose our home for your wedding."

"I hope we're not too much of an imposition, Your Grace." Sylvia made a curtsy, but her smile faltered.

"Not at all. Though, I do insist you call me Michael. You are a welcome distraction. Perhaps Tony told you marrying at Kerburghe has become a bit of a tradition. It seems none of my friends are patient enough to wait on English law." Michael shook Anthony's hand then greeted the rest of the party.

Elinor ran over and hugged Sylvia. "I'm so happy for you. You each received a few letters this morning by messenger. I have put them in your rooms. Is the ceremony urgent? I can call the vicar immediately if you like."

Anthony kissed her cheek. "I think that will depend on what is in those letters."

"Oh, I see." She winked. "Well, we'll have some tea in the parlor, and you two can go up and read your mail before you join us."

Waiting was torture, but Anthony sat on his bed in the guest room and bided his time until he heard the last of their party traipse downstairs. He went down the hall and knocked on Sylvia's door. "Sylvie?"

She opened the door with unopened letters in her hand. "I'm afraid to open them. Isn't that silly?"

He held up three letters. "Perhaps we can read them together."

Backing up, she let him enter, and they sat on the edge of the bed. "You go first. Who are your letters from?"

"I have one from my mother, one from Aunt Daphne and one from your father. Who are yours from?" He slid his finger under the seal of Mother's letter.

"My father and Serena and Lady Jane." She broke the seal on Serena's letter.

Anthony opened the one-page letter. It was in Italian, and so he scanned it before translating. His trepidation eased. "Mother is thrilled. She is coming here with Mr. Condon as her escort."

She took his hand. "Are you all right with this relationship between your mother and Mr. Condon?"

Oddly, he was. "You were right. My mother shouldn't have to be lonely. Father has been gone a long time, and she is a beautiful woman who is full of life. I will not make her unhappy if I can prevent it."

Kissing his cheek, she said, "I'm proud of you."

He loved that she meant those words. It meant more than anyone else saying them. "Read Serena's note."

"She says she knew we would suit and she will come immediately." Sylvia giggled. "The rest is just girl talk."

She tore the seal on Jane Everton's letter. "Lady Jane is sorry to see me leave the Society but delighted for us both."

"That's three with only good news." He gave her a wink.

"Yes well, we were cowardly and went for the good news first." She bumped him with her shoulder playfully.

Opening the letter from Aunt Daphne, he wondered which version of his aunt would be on the page, the cutting society dame or the loving aunt? He took a breath. "My dear nephew, I am happy for you and Miss Dowder. Kerburghe is too far for me to travel on such short notice at my age. When you return to London, I hope you will allow me to give you and your new bride a proper breakfast. It would please me to do so. Warmest regards, your aunt, Lady Daphne Collington."

"From her ladyship, that is quite a positive response." She drew a deep breath and let it out. "Shall I read Father's?"

"Let's open them together." He broke the Dowder seal.

Sylvia opened her letter. "It's not as bad as I thought. He said he will bring my mother and sister to Scotland. It says it's very inconvenient, but at least I found a nobleman with ample funds to marry. Not exactly swimming with affection, but more than I expected."

"Mine just states that he approves of my request to marry his youngest daughter, and he and his family will arrive in two days."

They sat in silence until Anthony leaned over and kissed the top of her head. "I told you it would be fine. We will marry when they all arrive."

Sylvia pushed his cane to the floor, turned and straddled his lap. "I'm happy my family will come, but I'd have married you in a shack with no one to witness the event."

Her intense gaze and sweet words humbled him. Gripping her with his good arm, he pulled her center in close until she could feel what she did to him. "And I you, my love."

Wiggling closer, she pressed her lips to his. "I wish we didn't have to go down for tea."

This woman would drive him happily mad, and he couldn't wait for their life to begin. Standing on one leg, he let her body slide down his, which forced her skirts up between them. He wrapped his hand around until he caressed her bottom. "We have a lifetime to make love a hundred different ways." He found the sweet spot wet and willing, and he slid his fingers along the crease until she cried out.

"Anthony, you said we had a lifetime." She pressed against his hand.

Longing to slip inside her and find his own release, he closed his eyes against the urge lest it overtake him. "That does not mean I can resist that look on your face when you come, sweet Everton lady."

She wrapped one leg around his waist, drawing her center tighter to his bulging shaft. "Don't you think the others will wait a few minutes?"

Light as she was, he carried her and hobbled to the wall, where he kissed her throat. "I think they will have to wait. It seems my wife-to-be is the most delicious wanton, and I am helpless to resist her."

She opened her mouth as he kissed her. Tongues, teeth and lips collided in almost violent passion. She muttered against his flesh, gripping his hair and spreading kisses on his cheeks, ears, and throat. "I'm so glad to hear it."

He'd never wanted anyone so desperately. Sure that this was the only person who could make him happy, Anthony gave himself over to her. She was his world, and fears aside, he would see to her happiness.

Meet the Author

A.S. Fenichel gave up a successful IT career in New York City to follow her husband to Texas and pursue her lifelong dream of being a professional writer. She's never looked back. Multi-published in erotic paranormal, erotic contemporary, Regency historical romance and historical paranormal romance, A.S. will be bringing you her brand of romance for many years to come. A.S. loves to hear from her readers. Be sure to visit her website at asfenichel.com, find her on Facebook, and follow her on Twitter.

A Lady's Escape

Read on for a sample of the first book in A.S. Fenichel's Everton Domestic Society series

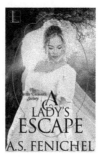

The perfect match may be closer than they imagine...

Despite her disastrous London debut, Millicent Edgebrook has proven skilled at securing matches—for every young lady but herself. Resigned to spinsterhood, and eager to gain independence from her lovable but eccentric uncle, Millie joins the Everton Domestic Society. Her first assignment: find a bride for Preston Knowles, Duke of Middleton. How difficult can it be to secure a match for a handsome, eligible aristocrat? As difficult, it seems, as resisting her own attraction to the duke...

Preston has promised himself not to be ruined by love. After being rebuffed by two perfectly respectable candidates, he'd rather remain happily single for the rest of his life...if only his mother would let him. Yet suddenly, he's fantasizing about the lovely matchmaker she's hired—the least suitable bride imaginable. Millie's past is shrouded in scandal, and the Everton Society forbids relations between employees and clients. But even with so many obstacles against them, Preston longs to convince the woman he adores that love trumps rules every time...

Chapter 1

Everton House was not grand by any standards, but it was formidable. Standing at the bottom of the stoop, Millicent Edgebrook was nervous for the first time in a long time. If Lady Jane rejected her, she'd be right back where she started with no options but to spend the rest of her life being blown up, smoked out and poisoned by every manner of stench. No. This had to work. It was the first step in her plan for independence, so Millie strode up the steps and knocked.

Mrs. Doris Whimple, Millie's hired companion and lady's maid, fidgeted next to her.

"What are you nervous about?" Millie asked.

"I have heard that Lady Jane Everton is terrifying. Mary McGinty told me that just a look from Jane Everton has sent more than one woman crying from the room." Mrs. Whimple shivered.

"I'm certain that is an exaggeration. Be calm. Besides, she is interviewing me, not you." Despite her brave words, a knot formed in the pit of Millie's stomach.

The door opened, revealing an ancient butler with tufts of white hair poking out from his head. "How may I help you?"

Millie handed over her card.

"Miss Edgebrook, please come in. My lady is expecting you." He opened the door wide and stepped aside, allowing them into the foyer.

Aside from a large vase of flowers adorning a round entry table, the hall was mostly wood and gave a masculine feel.

"I am Gray," the butler intoned. "Your companion may wait here. Lady Jane will see you alone."

Mrs. Whimple stiffened.

"It's all right, Doris. I'll be fine." Millie sounded braver than she felt. Her stomach was in knots, and her palms began to sweat as she followed Gray down a narrow corridor next to the stairs.

He stopped at a set of double doors. "My lady waits for you in the office." He gestured toward the door then ambled back the way they had come.

The butterflies in Millie's stomach turned to dragons at war. Drawing her shoulders back, she took a deep breath and knocked.

"Come in, Miss Edgebrook." A strong feminine voice came from within.

Millie stepped inside a well-appointed office complete with a wall of books to the right and tall windows out to the garden on the left. Millie stifled a sigh and pulled her pelisse tighter against the cool night. Another vase of flowers stood on a small table to the right. The woman behind the desk sat straight as a board with her dark hair pulled back severely and her hands folded.

She stood. "I am Lady Jane Everton."

Both curtsied, and Millie said, "I am honored to meet you, my lady. I am Millicent Edgebrook."

A warm smile softened Lady Jane's face as she gestured toward the chair in front of the desk. "Please have a seat and tell me what brings you to the Everton Domestic Society."

Heart in her throat, Millie gulped for air. "I'm not sure what you want to know."

Raising one curved brow, Jane cocked her head. "The truth would be a good start. How did you come to the decision that a life as an Everton Lady might suit you?"

Best to start at the beginning. "I was orphaned ten years ago and taken in by a kindly uncle. Perhaps you know of him? Francis Edgebrook?"

"He does have an odd reputation," Jane admitted, her expression bland, and no disapproval rang in her tone.

A long exhalation lodged in Millie's chest. "Yes, well, my uncle is a good man. However, as a man of science, he can get caught up in his laboratory, and on occasion there have been accidents. My family home is in Devonshire, and while it is entailed to me, it has been vacant for a decade and I have little income with which to open the house. I no longer wish to be a burden on Uncle Francis. It is time I make my own way in the world. Also, I'd like to do some good."

Elbows on the desk, Jane rested her chin on her hands and leaned in. She narrowed her eyes and stared at Millie. "What is it that you feel you can offer to the clients of Everton?"

The dragons returned to her belly. "I'm not exactly sure. I can run a house, I've been to hundreds of balls and know my way around the ton better than most. After all, this is my ninth season. I did remove myself from society for what would have been my second season. I surely can assist someone needing to get over a scandalous broken engagement."

Jane returned a sad smile. "Yes, I remember you had troubles early on. But, you are an attractive landed woman, Miss Edgebrook. Why have you not found another? You surely could have married if you wanted to."

Millie released her pent-up breath and glanced out the windows at the clouds rolling in. It would rain soon. A fitting end to the day. "It always seemed the men who were interested in me were better suited to my friends."

Sitting back, Jane asked, "How so?"

"For example, Joseph Wattsby took an interest in me last season. He is kind and smart. He loves the opera and goes as often as he can. I went to finishing school with Sarah Jessep, and she too is an avid lover of opera. It seemed a shame for the two not to meet, so I made the introductions. The next month they were engaged, and now they are expecting their first child."

"I see," said Jane. "And have there been other friends you found more suitable for your admirers?"

"A few." She realized too late she had said too much. Jane must think her an imbecile.

"How many?"

"Mrs. Whimple, my companion, tells me it is seven."

"Goodness. You must have a knack for matchmaking, Miss Edgebrook."

"I suppose I do. It seems quite obvious when I meet two people with common interests, they should meet. Mrs. Whimple has told me many times I should keep them for myself. I suppose if I ever loved one of them, I would."

"Indeed." Jane stood. "This puts me in mind of something, my dear. Thank you for coming to see me."

Resigned to her fate of being smoked out and blown up for the rest of her life, Millie's hope died as she rose to bid Lady Jane good day. She'd been a fool to think she had anything to offer the Everton Domestic Society. What would they want with her when they had so many accomplished ladies already? "I appreciate you allowing me to come, my lady."

"If you are amenable, and available, you should settle in then go to see the Duke of Middleton as soon as possible. He has recently had another romantic setback, and his excellent mother has contacted the society to help him find a bride. It seems to be just the first assignment for someone with your qualifications."

Millie's mind spun. She must have heard wrong. The Duke of Middleton? No, it must be a mistake. "You mean, you want me to be an Everton Lady?"

"I thought that was your wish as well, Miss Edgebrook. Have I misunderstood?" Jane cocked her head.

"No. I… Yes. I can move in tomorrow and start right away." Excitement warred with those darn dragons, and a jolt of energy filled Millie with hope.

"Very good." She reached in her desk drawer and pulled out a booklet. "You should read through the *Everton Companion, Rules of Conduct*." She handed the book to Millie.

The off-white book was sturdy in her hand and made the entire thing real rather than a dream. "I shall study it completely."

"It is a guide for success, but we trust our Ladies to make smart decisions during their assignments. We will have rooms made ready for you and your companion by midmorning tomorrow. I assume Mrs. Whimple will be a sufficient chaperone for you. We do have dowagers for instances when our Ladies must be alone with the male clients, but I assume you will be more comfortable with your own. That way she will not be put out by your uncle." Jane led her back toward the foyer where Mrs. Whimple sat waiting, with Gray standing nearby.

"Gray, have Mrs. Grimsby make two rooms ready for these ladies. They will join us tomorrow."

Mrs. Whimple popped up from her chair wide-eyed.

"Of course, my lady." He made his way to the door and pulled it open.

Millie wasn't sure what to say. Making a curtsy, she said, "Thank you, my lady."

"No thanks are necessary," Jane said.

Millie should run before Lady Jane changed her mind, but the flowers caught her eye. "My lady, how is it you have such beautiful flowers at this time of year?"

"Everton's has a greenhouse, and his lordship gifts me with fresh flowers most days." Pink flushed her cheeks though her expression remained stoic.

"How lovely," Mrs. Whimple said on a breath.

With a nod of her head and the barest of smiles, Lady Jane turned and strode back toward her office.

Unable to fathom what had just happened, Millie walked out of Everton House in a daze. She had done it. She was going to be an Everton Lady and be paid for her services.

Her uncle's carriage remained in front of the house. Millie still couldn't believe she was an Everton Lady as she climbed up with the driver's help.

As they rolled down the street, she looked at her companion. Mrs. Whimple stared down at her gloved hands.

"Doris, I assumed you would want to come with me, but if the idea does not suit you, I will find you another post as a companion. I'm sure something can be arranged."

Looking across the carriage, Doris smiled. "Of course I want to go with you. I'm just so shocked that they want us, both of us."

Relief flooded Millie. While she would have done it anyway, having her friend along made things easier. "Not only that, but we have our first assignment. Once we move in, we are to see to the matchmaking of the Duke of Middleton."

"A duke?" Mouth gaping, Mrs. Whimple shook her head. "You'd think a duke could find a bride without the help of the likes of us."

A thread of doubt tugged inside Millie. "You would think so."

CPSIA information can be obtained
at www.ICGtesting.com
Printed in the USA
FFHW022209070619
52897126-58492FF